OBLIGATION

The Underground Kings Series

Kai

Aurora Rose Reynolds

Table of Contents

Dedication

To every single woman who has the courage to fight her demons. Your strength is astounding even when you fight in silence.

First moments

"*EVERYONE IS LOOKING for you.*"

I turn my head, pulling my hair out of my face as I watch a boy I've never seen before climb up the stairs and into my tree house.

"*Who are you?*" *I ask him as he sits across from me.*

"*Kai,*" *he smiles, looking around. He looks a lot different than the other kids I know. His hair is long, and his skin is a lot darker than mine.* "*Why are you hiding?*"

I shrug and look away from him. Daddy was yelling earlier; he was so mad that he was turning red. Then Mommy started crying, and Daddy started yelling louder. I heard Mommy telling Daddy that he had to send me away. I don't want to go away. I try to be good, but sometimes, I forget to listen.

"*Why are you crying?*"

I look up at him and wipe my face. "*I'm scared,*" *I whisper, wiping my nose.*

"*Come on. I'll protect you,*" *he says, holding his hand out to me.*

Then my mommy calls my name again. I look at his hand, move Mr. Bear under my arm, and put my hand in his.

"*Myla!*" *Mommy yells, running towards me.*

I can tell she has been crying again.

"*Where did you go?*" *Her hands grab my shoulders and she shakes me hard.*

"*It's my fault. I asked her to show me the tree house,*" *Kai tells her.*

She stops shaking me then looks at him. "*You shouldn't have done that. You knew we were looking for her,*" *she says angrily her head.*

"*I'm sorry. I wasn't thinking,*" *Kai says softly, putting his hands in his pockets and looking at the ground.*

I look back at Mommy, and she shakes her head before grabbing my hand and pulling me with her. When I look over my shoulder at Kai, he smiles, making me smile back.

Prologue

"TIME FOR BED, *zvyozdochka*," Papa says as he walks into my room. I run to my bed and jump in, making all of my stuffed animals fly out of the bed before standing up, jumping once, and falling to my back, which makes him laugh.

"Your mama has told you about jumping on the bed, Zvezdochka."

I know that Mama doesn't like it when I jump on the bed, but it always makes Papa laugh.

"Will you sing me my song?" I ask him as he move towards the bed.

"Have you brushed your teeth?"

"*Da*," I answer affirmatively in Russian, making him smile.

"Did you wash your face?"

"*Da*," I repeat, giggling.

"Did you wash your smelly feet?" he asks while bringing my feet towards his face.

"*Nyet.*" I giggle harder, wiggling my toes.

"Ah, *zvyozdochka*, what should I do with you?" he asks, calling me his "little star" while tickling me.

I roll around on the bed, trying to get away from him as I cry out in laughter. When he stops tickling me and I stop laughing, he picks me up and pulls my covers back before laying me back down.

"Now will you sing me my song?" I ask him again, tucking Mr. Bear under my chin, feeling my eyes start to close.

"*Da.*" He kisses my forehead before sitting down on the side of the bed. His fingers run over my eyelids, causing them to close completely before he starts to sing quietly. "*Zvyozdochka, zvyozdochka,* you outshine the sun. *Zvyozdochka, zvyozdochka,* nothing compares to you.

1

Zvyozdochka, zvyozdochka, the holder of my treasure. *Zvyozdochka, zvyozdochka,* I will always love you dearly, for you are my star who guides me from far and will always lead me home.,"

Then I fall asleep.

"YOU KNOW WHERE to take her," Papa tells Philip as he carries me outside.

I cling tighter to Papa. Mama ran out of Papa's office soon after she woke me up, telling me to get dressed, and then took me to him.

"I don't want to go!" I cry, kicking my legs and wrapping my arms tighter around Papa's neck as he tries to hand me to Philip. I don't want to go away. I want to stay with him and Mama.

"*Zvyozdochka,* you must be a big girl and go with Philip."

"I won't be bad anymore!" I sob, screaming out as he pulls my hands from around his neck.

Philip's hands wrap around my waist, pulling me from my papa.

"You're our greatest treasure, Zvezdochka. We love you," my papa says as he opens the door for Philip, who sits down in the back of the limo, holding me in his lap.

"I love you, Papa!" I cry and see that my Papa is crying too before he turns his back on me.

"*Pah idiom!*" Philip says, and the limo begins to move.

I turn in Philip's arms and look out the back window, watching as Papa pushes the front door of the house open. Then I see Mama on the floor. Papa picks her up, and I hear her scream my name as the door closes.

Chapter 1
My Husband

I FEEL THE sun on my closed eyelids and something sharp poking me in the face. Moving my hand, trying to get away from the pain and whimper when it scrapes against my cheek. I lift my head and run my fingers along the side of my face, feeling wetness. Opening my eyes to see a light smear of blood on my fingers. I flip my hand over, and then I see the gaudy ring that is now taking up residence on my ring finger.

"Great," I whisper, closing my eyes and laying my head down again.

I prayed earlier, before I went to sleep, that when I woke up, the ring I'm wearing now and the man who put it there would be nothing but a bad dream. No such luck. I roll over and take a shaky breath, wanting to close my eyes for a few more seconds, wishing I could just sleep until everything was back to normal.

"Time to get up."

I turn my head and meet my new husband's eyes as he looks at me through the open bedroom doorway. He looks like an ancient Hawaiian warrior. His long, wavy hair is tied into a ponytail at the back of his neck with a piece of leather cord. His wide nose and square jaw make his full lips and long eyelashes somehow appear masculine. At five eight, I have never felt short, but next to him, I feel minuscule. He must be at least six seven. His shoulders are so broad that I wouldn't be surprised if he had to turn slightly to fit through most doorways.

"If we didn't have to meet with my lawyer, I would let you sleep," he says, bringing me out of my perusal.

One thing I have to be grateful for is that, ever since the moment he saved me, he has been kind and surprisingly soft with me.

"I'm getting up," I tell him quietly and start to sit up, but pain slices through my side, causing me to inhale sharply.

"I thought you said you weren't hurt?" he growls.

I'm gently lifted to a sitting position on the side of the bed. I'm so focused on trying to breathe that I don't even notice his proximity until I feel his hand on the bare skin of my shoulder.

"I'm fine," I mumble, trying to breathe through the pain and the feelings that are swimming around in my stomach.

"You're going to the doctor."

"I'm not," I say, lifting my head and meeting his eyes.

"Myla." His eyes go soft as my name leaves his mouth, and his hand comes up, causing me to flinch and his jaw to go hard.

"Sorry," I whisper while standing.

"We need to talk about what happened," he commands as his hand drops to his lap.

"How long do I have to get ready?" I ask, walking towards the bathroom.

"Thirty minutes," he replies as I turn to face him.

When our eyes connect again, his flash with annoyance as he stands.

"We will talk," he declares, walking out of the room, shutting the door behind him without saying another word.

I stare at the door for a moment before turning around and walking into the bathroom, where I turn the faucet on, place my hands on the counter, and look at myself in the mirror, watching as tears begin to fill my eyes.

"You're strong, Myla. You can do this," I whisper to myself, taking a deep, shaky breath and then letting it out as I splash cold water on my face.

When I look at myself again, the tears have been washed away with the water, no trace left behind. I grab a towel out of a built-in shelf and bury my face in it, muffling the sound of the sob that climbs up my throat.

My soul feels like it has been blackened by not only what I witnessed, but what I did. I have no idea how I'm supposed to get over seeing people die right in front of me or knowing I'm the reason they are dead.

I wipe my face on the towel and go to the glass shower door, sliding it open before turning the water on. Once I feel that the water is warm enough, I carefully remove my clothes and step into the shower, letting the water from the showerhead pour over me. I really want to sit on the shower floor and cry, but right now, that is not an option.

I wet my hair then look around the shower stall, finding a shelf full of bottles of different body washes. I quickly sort through them, find one for women, and then pour a big glob onto my hand and lather up. I don't know for sure if this is Kai's bathroom, but if by chance it is, I don't want to use something of his and smell like him for the rest of the day. As it is, it's difficult to be around him.

I rinse off and get out of the shower before drying off and picking my clothes up off the floor. When I step back into the room, I take it in for the first time since arriving here last night. The room is huge, with large, glass doors that look out over the ocean. I walk toward the doors and look out at the water.

In Seattle, I live in a beautiful two-bedroom condo. I chose my condo because of the ocean view I have, but the view I have back home is nothing like this. Other bodies of land block my view, and the water is so dark that it's almost black. Here, the water is a blue I have never seen before. So blue that it almost looks like the sky on a crystal clear day.

My eyes travel from the view outside to the giant bed that is covered with a set of pure-white sheets. It's even bigger than the California king a friend of mine has, and it would be a perfect fit for a man Kai's size. On each side of the bed, there's a table with a lamp that looks like a piece of driftwood on it. The lamps match the dresser in the room, which is long with a few odds and ends on it. There's another tall one, but it's completely clean.

The room has no paintings or anything else to give it life or say whose room it is. I shake my head at my own thought and look at the clothes I had on earlier, scrunching up my nose. Even though I was exhausted enough to fall asleep in them last night, I do not feel like having them on again today. I walk to the long dresser, pull the top drawer open, and find men's boxers. I pull a pair out and slip them on under my towel. When I open the next drawer, I find socks and slip them on as well before searching through the rest of the dresser and finally finding a shirt, being careful of the bruises on my side.

Once I'm dressed, I take towel into the bathroom and hang them up. I find some toothpaste and use my finger to brush my teeth before taking a breath, preparing myself to face Kai and his lawyer. Yesterday, when we got married, I didn't sign a prenup even though the men with Kai had insisted. I really didn't understand why they were so adamant until after we were married and at the airport.

I'd expected us to just get on a flight. I was shocked when we were escorted to a private plane. I was more surprised when the name on the plane happened to be my new husband's. I had somewhat gotten myself under control by the time we arrived in Hawaii, but I was shocked again when a Bentley picked us up at the airport and took us to a mansion. I have been around people who have money, but I have never been around anyone with the kind of money Kai obviously has.

I go to the door and run my fingers through my wet hair before turning the knob and opening it an inch to peek out. It takes a second for my eyes to adjust to the darkness of the hall, but when they do, they connect with a set of hazel eyes surrounded by dark lashes.

"Myla," the man says.

I double-blink and take in his features. His hair is dark brown, his nose is wide, and his skin color is similar to Kai's. My eyes drop to his mouth, and he smiles, making my eyes narrow before they lift to meet his again.

"Who are you?" I ask, opening the door the rest of the way and crossing my arms over my chest.

His eyes move to my arms and then back up, and his smile gets wider. "Aye."

"What?" I frown when he chuckles.

"Name's Aye."

"Like when a pirate says yes?" I inquire. Then I growl, "What's so funny?" when he bends over, holding his stomach and laughing.

It takes a moment, but eventually, he pulls himself together and stands back up to his full height.

"My name's Aye, but my friends call me Daddy. How about you just stick with that?" he asks, sticking out his hand.

"I'm not calling you Daddy," I frown, watching his lips twitch.

"You don't have to call me Daddy." He smiles, reminding me of a little boy. "You can call me Aye."

My frown grows deeper. "Do people really call you Daddy?" I narrow my eyes, daring him to lie.

"Sure do," he smirks, wrapping the hand he had out for me to shake around my upper arm. Then he moves me from the door and closes it before putting his arm around my shoulders and leading me down the hall.

"What are you doing?" I step out of his hold.

His eyebrows pull together and he looks down the hall to where we are heading. "Kai didn't tell you I'll be your security?" he questions, and I shake my head. "Well, me and Pika will be, but he is not here right now, so it's just me until he gets back."

"I thought I was safe now?" I murmur, wrapping my arms around myself.

"You are safe," he says, concerned, looking me over. "No one will get to you."

"Can you just take me to Kai?" I ask softly, feeling anxious. Even though I don't really know Kai, he is the one person I trust right now.

"Of course," he says quietly, taking my hand and leading me down the hall.

When the hall opens up, we are on the third floor. A glass banister that gives a clear view of a large, wooden staircase is in front of us. The stairs lead down to a level with wooden floors. Then another set leads to the beach below. I have never seen something so amazing. The ocean is just yards away, but the beach is literally inside.

"It must be expensive to keep this place clean," I mutter to myself, looking out at the ocean and the sand that is spread across the bottom level of the house.

I hear Aye chuckle again before he tugs on my hand and begins leading me over a bridge, down another hall, and into a large dining room, where Kai and another man are sitting with papers spread out in front of them. As soon as we enter the room, both of their heads turn towards us. Kai's eyes travel from my still-wet hair to my sock-covered feet before he holds a hand out in my direction, nodding his chin ever so slightly. I don't want to go to him, but something in the look he's giving me tells me to do it. I walk to him and take his hand, not even flinching when he pulls me down onto his lap.

"*Makamae*," he whispers against the shell of my ear, placing a kiss there.

My stomach knots and I dig my nails into the palm of my hand as I turn my head to look at him. When our eyes connect, I try to silently understand what he's doing.

"You found some clothes," he says quietly as his fingers play along the edge of my shorts.

"I hope you don't mind," I murmur, grabbing his hand and stilling his movements.

"I would never deny my wife," he mutters, holding my eyes.

I fight to not look away, to not cower.

The moment I met him, I knew he was not someone I would ever want to cross, but he was my savior. Even knowing he promised not to hurt me, I still feel the urge to pull away from him and the energy that is wrapping around me.

"Are you feeling better, now that you have showered?" He searches my face as his fingers come up to run along the underside of my jaw.

"Yes," I mutter as that knot in my stomach loosens and another feeling begins to take root.

"Good," he murmurs, leaning forward and brushing his lips lightly over mine.

My hand goes to his chest, feeling the warmth of his skin and the beat of his heart through the material of his shirt. When he leans back, his eyes search mine for a moment before looking away. The moment the connection is broken, I pull in a breath and turn on his lap to face the man across the table.

"Myla, I would like you to meet detective, Nero Wolfe. Nero, this is my wife, Myla Kauwe." He squeezes my thigh when my nails dig into his.

"Nice to meet you, Myla." He smiles, showing off a dimple in his left cheek, which is highlighted by his tan skin. His dark-brown eyes look between Kai and me as he shakes his head, causing his shaggy, dirty-blond hair to slide against the collar of his dress shirt. If he weren't wearing a suit, I would've guessed he's a surfer, not a detective.

"Nice to meet you," I murmur, shifting slightly under his gaze. I knew we would eventually need to talk to the police about what happened, but I was hoping I would have a few days for myself to accept everything.

"Kai has filled me in on most of what occurred, but I do have a few questions for you. If that's okay?" he asks softly.

I war with myself on turning to look at Kai for permission. I was not prepared for this, and I feel like I have been put on the spot.

"Of course." I nod and pull away from Kai, moving to my own seat.

I need to remember that this is all a lie; we may be married, but it's not out of choice—it's out of necessity. I can't let my personal vulnerabilities affect this situation. And as much as I hate to admit it, Kai has an enormous effect on me.

"Well, let's get started, then," Nero says, rearranging some papers on top of the table. "I know you and Kai were married yesterday in Vegas, but can you tell me what happened the day before?"

I wrap my arms around myself and look over my shoulder towards the door, where I want to escape, but my eyes land on Aye, who nods and gives me a small smile. Then I feel a squeeze on my thigh and the roughness of Kai's palm as it moves along my skin.

I turn my head back towards Nero without acknowledging Kai. "What would you like to know?"

"Start from the beginning." He gives a slight smile, picking up a pen.

I nod again and pull my feet up under me on the chair, trying to get my thoughts in order before I begin.

"I own a bakery in downtown Seattle called Raining Sprinkles." I swallow, remembering that my bakery is nothing but ash and rubble now.

"Take your time," Nero says comfortingly.

"Like I said, I own a bakery, and on Sundays, I open the bakery alone and give my girls the day off because it's normally pretty slow in the shop. Really, the day started out like any other day. I got there around five, made a pot of coffee, and took care of some stuff in the office until around six. At six, I went to the kitchen and threw together a few batches of muffins, put them in the oven, and then went out to start stocking the display cases. At eight, I flipped the sign from closed to open, and not long after that, my first customer came in."

I pause, taking a breath while wrapping my arms a little tighter around myself. "The rest of the day was uneventful. There was nothing out of the ordinary. I was busy because I was on my own, but I expected that. At around two thirty, I went to the back and pushed a load of dishes through the dishwasher, and when I got back out front, I realized the man from that morning was still sitting at the same table he had been when I first opened."

I close my eyes and open them slowly. "I went and made sure he was okay and that he didn't want anything. Then I told him I closed at three. When three o'clock came around, he was gone. I took care of a couple of customers who had been waiting for me to box up their items and walked them to the door to leave. As soon as they were gone, I shut the door, and I was flipping the sign over when the man from earlier came running up to the door, telling me through the glass he thought he left his phone in the bathroom."

I bite my lip and, without thinking, look at Kai and then back at Nero before speaking again. "I got a weird feeling, so I stood by the door while he looked around for his phone. I was watching him when the door was shoved open and I stumbled back. I thought it was a customer, but that's when I looked up and saw my brother, Thad." I shudder as bile crawls up my throat and nausea rolls in my stomach.

"Are you okay?" Nero asks as I pull in a deep breath.

"Fine," I whisper, putting my feet on the floor while sliding away from Kai's touch. "I was taken aback when I realized who it was. I had not seen him since I was eighteen and moved away from home. He pushed his way past me and then let in a few other men," I say, and I feel Kai's hand on my lower back as he lifts my shirt slightly. Then his fingers begin to move over my skin. I wonder if he is trying to remind me of the things I'm not supposed to talk about.

"Then what happened?" Nero questions softly, and I lean back slightly into Kai's hand, who pauses his movement before resuming.

"He forced me into the back room. My brother said he owed some men money and that I needed to give it to him. I don't know if he was on drugs or what, but he seemed really afraid. I told him I didn't have the kind of money he was asking for, and he proceeded to tie me to a chair."

"Then what?"

"I don't know," I say faintly. "I was hit over the head, and when I woke up, Kai was pulling me out of the burning building," I look over at Kai, and even if I never tell anyone every detail of what really occurred, I do know that that part is not a lie, and I will forever be indebted to him.

"Then you went to Vegas and got married?"

I pull my eyes from Kai to look at Nero. "Yes. Well…we had been planning on getting married," I lie.

Kai's hand pauses on my back. We never discussed what exactly happened to me or what we would say if someone asked me about this, so I was trying to think on my toes.

"After what occurred, I realized how short life is, and I told Kai I didn't want to live another day without him and that I was tired of putting off our relationship. So we stopped in Vegas on the way here and got married," I tell him.

Nero searches my face. Then his eyes drop to the pad in front of him, where he begins to write again.

I bite my lip, feeling like I have done something wrong. I have no idea what I should have said. I don't think, "*I met him for the first time yesterday, and I married him because he told me that was the only way he could keep me safe at this time,*" would have gone over so well.

"And you don't remember anything else?" he asks, lifting his head to look at me.

I shake my head and pull my feet back up under me. "Nothing," I mutter, pressing my lips together.

"Can you tell me a little about your brother?"

My body stills and I feel all the blood drain out of my face. "There is nothing to tell," I whisper, hating myself a little bit for being so weak when it comes to him.

"Are you okay?" Nero asks, reading my face.

"Fine. Just tired." I sit up, putting my elbows on the table, holding my hair back from my face as images from my past flash through my head.

Being taken from my parents when I was little and told that they were dead.

Moving in with Modesto and Ida Akskvo and their two sons, Thad and Royce.

Being told that, if I ever spoke of where I really came from, I would die.

Having happy memories of my life with my new family.

Working in my dad Modesto's bakery. Shopping with my mom Ida.

Hanging out with my brother Royce.

But then everything changed when I turned sixteen and Thad started sneaking into my room at night, showing me that Hell can exist on

Earth.

The memories alone of the things he did to me, the things he took from me, cause me to gag. I stand from the chair and run out of the dining room. I have no idea where I'm going and begin opening and closing doors along the way until I finally find one that leads to a bathroom. I slam the door behind me, fumble with the lock on the door until I hear it click, and then feel along the wall, finding the switch and turning it on.

The moment my eyes adjust to the light, I see my refection looking back at me. My face is pale, my dirty-blond hair looks stringy, and my lips are a darker pink than normal. Another wave of nausea hits me, and I lunge for the toilet. It takes a few minutes to get myself under control, and when I do, I realize someone is pounding on the door so hard that the painting on the wall is shaking.

"I'm kicking it in!" Kai yells from the other side.

I'm about to tell him that I'm opening it when the door crashes in, banging against the wall, and wood flies everywhere. Kai appears in the bathroom doorway. Our gazes lock, and I see something flash within his eyes as he storms towards me.

"I'M GOING TO carry you so you don't get anything stuck in your feet," he says softly, picking me up. "Aye, tell Detective Nero we're going to have to reschedule. My wife isn't feeling well," Kai mutters, carrying me into the room I was in this morning and shutting the door with his foot before carrying me to the bed, where he gently lays me down. "Let me get a washcloth for you," he says, walking into the bathroom.

I hear the water turn on, and a moment later, he comes back carrying a rag.

"You need to tell me what happened at the bakery before I showed up."

He sits on the side of the bed and holds the wet cloth out for me. I take it from his hand, trying to control how badly I'm shaking. What happened begins to play in my head like an old movie.

"Myla, I've missed you," Thad said, wrapping an arm around my waist, walking me backwards into the shop.

His body bent, his face went to my neck, and I felt his tongue touch my skin. My body froze and I instantly hated myself for not screaming, for not fighting, but like all those years ago, my body had stiffened in fear.

"What are you doing here?" I whispered as two more men walked in. My stomach dropped as I watched one of the men close the door and turn the lock.

"It's your birthday," he said as he began to pull me with him towards the back of the shop.

I cried out and tried to pull away, and he smiled evilly and started to laugh. His fingers dug into my skin so hard that I knew I would be bruised.

"Please let me go." I tried to pull away again, but his grip tightened, and he dragged me to the back room, shoving me into a chair.

"Shut up," he ordered with a finger in my face. Then he looked over at one of the men who had just walked in. "Go to her place and get all of her shit. Then meet us here," he said, tossing my purse at the guy.

"Got it," he said, digging my keys out of my bag and leaving the room.

"What's going on? Why are you here?" I whispered.

Thad turned towards me. His hand went to my jaw, his thumb and middle finger on either side, where he squeezed hard.

"I'm taking you home and you're getting married. Mom is going to be so happy," he smiled.

I felt bile fill my throat, making it hard to breathe. "What are you taking about?" I finally got out through my fear.

"Oh, princess, there is so much you don't know." His hands went to each arm of the chair and his body caged mine in. "Don't worry though. We'll have plenty of time to talk about it." He licked my neck, making my stomach roll.

When he pulled away, my eyes locked on the man's across the room, the man who had been in my shop all day. Something flashed in his eyes, but he turned his face away from me before I could catch it.

"We have a busy day ahead of us," Thad said.

I looked around, trying to plan my escape.

"Myla? Myla."

I realize I'm being shaken. My eyes focus in on Kai's face above me, and I quickly scoot back in the bed, hitting my head on the headboard in the process.

"Careful," he complains as I rub the top of my head.

"Sorry."

"Don't apologize." He looks away from me to the view outside. "Do you want to talk about what happened?"

I shake my head and then realize he's still looking out the window. "No." I lean my head back and close my eyes. "I'm sorry about telling the detective we were dating. He caught me off guard and I was already flustered, and honestly, I had no idea what to say. We probably should have talked about that. I mean, I don't even know if you have a girlfriend." My eyes fly open and connect with his, and I can see laugh lines around his eyes and a smile on his lips. "Do you have a girlfriend?" I hiss, watching as his smile gets bigger.

"You talk a lot," he chuckles, shaking his head.

"Well, do you?" I growl. I never even thought about that for one moment, and something about the thought of him having a girlfriend makes me feel a different kind of nausea.

"No."

"Good." I nod, and his smile gets bigger. "I just mean good because I would feel horrible if you were dating someone and then got married to someone else."

"Myla, I know." He rubs my knee, and a tingling sensation begins to fill my lower belly.

"How badly did I mess up with Nero?" I question, sitting up farther and moving away from his touch.

"You did fine. We spoke before you came in, so he understands you're still trying to deal with what happened."

I bite my lip while wrapping my arms around myself. Then I look out the window. "So, now what?"

"Now what?" he repeats, and my eyes travel back to him.

"Yeah. Now what do we do? You said we needed to talk to your lawyer."

"You do nothing. I canceled the meeting with my lawyer when Nero showed up, and now, I have business to take care of. If the gods are working in my favor, we can get everything resolved and things can get back to normal," he says softly.

I dip my head slightly in agreement, even if my normal was lost a long time ago.

Chapter 2

I Know You

I LOOK OVER my shoulder at the house behind me when I hear Kai yelling. I push my sunglasses up to the top of my head and put my Kindle down on the table next to my lounger.

"Stay here," Aye says, taking off towards the house.

When the voices begin to get louder, I get up and head inside. I walk softly down the hall and peek around the corner, seeing the guy who let Thad into the bakery. He's standing in the kitchen alone, his body pressed close to the wall, his head tilted back like he's waiting for the moment to strike.

My gut twists with anxiety, but I battle it back, head down the hall, and open the bathroom door, looking for anything to use as a weapon. It's a half-bath with a pedestal sink and a mirror; there are no drawers or cabinets. I'm about to give up and go search out somewhere else when the plunger catches my eye. I pick it up and test the weight in my hand. It's a heavy, wooden one with a large, black, rubber end. I take it with me down the hall and wait just outside the kitchen.

The guy is no longer there, but Aye is standing next to the counter. I start to walk towards him, but the guy begins to sneak up on Aye. Without thinking, I charge at him with the plunger over my head and bring it down hard on his head. The rubber end flies off and bounces across the kitchen floor as the guy crumples to the ground.

"Wh—" Aye looks down at the guy, who is now knocked out, then looks back at me with wide eyes. "Why did you do that?" He takes the plunger stick from my hand and looks at it then back down at the guy.

"He was sneaking up on you," I tell him, turning the guy onto his stomach then pulling his hands behind his back, using the skills I learned in a self-defense class I took, to make sure he is immobilized. "Do you have cuffs or something?" I ask, looking up at Aye from my bent position.

"We're not cuffing Pika," he mutters, shaking his head while looking at me like he has no idea who I am.

"This is one of the guys from the bakery," I tell him.

His eyes flash with understanding, and Pika starts to moan, so I grab the stick from Aye's hand and start to hit the guy again, but then it's snatched away from me.

"Myla?"

I turn my head towards the kitchen opening when Kai says my name. His eyes travel down my body, over the bikini I'm wearing, making goose bumps break out along my skin. When his eyes reach my toes, they widen at the sight of the guy lying at my feet.

"What's going on?" He steps into the kitchen and over to my side.

My belly dips as his smell surrounds me. He smells like spice, coconut, and the hot sun. Every time he's near, I have to stop myself from leaning closer.

"This is the guy who let Thad into my bakery. The one who said he left his phone," I tell him.

His eyes go soft, and he unbuttons his shirt so he's wearing nothing but a pair of black dress pants and his shoes. I watch as his abs flex. Then he opens the shirt and slips it around my shoulders. I pull away slightly and push my arms through the holes, holding my breath for a moment, keeping his scent in my lungs as long as I can.

"This is one of my guys," he tells me, crouching down and rolling the guy over.

"He was at my bakery. He...he is the reason Thad got inside," I repeat in a stammer, watching as the guy's eyes open and then focus on me.

"He was my inside source for the men Thad was working for," Kai says, helping Pika sit up.

"What do you mean he was working for you?" I look at the injured man then at Kai.

"Why don't you come with me?" Aye suggests softly, grabbing my hand.

"No." I shake his touch off and cross my arms over my chest. "Why didn't you tell me that before?" I glare at Kai.

"There was no reason to," he says, looking at me like I'm crazy for even asking.

"No reason?" I shake my head in disbelief. His audacity is absolutely ridiculous.

"He was doing a job," Aye chimes in.

My head swings his way and his hands go up in front of him to warn me off.

"I'm sorry," Pika says as Kai helps him to stand.

"You're sorry? You're sorry you allowed men to follow you into my shop, or are you sorry you watched as Thad kicked me in the ribs while I was curled up in a ball and begging him to stop? Or are you sorry that you set my bakery on fire? Please clarify which part you're sorry about!" I yell, and my chest heaves as I attempt to take a full breath.

"All of it," he whispers, unsure, looking at me then Kai.

"Thanks. I feel so much better now that I know you're sorry," I say, shoving through the three of them and walking down the hall towards the living room.

I need to go clear my head. I can't say that I have gotten over what happened, but since being here, I've found it easy to pretend like I'm safe. Now, seeing him makes me realize how much I have let my guard down, and that is something I never want to risk happening again.

I rush out of the house and walk out to the water's edge until the waves rush over my feet.

"If he could have helped you, he would have."

I look over my shoulder, toward the sound of Kai's voice, and watch him walk up to me wearing another shirt.

"He would have, but he knew he couldn't risk them finding out he worked for me."

I feel my throat clog, turn my head away, and look back out over the ocean, not wanting to acknowledge his words. "He watched." I take a deep breath, letting the smell of the salt water clear my head. "He watched and did nothing," I murmur, wrapping my arms around myself as my words get lost in the sound of the waves crashing against the shore.

"I've known him since I was seventeen," Kai says closer to me than I expected, surprising me by wrapping an arm around my shoulders. "If he could have stopped it, he would have."

I stiffen slightly before forcing my body to relax and lean into his embrace. Deep in my soul, I know he's right, but I'm still angry. I'm angry that Pika saw me in a moment of weakness, angry I couldn't do anything even when I had done everything to make myself stronger. Angry that I never took into consideration the amount of fear I would feel when I came face-to-face with a part of my past that had terrified me for so many years.

"I forgot," I whisper, shaking my head, watching as the sun turns the sky orange and red.

"Forgot what?" he asks softly, his fingers sending tingles down my arm through the fabric of his shirt.

"That I'm in danger. That I need to watch my back," I say, and his arm tightens around me.

"You're safe here."

I tilt my head back and look up at him as he towers over me. His chin dips, and our eyes connect.

"I promised you I would protect you. Trust me to do that," he says softly as his eyes search my face.

My eyes focus on his, and I notice for the first time that he has a dark ring of brown around the outside and an almost-copper color that shoots out from around the center.

"Trust me to do that," he repeats.

I feel his warm breath against my skin. And I wish in that moment that I were someone worthy enough of someone like him.

"I'm trying." My eyes close. I pull away from him and then step farther out into the water.

"I need to go meet someone," he says regretfully after a moment.

"Sure," I murmur without taking my eyes off the sea.

"I'd like it if you'd go with me."

I turn my head to look at him. His hands are in his pockets and his shoulders are slumped forward. The vulnerability I see on his face makes me nod in agreement immediately. The only time we have spent together is when we have met for meals or when he has needed me to talk to someone with him. I only recently found out that the room I have been staying in is his. He claimed that the bed is much better than the others in the house and refused to take the room back even after I insisted. And something about sleeping in his bed has made me feel closer to him—and safer in a strange way.

"Where are we going?" I ask after a moment.

"You'll see. Dress casual." He smiles, and a piece of hair blows onto his lip.

I fight the urge to close the space between us and remove it with my finger, using that as an excuse to see if his lips are as soft as they look.

"Did you hear me?" he asks.

My eyes focus on his. I feel my cheeks get pink when I notice the small smile on his handsome face.

"Sorry. No," I admit.

"I asked if you could be ready in the next hour."

"Oh, yeah... Sure," I say, hoping I don't sound as anxious as I feel.

He watches me for a moment before nodding once, turning away, and walking back towards the house. I watch him go, wondering what exactly I'm feeling. Since the moment I met Kai, I have felt some kind of strange pull towards him. But as much as he entices me, he scares me.

The only men I have been with have been lanky and soft-spoken, men I knew I could get away from if I needed to. I hate to say it, but I was very promiscuous for a while. It was like something in me had flipped and I realized the power I had. I realized I had the ability to say yes or no when it came to sex, and I wanted to prove to myself I could be intimate with someone—and maybe not completely enjoy the act—but it would be my choice.

I'm not proud of the way I acted or the way I used men. But like most things in life, it's something I learned from, and it helped me grow and become a better person.

Kai is like none of the men I've been with. He's large and intimidating. Though he is soft with me, I have seen him speak to some of the people who work for him, so I know that his gentleness is not always his way. I also cannot imagine him letting me be in charge the way I'm used to.

I haven't been intimate with a man since my last relationship, and that was a few years ago. After Fredrick broke up with me, I was left confused. He was the person I'd planned to spend the rest of my life with. We'd met when I bought my bakery, and he'd helped me get my loan.

He was so funny; he had the ability to make me laugh at nothing. He was not much taller than I am and cute in that nerdy-guy kind of way. He was soft-spoken and gentle, and he said all the right things. After six months of dating, he asked me to marry him. I, of course, said yes. Our wedding was set for the fall, and we were planning on having a baby right away, hopefully with conception occurring during the honeymoon. Everything was perfect. I was getting the one thing I had craved since moving away from home: a family of my own, people who loved me, and somewhere I belonged.

Then, like everything in my life, it came crashing down around me.

Fredrick had been away for a week at a conference, and when he arrived back in Seattle, he asked me to meet him for dinner. I got dressed up, packed an overnight bag, and met him at one of my favorite seafood restaurants.

The moment I saw him, I knew something was off. He didn't greet me with his normal hug and kiss. He took my hand and helped me sit down across from him. Without a word from him, I knew we were over. I remember sitting there, looking at him sitting across from me, wondering, *Why?* That's when he told me that he believed our lives were going in two different directions and he wasn't ready to settle down.

I told him that I would wait for him, that we didn't need to get married, that we could put off the wedding until he was ready, and that was when it seemed like I was begging to be with him. That was the moment I realized he didn't love me the way I loved him, so I lifted my chin, scooted the chair away from the table, and walked out of the restaurant, never looking back.

I loved him, but there was no way I would ever feel like I was begging someone to be with me again. I wouldn't ever let someone have that much power over me.

I come out of my thoughts when the sound of seagulls fills my ears. I lift my face towards the sun, letting the rays warm my skin for a moment before turning and heading to the house to get ready.

"LET'S GO." I look at Kai, who is leaning against the side of a black convertible, dressed more casually than I have ever seen him.

Even when he comes to breakfast in the morning, he is normally wearing a suit, so seeing him in a pair of khaki shorts and a white, linen shirt with the top two buttons undone and the sleeves rolled up—showing off a tattoo I never noticed before that wraps around his forearm—has stunned me.

I start down the steps, my eyes meeting his, and my step falters slightly when his eyes sweep me from top to toe before locking on mine.

"You look nice," I say, immediately feeling like a fool when he gives me a slight smile and opens the door to the car without telling me something relatively the same.

I know this isn't a date, but I took extra care in getting ready. I have no idea where we are going, but I wanted to make sure I looked nice. I chose a dress I had gotten from one of the few shops in town. The strapless, cotton dress covered in bright, tropical flowers looks nice against the creamy color of my skin, and the sandals I chose are black and wrapped around my big toes then up and around my ankles. I thought I looked attractive, but as Kai gets behind the driver's seat, I'm beginning to have doubts about my choice.

"It's about an hour drive," he mutters as the car roars to life.

I nod then realize he can't see me, so I clear my throat and murmur a quiet, "Okay," as we pull away from the house. "Is Pika okay?" I ask, wanting to fill the silence. I turn my head to look at Kai.

His eyes come to me for a moment before he focuses on the road again. "He's fine. He has a bump, but he's had worse."

"OH," I MUTTER as my eyes drop to my lap, and I begin to turn my ring around on my finger, watching as the light bounces of the diamonds. "Why did you have him working with Thad?" I ask when he doesn't say anything else.

"Your father was a very good friend to my dad." He lets out a breath, and his hand wrings the steering wheel. "Before your father passed away, he told mine his plan for keeping you safe." He pulls his sunglasses over his eyes, turns his head, and looks at me before turning towards the road. "Your father asked mine to help keep an eye on you. He knew that, even with everyone believing you had also been killed, there would still be some who would be looking for you."

"What do you mean they believed I was killed?" I whisper.

"Your parents' remains and the remains of a child were found after they put out a fire in your parents' home," he says, and I turn my head to look out the window as a loan tear slides down my cheek.

I have small memories of my real parents. Every time I pull a batch of snickerdoodles out of the oven and the smell of vanilla, cinnamon, and sugar hits my nose, I think of my mom. I can remember her baking them often when I was little and the way she would yell at my dad when he came into the kitchen to steal them off the counter when they were fresh out of the oven. I can remember laughing when he would quiet my mom with soft words and a few kisses before leaving and going back to his office.

I remember the way my dad was so large and everyone seemed so afraid of him, but to me, he was so gentle. He always smelled like mint, and if I were around, he would pull me up against his chest and kiss my hair no matter what he was doing.

I know that my mom and I were his whole world. Even if I can't remember much from my childhood, the memories of my parents always bring me comfort. So even though I have known for years that they are gone, hearing that their bodies were found has the already-shattered pieces of my heart crumbling a little bit more.

"Who was the child?" I wonder out loud as I watch a group of seagulls fly off in the distance.

"I would guess they got a body from a morgue," he says easily, and my stomach turns as I wonder what kind of people would do something like that.

"My dad was a bad guy, right?" I ask as some puzzle pieces begin to fit together.

The car slows down suddenly and veers off to the side of the road. My head turns and I look over at Kai, who now has his sunglasses up on top of his head and his eyes on me.

"Your father was a good man. He was a man of honor and a man who loved his only child enough to make sure she'd have a future. He may not have been a man who lived on the right side of the law, but he was not a bad man," he says firmly, making me feel instantly relieved.

"Why is this happening now, then?" I don't realize I ask that question aloud until Kai's eyes soften, his hand comes up to my face, and his thumb runs over my cheek, sliding away another tear.

"There is so much you don't know, Myla."

"Like what?" I whisper.

"When the time is right, I will tell you."

A part of me wants to demand him to tell me what he knows, but there is another part of me that wants to ignore everything happening around me and leave all of this behind.

"How difficult is it to get a new identity?" I mutter, surprised when I hear a chuckle come from Kai. "I'm serious," I complain, turning my head to catch a smile that makes my heart constrict from how beautiful it is on Kai's face. I swallow hard and look back out the window, trying to ignore the feeling I have from knowing I made him smile.

After a moment, the car fills with music, and my body relaxes into my seat as The Fugees' "Killing Me Softly" fills the air. When I peek at Kai out of the corner of my eye, I wonder if he's hearing the song like I am in that moment and if he knows that the lyrics of this song say so much more than I ever could.

Chapter 3

Looking in a Mirror

"MYLA."

My shoulder is nudged. I lift my head just in time to see a group of laughing kids run in front of the car.

"Where are we?"

"A luau."

I turn and look at Kai, who is watching out the front window of the car. When his head turns and his eyes meet mine, he smiles, and then his hand lifts and his finger runs down my cheek.

"You need to learn not to sleep on your hand. Every time you wake up, your ring is imprinted in your cheek," he mutters.

My hand goes to my face, my fingers running over the skin. I swear I can still feel the tingle from his touch.

"It's a big ring," I point out and glimpse at him when he doesn't say anything. His eyes are on the ring on my hand, and regret is bright as day in his eyes.

I pull my eyes from him, tug the visor down, and look at myself in the mirror, wanting to ignore the feelings seeing that look on his face caused. I thought at first that the ring was just something he had picked up in Vegas, but then I noticed an inscription on the inside of the band that reads, *In this lifetime and the next,* with the initials *B* and *N*.

After I saw the engraving, I knew that the ring that now sits on my finger had once meant a lot to someone, and even if I had hated it at first, there was something beautiful about it now. I also understood why Kai hates that I have the ring. Before me, the ring was a representation of love, and now, it's the symbol of a lie.

"Are you ready?"

Without looking at him, I nod and unbuckle my seat belt, and once I'm out of the car, I look around. Kids are playing in the sand, building sand castles, or chasing each other near the water's edge. There are teenagers in small groups scattered along the sand, some sunbathing, others talking in groups, while the adults stand around chatting and laughing. I run my hands down my dress, feeling a little overdressed since a lot of the women are only in their swimsuits while the men are dressed similar to Kai.

"Ready?" Kai asks again when he reaches my side.

"Yep," I tell him with more certainty in my voice than I actually feel, shocked when he takes my hand. "What are you doing?" I ask, trying to pull my hand free from his grasp.

"Holding your hand," he replies, entwining our fingers.

"We're in public," I hiss.

His head dips, his sunglass-covered eyes meet mine, and his energy changes, beginning to beat against me. "What does that have to do with anything?"

I look at him like he's crazy and then around at the people on the beach. "All of these people can see us."

His frown grows deeper. Then he drops my hand, lifts his sunglasses to the top of his head once more, and turns his body so he's standing right in front of me.

"You're my wife."

"Pretend wife," I remind him quietly.

His eyes flash with something I haven't seen before and his jaw goes hard, making my breath catch.

His face dips and he whispers against my ear, "None of these people know that it's pretend."

It wouldn't be so bad if the effect he has on me was also pretend, but when he's touching me in any way, it's difficult to keep things separate.

I let out the breath I was holding and pull back so I can look into his eyes. "You're right," I acknowledge, hoping he will let me go.

He searches my face, and without another word or giving me any other option but to walk with him, he takes my hand, intertwines our fingers, and leads me towards a giant fire that is set up in the middle of the beach. As we approach the bonfire, I notice the men lifting their chins to Kai. He does the same in return. I also notice that the women we pass all devour him with their eyes before shooting daggers at me.

I'm so caught up in watching the people we pass that I don't notice that Kai has stopped until my hand is tugged. I turn my head to see what's holding him up.

"Kai!" a beautiful woman wearing a gold bikini yells, running up to us, looking like she just stepped out of an episode of Baywatch. Her hair is dark brown and down around her shoulders. Her body looks like she spends her days counting calories and working out. Even from just looking at her, I feel insecure.

As she nears us, a smile lights Kai's face up, and he drops my hand just in time to catch her as she throws herself into his arms. Jealousy like I have never felt before ignites in my stomach as I watch them embrace. She is the first to release him, but even then, his arm stays around her. I have never been one for violence, but the urge to rip his arm off and beat him with it causes me to fist my hands at my sides.

"Myla." Kai says my name and the woman's face lights up again.

She catches me off guard when she steps away from Kai and throws her arms around me. My hands go out to my sides, and I stand there awkwardly, not knowing what I should do.

"I'm so happy to finally meet you," the woman tells me as she releases me and steps back to stand near Kai.

"I—" I look at Kai when I have no idea what I should say or who this woman is.

"Meka," Kai says warningly, grabbing my hand again and pulling me closer to his side.

The woman looks up at him, and I realize she is not quite as old as I first thought she was. And she has the same lips and eyes as Kai.

"Myla, this runt here is my sister, Meka. Meka, my wife, Myla," Kai says, making me feel instantly nauseated.

I didn't realize I would be meeting his family, let alone meeting them as his wife. I can't imagine that this will be easy to explain or easy to undo when the time comes, and having other people involved will only make it that much more difficult.

"It's nice to meet you, Meka," I finally get out.

Another smile lights Meka's pretty face up as she looks at her brother then back at me and shakes her head. "You said she was pretty, but you didn't tell me *how* pretty," Meka says, making butterflies erupt in my stomach as Kai's fingers flex around my hand. She takes a step back then holds up her hands in front of her, forming a box with her fingers before squinting and closing one eye. "You guys look perfect together—her with all that blond hair and you with that long, womanly, dark hair." She giggles, and I cover my mouth when an unexpected laugh explodes from it.

"Don't encourage her," Kai grumbles from my side, but I can see the side of his mouth tip up slightly in a smile.

"Seriously, you guys look good together," she says as she looks at her brother, her eyes going soft.

"All right, kid, If you're done annoying me, tell me where Kale is."

"You're never any fun." She pouts, putting her hands on her hips.

"And you're always a brat," he tells her, but his tone is loving.

I have seen Kai be soft before, but I have never seen him the way he is with her.

"He was near the barbeque pit the last time I saw him." She shrugs then waves off in the distance when someone calls her name.

"Thanks, runt."

"Anything you want to know, Myla, you call me. I know all of his dirty secrets," Meka says, making me smile before she walks off towards the water.

"I might do that," I say under my breath as Kai begins walking again. "I didn't know I was going to meet your family," I tell Kai as my feet move double time to keep up with him through the thick sand.

"It's not a big deal." He shrugs.

I can feel myself frown at his words. I have no idea how he can say that it's not a big deal when, to me, it's huge.

"They know we're married. We're not staying married, so I think it *is* a big deal," I say, tugging his hand and forcing him to stop.

"Myla, I've told you from the beginning that I wouldn't let anything happen to you. I know what I'm doing."

"This isn't about you keeping me safe, Kai. This is about you lying to your family."

"My family knows me. They trust me to always make the right decisions. So, no, it won't be easy, but in the end, everyone will know I did what I had to do," he says adamantly.

"Why don't you just tell them the truth now? Be honest about it. That way, they're not surprised."

"I can't. If that information falls into the wrong hands, then this whole thing was for nothing. Our marriage needs to seem as real as possible. Only my closest men know the truth," he informs me.

"But it's your family. Don't you trust them?" I ask, feeling my eyebrows pull together in confusion.

"I do, but I also know they are not my employees. I can't kill them if they disobey me."

I feel my eyes widen and my mouth drop open with shock at his words.

"I'm kidding, Myla." He shakes his head.

I search his face, but he doesn't appear to be joking, and all of a sudden, I feel like Alice when she fell down the rabbit hole.

"All you need to know is you're safe. Trust me to keep you that way."

"Alrighty," I mutter, rolling my eyes.

"Are we done?" he asks impatiently, but I can tell that, if I wanted to talk, more he would put off whatever he needs to do and take some time to talk to me. I would be lying if I didn't admit that that makes my heart lighten towards him.

"Well, it's your soul, so sure." I shrug.

His lips twitch, and I notice a small scar that slices through the middle of his full bottom lip. I also notice how his lips look so smooth. I have never been one who really enjoyed kissing, but I could imagine myself really enjoying kissing him.

"Myla?" he rumbles.

My eyes lift to his, seeing that they have darkened. I swallow and take a step back, needing to put some space between us. He clears his throat and lifts his hand to the top of his head, pulling his sunglasses down over his eyes, and I immediately feel like I have been blocked out.

Without another word, he takes my hand again and begins to lead me across the beach. This time, his pace is slower, like he's more aware of me. As soon as we reach the bonfire, he pauses and begins to look around. I don't know who he's looking for, but my body is wound tight and the butterflies that erupted in my stomach earlier have not lessened. Plus, it's not helping that his thumb is continuously moving in circles over my skin, causing my awareness of him to never calm.

"Kale!" Kai shouts, and I follow the direction of his gaze.

My eyes land on a man with short hair who is almost as handsome as Kai. He's wearing a pair of swim trunks printed with large Hawaiian flowers on them. He starts towards us, his eyes locking on our entwined hands, and I can see trepidation in his gaze as he comes to stand in front of us.

"Mom and Dad are here," the guy named Kale says.

I feel my body freeze, and I begin to look around, trying to pick people who also could be related to Kai out of the crowd.

"I thought they weren't going to be home for another week," Kai mumbles, holding my hand a little tighter.

"Did you really believe you could call Mom with news that you got married and she wouldn't rush home to meet her new daughter?" The guy scoffs like Kai's an idiot, and I'm beginning to believe that that might be the case.

"They were in Australia," Kai says.

I twist my hand slightly to pinch his skin between my fingers as hard as I can, needing to get some of my frustration out. If I could knee him in the nuts without causing a scene, I would do it without a second thought.

"You got married," Kale repeats.

I stop pinching and begin digging my nails into Kai's palm. I'm so angry that I could spit fire. I can't believe he brought me here knowing his family would be here, and I really can't believe he at least didn't tell me that he'd told his family we got married.

"Where are they now?" Kai asks, forcing me to move in front of him, wrapping his arms around me, and causing me to become immobile.

I try to wiggle away, but Kale looks between us, frowning, so I instantly wrap my arms around Kai, making it look like we're embracing.

"I'm not sure," he mutters, looking around, and I do the same even though I have no idea what his mom and dad look like.

"Well, before they get here, let me introduce you to my wife," Kai says as I return my gaze to Kale.

"Nice to meet you," I tell him softly.

"You too," he grunts then glances behind us, a smirk appearing on his face. "Good luck. You're going to need it," he says, looking at Kai before disappearing.

I'm just about to open my mouth and yell at Kai about how giant of an idiot he is when I hear someone take a sharp inhale. I turn my head to look over my shoulder and see an older woman who's wearing a swimsuit with a sarong tied around her waist and a handsome older man wearing a linen shirt and shorts.

"Fuck," Kai groans under his breath while turning me in his arms and wrapping his hands around my waist.

"Zvezdochka," the woman whispers, looking at me. Then confusion fills her eyes as she looks at Kai.

"Mom, I would like you to meet Myla. Myla, my mother and father, Leia and Bane Jr."

Kai's mother's eyes travel from Kai to me then back again, and I can see hurt in her eyes, which I don't understand.

"Nice to meet you," I tell her, putting my hand out in front of me.

Her eyes drop to my hand then lift to meet mine again. "Bane?" she gasps quietly, looking from my hand to her husband.

I take my eyes off her and look at him just as he's pulling his eyes off me, but I still catch the look of sadness in his gaze.

"Kai?" I ask as his father tucks his wife into his chest when she begins to sob.

"My mom and yours were very good friends," he tells me softly in my ear, "and you look a lot like her, so I think it's just a shock for her to see you here."

"My mom?" I whisper back.

I don't have any pictures of my family. I remember my mom having long, blond hair, but that's all I can recall about her appearance. So thinking about the fact that I might have been seeing my mother every day when I looked in the mirror is shocking.

It takes a moment for Kai's mom to pull herself together, but when she does, her head turns towards me, and she takes a deep breath before stepping away from her husband and coming to stand in front of me. Her hand lifts and she cups my cheek as tears fill her eyes.

"I didn't know." She inhales and closes her eyes when her gaze meets mine again.

I'm confused by the look on her face until she speaks.

"Your mother would have been thrilled. We would joke often when you were young that you and Kai would get married. At the time, it was just wishful thinking, but seeing that her wish has come true, I know she is still watching over you." She whispers the last part, and I hate myself a little more.

I swallow over the sudden lump in my throat and notice that Kai's hands have tightened around me so much that I can feel every one of his muscles against my back. I try to speak, but there are no words to describe the emotions I'm feeling right now. I can't believe that his mother and mine were friends, and I can't believe he knew the kind of effect this situation would have on everyone yet still followed through with it. He never even gave me a choice in the matter, and I feel worse now than I ever did.

"You knew my parents?" is the first thing that comes out of my mouth, and then I feel horrible when silent tears begin to fall from her eyes.

"I did. *We* did. I thought…" She pauses and looks over her shoulder at her husband then brings her gaze back to me. "I believed you were dead. If I had known, I would ha—"

"Leia," Kai's father says, cutting her off, and comes to stand next to her. "Maxim didn't want that."

"But—" she tries to argue.

"No, love. It wouldn't have been safe," Bane says firmly, and Leia dips her chin then looks up at Kai through her long lashes.

"How did you know?" she asks him quietly.

I tilt my head back to look at Kai. His sunglasses are now sitting on top of his head again, his eyes focused on his mother.

"We always knew," Kai tells her.

I instantly wonder what else he could be keeping from me. I first believed he was doing this to help me, but a nagging feeling in the pit of my stomach is leading me to believe that this has more to do with him than me. I just can't figure out why.

"I know you have a lot of questions, but let's put them off for another time. Myla hasn't eaten."

"I'm fine," I tell him, hoping he will relent. I have a lot of questions of my own, and maybe his mom will be able to answer them for me.

"You need to eat," he tells me on a squeeze.

"He's right, honey. And we'll have plenty of time to talk when we're planning your real wedding."

At her words, the nausea I was feeling earlier comes back in full force, making it hard to breathe.

"That's not necessary," I wheeze out.

"Of course it is. I don't understand kids these days, all of you in such a hurry to get things done that you forget you need to remember the little moments. Don't get me wrong. I'm happy you have fallen in love with my son, but as a friend of your mother's, I know she would have wanted a big wedding, with you in a dress. I want to make that happen for her."

I nod because I can't say anything.

"We should find your sister. I know she will be excited to meet Myla," Kai's mom mutters, looking around.

"She met her earlier," Kai states, wrapping an arm around my shoulders.

Her eyes come back to us and go soft when she sees Kai press a kiss to the side of my head, which I stupidly feel all the way down to my toes.

"We're both glad you're here, Myla," Bane says, looking between Kai and me. "I'm sure we will be seeing a lot of each other."

"We will," I agree, and he puts his arm around his wife.

"I'm glad you're here, Myla. I will come over soon and visit with you," Leia promises.

"I would enjoy that very much," I tell her, feeling my face brighten.

Without thinking, I take a step towards her and give her a hug. When her arms close around me, I feel like she is somehow a link to my parents, and I will be able to find out whatever it is I need to know. That feeling alone is worth whatever messed-up crap is going to happen.

"Do you have any photos of my mom?" I quietly ask her when I pull away.

Her face goes soft again, and she gently slides her finger across my forehead, moving a piece of my hair. "I do. I'll bring them when I come visit you." She smiles slightly then looks at Kai. "Take care of her."

"You know I will," he tells her, and I can hear the sincerity in his tone. "Are you guys going to stick around for a while?"

"Yes. Your uncle Frank is here," his mom says.

Kai mutters, "great," under his breath.

"I heard that," she scolds then looks at me. "You'll like Frank." She smiles. "Your mom loved him. He's funny."

"NO ONE THINKS Frank is as funny as Frank thinks he is," Kai's dad says, shaking his head.

"He's funny," his mom tells me with a wink. "We will see you guys before we head home."

"Sure," I concur, watching them walk away. Once they are out of earshot, I turn in Kai's arms, get up on my tiptoes, and pull his head down so I can whisper in his ear, "You have a lot of explaining to do."

He leans his head back and looks down at me. His arms wrap around my waist, and he hauls me flush against him, making me inhale sharply at the feeling he ignites between my legs.

"You told me you would trust me."

"You keep making that task very difficult," I tell him honestly.

"Sometimes, the things that seem the most difficult end up being the most extraordinary," he tells me quietly, dipping his face and running his nose across mine.

My breath pauses as his lips barely skim mine. "Please stop," I murmur, dropping my forehead to his chest.

He is making it so difficult to separate real from fake, and I cannot let myself be pulled down any further than I already have been. Regardless of how much I want to get lost in this thing with him, I know I can't.

"Myla?"

"No, Kai, please. This is already hard enough."

"All right, *makamae*," he says gently, letting me go, but not before I can feel his arousal against my belly, which makes my stomach dip.

"What does *makamae* mean?" I question as he takes my hand again, making a tingling sensation shoot up my arm.

"One day, I'll tell you," he says, leading me through the sand back towards the fire pit.

"Why not now?"

"Now, you need to eat," he says, giving my hand a tug when my feet stop moving, because in front of me, on a table, is a pig that looks like it has been cooked whole. The outside is golden and glossy, and in its mouth is a bright-red apple.

"I'm not hungry," I tell him immediately.

I love meat; hell, I love bacon as much as the next person. But seeing a pig whole like the one sitting in front of me makes my stomach turn over.

"You need to try it."

"I can't," I whimper.

"I know you eat meat. I've *seen* you eat meat, including bacon."

"I know," I swallow as saliva fills my mouth.

"I'm going to make a plate for myself and one for you without the *kalua,* and if you feel like it, you can have some of mine," he tells me, which makes my body relax. I don't want anyone to think I'm being disrespectful of their culture, but I cannot imagine myself eating that.

After making our plates, he leads me a little ways down the beach, away from most of the crowd. He takes a seat in the sand, and I follow his lead, slipping my sandals off before sitting down next to him. Once I'm situated, he hands me my plate and I begin to eat, enjoying everything he chose for me.

"It's really beautiful," I say, looking out at the ocean.

"It is," he agrees.

I turn my head and see that he's not looking at the water, but at me, and there is a dark look in his eyes that makes my pulse speed up.

"Would you try something with me?"

"Like what?" I ask, turning slightly towards him.

"I want you to close your eyes and I'm going to feed you."

"Kai." I shake my head but then realize this might be the perfect opportunity for me to get some answers. "If I do this, then you have to do something for me," I tell him.

"Like?"

"Answer a question for me."

His expression closes off, and I can tell he is going to say no.

"One question, Kai," I plead, sitting up a little taller.

His eyes search my face, and then he nods, making me feel like I just accomplished a huge feat.

"Turn towards me and close your eyes," he orders, taking my plate.

I shift slightly and sit cross-legged in front of him. His eyes drop to my chest and then my legs, and I pull my dress down slightly so it lays over my thighs.

"Close your eyes."

The rough, deep tone of his voice makes the butterflies erupt once more, and my pulse pick up. I bite my lip and close my eyes, feeling the intimacy of the moment wrapping around me.

When I hear a low growl from him, my eyes fly open and I see that his are locked on my mouth.

"Close your eyes."

I do and inhale sharply when I feel the touch from one of his fingers on my bottom lip.

"Open," he says, pulling down slightly on my chin.

My lips part, there is a cold, sweet taste on my tongue, and the flavor of ripe pineapple fills my mouth.

"Do you like it?" he asks, and I nod.

I have always enjoyed pineapple, but since coming to Hawaii, I have found out that it's nothing like what I used to buy at the store back home. Here, it's sweeter, and there are times when I swear I can taste the sun when I take a bite of it.

"Open again," he tells me as soon as I swallow.

I do, and this time, the taste of ginger and chicken hits my taste buds. I chew slowly, enjoying the texture.

"Do you like that?" he asks.

"Yes," I whisper as soon as I swallow.

"Again," he instructs, pulling down on my bottom lip.

My lips part, and the taste of smoked meat fills my mouth. I block out what I saw and just enjoy the flavor.

"That is the taste of years of tradition. Men are taught at a young age how to properly prepare and cook the *Kalua* pig."

I feel his finger on my bottom lip again, and my eyes open. I look at him and suck in a breath. His face is inches from mine and his dark eyes are on my mouth.

"I'm going to kiss you."

I can't say anything. I can't even breathe. His lips brush lightly over mine at first. I turn my head slightly, not wanting it to be over, and he groans as his hand tangles into the hair at the side of my head, making me gasp. Then I feel his tongue on my bottom lip, and I open my mouth, losing myself in his taste and smell. He pushes me back into the sand, his body lying half on me. His hand not in my hair holds on to my waist, his thumb close to the edge of my breast.

"Kai," I moan into his mouth as my hands find the hard, smooth skin of his back under his shirt. My nails dig in and my hips lift as he slides one of his large thighs between my legs.

"*TU Kai*," he groans when he pulls his mouth from mine and presses his forehead against my shoulder, ending what was one of the hottest make-out sessions of my life. "Ask your question," he says as his chest moves rapidly against mine.

My mind is in such a haze that it takes a moment to decipher what he said. My brain goes over all the questions I have to ask, trying to pinpoint one that will help me the most.

"Why are you doing this?" I whisper, not realizing I spoke out loud until his body stiffens and his face rises above mine.

"When you were little, I found you crying in your tree house. I wasn't very old then, but the moment I saw you with tears in your big, blue eyes, I knew you were something that needed to be protected." He looks above me and out into the water before bringing his gaze back to mine, pulling his hand out of my hair, and running it down my hairline. "I have always needed to protect you," he says softly.

I feel my world tilt once again. Without thinking, I lift my head and press my mouth to his. He groans, and his hand slides behind my back, pulling me deeper into his embrace. The sound of the ocean off in the distance and the feel of the warm sun on my exposed skin makes the moment feel even more surreal.

He slowly pulls away, placing one last kiss on my lips before lifting his head and looking down at me. There is something in his eyes now that I didn't notice earlier, but before I can read it, he looks away and sits up, pulling me along with him.

"I DON'T THINK we can eat that," I say, laughing when I see that our plates have been sprinkled with sand.

"I think we should head home," he says, ignoring my comment.

As I watch him stand, I suddenly feel awkward when he doesn't look at me. I get up, dust myself off, and then pick up my sandals and my plate, heading towards a trash can. I have no idea how he can create such a tornado of feelings inside me.

I don't like that he has the ability to make me melt with a kiss or become so mad that I swear I could spit fire. With him, I feel like he causes me to become two different people. And I don't even know if I like one of those people.

"Are you ready?" he asks when his hand takes mine as soon as I have dumped my plate into the garbage.

I look around and notice once again that people are watching us, so my stomach drops when I realize that, to him, this is probably all just a show.

"Sure." I shake my head and wish I had a pair of sunglasses so I could block him out. I know that, if he were to look into my eyes, he would see much more than I want him to.

Chapter 4

Popcorn

"**H**OW LONG ARE you going to pout for?" Aye asks.

I look over at him and glare. It's been a week since I went with Kai to the beach and met his family. One would think that things would have been different after our awkward moment, but they haven't.

The man confuses the hell out of me. One moment, he is kissing me senseless, and the next, he is standoffish and making me feel like I had made a giant mistake. But then he's back to being his regular charming self while acting like he didn't rock my world.

"I'm not pouting," I sigh.

"Your bottom lip tells a different story. Now be a big girl and tell Daddy what's wrong," he says, taking a seat next to me on one of the oversized loungers as I fight back the smile threatening to take over my face.

"Please stop referring to yourself as Daddy," I say, but I end up laughing at the end, which makes him smile.

"Please stop telling my wife to call you Daddy," Kai growls, walking up behind us, which makes me jump.

"Yes, sir," Aye says, standing quickly as I tilt my head back and put my hand above my eyes to block the sun so I can look at Kai.

"Are you still upset?" he asks then looks at Aye and flicks his head in a sign for him to leave us.

"No," I tell him, watching Aye go, even though I still feel a small amount of anger over the news he gave me this morning.

"It's for the best," Kai assures me.

"Is it?" I ask, tilting my head when he comes over to sit down at my side.

"Yes. Your mother and father have been worried, Myla."

"So *you*"—I press my finger into his chest—"took it upon yourself to tell them that I ran off and got married, and then you paid for their plane tickets to come visit. So now, not only am I forced to lie to *your* family, but I have to lie to the people who raised me since I can remember. Not to mention, their son is Thad, so you have just told him where I am," I say, trying to keep the fear over the last part out of my voice.

"Thad won't get near you," he growls, grabbing my thigh.

"Okay, Kai. You know everything." I shake my head and look out at the ocean, trying to ignore the feelings his hand on my skin is giving me.

"It's a few days, Myla," he says gently.

"It's a few days of lying to their faces," I clarify. "How are we going to explain sleeping in separate rooms?" I question, raising a brow at him.

"We'll be sleeping in the same room while they're here." He shrugs like it's no big deal.

"What?" I whisper, feeling the color drain out of my face. It's difficult enough seeing him every day. I have no idea how I will deal with him sleeping in the same room as me, let alone the same bed.

"It will be fine. You'll see."

"You're delusional," I breathe.

"Pardon?" he asks, taking on the same tone I hear from him when he's speaking to his men.

I gather some much-needed courage and look him dead in the eyes before repeating myself more slowly. "I said you're delusional. You actually believe this is going to turn out okay, when I know that it won't. Haven't you ever watched a movie before? There is always some huge lie that is being kept hidden, and in the end, the truth comes out." I suck in a breath. "I don't want to be there when this hole caves in."

"The difference is this isn't a movie, Myla, and I know what I'm doing."

"If you say so." I shake my head again and pull my eyes from him.

When we were just lying to ourselves, I was able handle all of this, but now that we have gotten people we both care about involved, I know that this is going to be something I end up regretting. I just hope I don't regret it for the rest of my life or that my choice doesn't have a negative effect on the people who are innocent in this whole thing.

"Your mom misses you," Kai says, breaking into my thoughts.

"I know, and I miss her too, Kai, but this isn't the time or place for a family reunion."

"You need to learn to trust me."

"And you need to learn to talk to me before taking it upon yourself to just do stuff you have no right to do," I argue.

"You're right," he says, and I'm completely taken aback by his words and the fact he just agreed with me. "You're right, but I'm also right."

I let out a defeated breath, realizing once again that he just doesn't get it.

"So much for that," I think and don't realize I've said it out loud until I see his lip twitch.

"It will all work out."

"You keep saying that, Kai, but you and I both know that your mother has built it up in her head that my mother's wish has come true. She is so happy that she has this relationship to reconnect her with her friend who is long gone that she is not going to be very understanding about the fact we have lied to her and everyone else."

His eyes search my face, and for the first time, I get the feeling that he finally understands what I have been saying all along.

"So we try to make this into a real relationship."

My lungs freeze and my mouth goes dry as I sit there in stunned silence, looking at him and trying to think of a way to come back from that.

After a moment, I sit up in the lounger. "Are you insane?" I screech.

"You're attracted to me," he states.

"I...I'm attra—attracted to you?" I stutter out.

"And I'm attracted to you," he says as his eyes travel over my body, and I feel my nipples pucker against the thin material of my bikini.

"Be serious." I cross my arms over my chest.

"I'm being very serious."

"It won't work," I argue.

"Why won't it? Every relationship starts with attraction. You're attracted to me, and I'm attracted to you."

"Stop telling me that I'm attracted to you," I growl, trying to stand up, but before I can, I'm down in the lounger and Kai is leaning over me with his face inches from mine.

"Why not try, Myla?"

"Because it's a very, very dumb idea, Kai." I roll my eyes.

"We don't even have to have sex until you're ready," he says, ignoring what I just said and moving his face closer to mine. "Let's try it while your family is in town. After they leave, we will reevaluate everything and then decide if we want to keep moving forward in our relationship."

"I can't believe I'm even considering this," I say.

A small smile appears on his face right before he lowers his head and takes my mouth in a kiss so hot that I feel it all the way to my toes. When he pulls his mouth from mine, his lips go to my forehead, my nose, then my chin. I'm surprised by the sudden feeling that ignites in my chest from his soft show of affection.

"We need to have a first date," he tells me, and I don't even try to fight back my smile this time. "What?" he questions as his eyebrows pull together.

"I get to pick our first date," I tell him and then bite my lip when his eyes narrow.

"All right, Myla. You get to pick the first date," he agrees.

I can tell he is trying to figure out what I'm up to, and it takes everything in me not to smile or tell him that he's in for it.

"In the meantime, would you like to watch a movie?" he asks, catching me off guard.

"I…" I pause and search his face before lowering my voice and asking, "A movie?" Aye, Pika, and I watch movies often, but Kai has never even *asked* to watch one with us. And he honestly seems annoyed when he finds us all lazing on the couch together.

"It's Saturday. There isn't much going on, and I don't need to work, so uh—"

"Okay," I agree, cutting him off, seeing how uncomfortable he is with asking me, "but I get to pick."

"No!" He shakes his head. "I'm not watching a chick flick."

"I never said anything about watching a chick flick. I said I get to choose the movie."

"Nope. I'm picking," he says firmly.

I roll my eyes and hop off the lounger before he can stop me again. I look over my shoulder when I notice he's not following me. "Are you coming?"

"Yep," he mutters with his eyes glued to the waist of my bikini.

"What's wrong?" I ask, looking down to where his eyes are locked.

"Your color is changing," he says, his eyes traveling up my body, making me feel like I'm not wearing anything.

"I've been using sunscreen," I tell him when the look in his eyes doesn't change.

"I can see that," he says so quietly that I almost don't hear him.

I'm just about to ask him what his problem is, but then his hand goes to my waist and he pulls the side of my bikini down.

"What are you doing?" I ask, stepping away from his touch.

"Your tan lines…" He shakes his head like he's coming out of some kind of trance.

"What?" I ask confused.

"Nothing. Are you ready?"

"Sure." I bite my lip and walk into the house in front of him. The whole way, I swear I can feel his eyes roaming over my exposed skin. "I'll be right back," I mumble, running up the stairs and into my room, where I quickly grab an oversized shirt and slip it on before I run back down to the movie lounge. "What did you pick?" I ask, plopping myself down onto one of the overstuffed sofas.

"You'll see." He smiles at me over his shoulder, and that image alone is enough to make me want to go to him and kiss the smile off his face.

For a man who doesn't smile often, when he does, it's always stunning. It astounds me that someone who gives off the energy of a person you wouldn't want to cross is the same man you would pray to spend a moment with just to see if you could get him to smile at you.

"Myla?"

"Hmm?" I ask.

"I asked if you would like something to drink?"

I feel my face heat up, realizing I was staring at him, and know that I need a moment to gather my wits before sitting alone with him in a quiet room. "Oh, I can get it." I hop up off the couch and make it to the edge of the movie room before turning around and asking, "Would you like something?"

"A beer." He smiles and I feel my already-hot skin become even hotter.

"Got it. Beer," I say under my breath, quickly going to the kitchen.

By the time I make it back to the movie room, it has been a good fifteen minutes. I got drinks, made some popcorn, and dug around in the cupboards until I found some gummies and chocolate. I was killing time, but I knew that, if I was going to be around him, I would need to have provisions that would keep my mouth and my hands full while I was in such close proximity to Kai.

"So, what did you pick?" I ask him again before grabbing a handful of popcorn and shoving it into my mouth.

"You'll see," he says once more, coming to sit down right next to me.

I try not to look at him, but I can't help it. I swear my eyes have a mind of their own. When I turn my head, he has what looks like an iPad in his hands and is pressing the screen.

I study him for a moment when I know he is completely caught up in what he's doing. His hair is tied back like it usually is, and his jaw is locked in concentration. The slight bump in the center of his nose is more pronounced with the downward tilt of his chin. My eyes lock on his lips, and even from his profile, they look full and completely kissable.

"You're staring at me."

"Am not," I tell him, putting popcorn into my mouth while turning my face towards the TV.

"I told you you're attracted to me," he mutters.

"Whatever." I smile then look over at him when I feel his eyes on me. "What?"

"Nothing." He grins, making my belly dip.

"So, what are you torturing me with?" I ask.

His eyes heat at my words, which makes me squirm in my seat. Without answering, he presses another button. Then the TV lights up and Die Hard begins to play.

"Oh my God! I love this movie," I beam at him, and his hand comes up, his finger running over my lips before he drops his hand and turns to face the television again.

I inhale a deep breath, letting it out slowly before turning back to face the screen. We spend the rest of the day watching movies and relaxing, and by the time we're both ready for bed, I have found something out about Kai that I never expected: he is definitely someone I can see myself falling head-over-heels in love with.

I also realized that, with him, it would never be as easy as just love. Love seems too simple of an emotion to describe what I'd feel for him if I allowed myself to go there.

Chapter 5

Swimming with the Sharks

"**A**RE YOU SURE about this?"

No, I'm not sure now that we're out in the middle of the ocean, but there's no way I'm backing out. When I woke up this morning, I was surprised to find Kai sitting on the side of the bed, watching me. I was even more surprised when he told me that we were going to have to have our date today because my parents would be here in two days and he wouldn't have much time to get away during the week.

Although I'm excited to see my parents, I still have a fair amount of anxiety about their visit. Even if Kai and I are going to be seeing where this thing goes, I have no idea how it will play out with two people who know me having a front-row seat at the start of our relationship.

I look from the ocean, where a cage has just been placed into the water, to Kai and give him a shaky nod. When I was around ten, I watched Jaws for the first time and instantly became obsessed with the ocean and all the creatures that live in it. One of the things I loved the most about the ocean was sharks, and I promised myself that, if I ever got the chance, I would go swimming with them.

This plan always seemed like a good idea. That was before I was sitting on a large boat, wearing a diving suit, getting ready to be lowered into the ocean in a cage, where fish blood and body parts will be tossed into the water with me, at which time I'll come face-to-face with one of the world's greatest predators.

"I promise you will love it," he tells me, grabbing my hand, running his fingers over my skin.

"I want to do it." I swallow thickly.

When I told Kai what my plan for our first date was, his face lit up and he looked like I had given him some kind of gift. He told me that shark diving is one of his favorite things to do, next to surfing. He said that he doesn't get to go often but his friend would be willing to take us out on his boat. I can't believe how fast everything happened. It felt like all I had done was snapped my fingers, and then I was on a boat, wearing a wetsuit.

"Do you remember what to do once we're in the cage?" he asks.

I nod again, my voice seeming to be lost. Luckily for me, I took diving lessons a couple of years ago, and when Kai and his friend went over everything with me and asked me questions, I still knew all the right answers and what to do in case of an emergency.

"All right. Let's get the rest of your gear on, *makamae*."

He takes my hand and leads me to the ledge, where I don the breathing mask and the rest of my gear. After Kai gets me ready and has checked me over at least three times, he quickly puts on his own, gives a thumbs-up, and then signals me to place the breathing apparatus in my mouth. I do and immediately feel the flow of air that will allow me to breathe underwater.

As soon as I'm set, Kai pulls me over to the side of the boat, where a set of stairs leads into the water and down into the cage. He goes ahead of me and waits at the bottom of the steps for me to follow him down. When I reach the step that has half my body in the water, I become fully aware he is there, his body caging me in. His hand gives my waist a squeeze of reassurance before he submerges himself fully into the water.

I follow him under and am instantly stunned by the serenity. The ocean is so blue from above, and the water is so clear from below that I swear I can see for miles. The silence is like nothing I have ever known. The only sound I can hear is the noise coming from my own concentrated breathing.

I spin around slowly and come faceto-face with Kai, who points to his eyes then up to the top of the water. Suddenly, the water turns red and there are specks of white, which I know are fish particles filling the area surrounding us. Even though I know what's coming, I'm still in awe when small fish swim near the cage and begin to eat up the smaller pieces of chum.

As I watch them, I realize they are almost moving in slow motion up until the moment their mouths open, and then they move suddenly, snatching up the food they were after. I don't know how long it takes— it could have been minutes or maybe even hours—but Kai taps me on my shoulder. When I look over at him, he's pointing to the far end of the cage, where there is a large, black mass heading towards us. I grab Kai's hand and try to keep my breathing even as the fuzzy image clears up and the black mass becomes a large shark. I know right away that it's a tiger shark, one of the deadliest animals on Earth.

I grab Kai's hand tighter as the shark swims around the cage a couple of times. The moment seems almost suspended in time, but before I have even really had a second to appreciate the beauty of the magnificent creature in front of me, he's gone. We float around the cage for a few more minutes, but when Kai taps his wrist, I know that it's time to head up.

Once we reach the surface, Kai's friend helps me onto the boat and begins getting my gear off me. When my mask is off, I take a deep breath of the salty ocean air and look around for Kai. When our gazes connect, I try to convey with my eyes how much this moment means to me. It's not every day you get to live out one of your childhood dreams, and I couldn't be more thankful that he is the one who gave this to me.

I finish getting everything off and put away while trying to understand the feeling I have in my chest. It's not until Kai comes over and drags me from where I was sitting to a large couch at the back of the boat when I realize what it is: *Happiness.*

I have always considered myself a happy person, but I didn't know that, deep down, I really wasn't, and since the moment I arrived in Hawaii, I have been truly happy. I miss my shop and my girls, but to me, I was just getting by before. And now that my life has evolved, I've been forced to do something I never would have done before, and I've left what I'd thought of as the security of my home, I'm finally, really, and truly happy. With that thought, I curl into Kai's side, lay my head on his chest, and drift off to sleep with the smell of the ocean and the rocking of the boat lulling me into dreamland.

I WAKE UP and attempt to roll over, only to find myself tethered to the bed by an arm over my waist and muscular, hairy legs tangled with mine. And then I remember that my parents are in Hawaii, sleeping a few doors down from our room.

"Go back to sleep," Kai rumbles against my neck, causing goose bumps to break out all over my body.

"I thought you were going to stay on your side of the bed?" I whisper, rubbing my legs together, which have suddenly become restless.

"It got cold. I needed your body heat to stay warm."

I smile at his reply and turn in his arms to face him, noticing that it is much colder in the room than it normally is. As soon as I'm facing him, he wraps an arm back around my waist, places his hip over mine, and begins to play with my hair. It has gotten easier over the last couple days to be this close to him, and if I'm honest with myself, I have come to crave his touch and presence. He's like a drug I know is bad for me but can't help wanting more of.

After a moment of enjoying the ease of the moment, I tilt my head back and ask, "Do you think it will be weird today, having my mom and dad and your parents here?"

His gaze travels from the piece of hair he's playing with to mine, and then he looks over my head before replying, "No. My mom and I talked. She won't even be bringing up the fact she knew your mother." He tucks my face under his chin, forcing me to inhale a lungful of his scent.

"I still think it's going to be awkward."

"I'll be with you for most of the day. I have to leave for a couple of hours around noon, but after that, I'm all yours," he tells me, and I ignore the feeling I get from him telling me that he's mine and pull my face out of his chest so I can look up at him.

"You know, if your mom brings up planning a wedding while my mom is here, we're completely screwed," I sigh.

"If that happens, we will deal with it when the time comes."

"You act like it's not a big deal, Kai. It was bad enough that I got married once and it wasn't real. I don't want to do it again, only this time wearing a white dress and doing it in front of my parents."

"Don't worry about that right now. Just enjoy the time you have with your parents while they are here," he encourages.

I bite the inside of my cheek to keep from saying more. It seems like, no matter what I say, he's not understanding that *that,* for me, is way more than I can handle right now. I have never been a good liar, and it's not something I want to become good at.

"We should probably get up." I pull away, take the blanket off, and shiver when the cold air hits my skin. "Did you turn on an air conditioner?"

I look over my shoulder, and though his back is to me, I hear him mutter, "No," under his breath as he stands. I try to pull my eyes away from him, but seeing the muscles of his back flex when he raises his arms above his head keeps my eyes in place.

"Do you need to shower?" he asks, smiling when he catches me staring at him.

"I do." *A cold one,* I think but don't add as I stand and go to the bathroom.

I shut the door, go to the sink, get my toothbrush, and see that Kai's toothbrush is next to mine in the holder. I ignore the feeling that gives me, squeeze some toothpaste onto the toothbrush, and brush my teeth before going over to the shower.

"What are you doing?" I ask him as he walks into the bathroom just as I'm turning the water for the shower on.

He ignores my question, walks over to the sink, and begins to load his toothbrush up with toothpaste.

"I'm going to shower," I say, looking at him through the mirror and frowning when he begins to brush his teeth. "Do you need to do that right this moment?"

Our eyes connect and he pulls the toothbrush from his mouth. "Feel free to get in," he tells me, and I can hear the challenge in his voice.

Something in me snaps, and I pull off the pair of panties I have on then rip my nightshirt over my head and get into the shower, keeping my back to him.

The glass doors are mostly fogged, but I know he can still see me. I honestly can't believe I did something so ballsy, but I feel like he is constantly pushing me, maybe even testing me. I peek over my shoulder and find his gaze locked on me through the mirror.

My nipples harden and I feel my pussy contract from the look in his eyes. I start to think I'm an idiot when all he does is stare, but when his body turns to face me, he starts to take a step in my direction. Instead, he stops and shakes his head, adjusting the bulge in his pants and then leaving the bathroom, shutting the door behind him. I let out the breath that was locked in my chest and turn the water temperature to cold for a moment, needing to cool down before switching it back to warm, quickly washing up, and getting out.

By the time I make it into the bedroom, Kai is gone, but the scent of his cologne is still lingering in the air. I put on a pair of navy-blue shorts that fold at the hem and a white, linen button-down shirt over my navy-blue bikini before toeing on a pair of white flip-flops that have rhine-stone studs across the straps and putting my hair into a quick braid. Then I leave the room.

"Hey, Pika," I say when I open the door to our room and find him leaning against the wall across the hall.

"Kai asked me to take you to the dining room."

I nod and begin to follow him down the hall. Things have gotten a little easier between Pika and me, but I still hate the look of pity I sometimes see on his face when he's looking at me. I guess it helps that he doesn't talk much, and honestly, half the time, I forget he is even around.

"Did you have a good night off?" I ask, trying to fill the silence between us.

His eyes come to me over his shoulder, and he shrugs. "Didn't do much," he grumbles then turns around and continues walking.

"Sounds like fun," I mutter then bite the inside of my cheek, wondering why the hell I said that.

Normally, Aye is with us, so it's easier to deal with Pika and his cold demeanor. He seems like an all right guy—if you like the silent, broody type who would be more inclined to watch paint dry than to talk to you.

We walk the rest of the way in silence, and as soon as we make it just to the entrance of the dining room, I hear my mom ask if I'm coming and Kai tell her that I was getting out of the shower when he left the room. I duck my head and fight back a blush that is getting ready to take over my face, remembering what I did.

When we enter the dining room, I take in my mom, who is sitting next to the large open doors that lead out to a balcony. If you didn't know any better, you would think I'm her biological child. We have the same blond hair and blue eyes, and she is also tall and lean.

My dad is sitting at the table with a newspaper open in front of him. He shaved his hair off when I was fifteen and hasn't grown it back since. He is also tall, but his body is larger, and where he used to be fit, his body has started to go soft with age. His dark-brown eyes meet mine and he smiles, pushing back from the table and coming towards me.

"There's our girl," he says quietly, wrapping me up in a hug.

"Hey, Dad," I reply just as softly, wrapping my arms around his back while soaking in one of his wonderful hugs—one of my favorite things in the world.

"You doin' okay this morning?"

"I am." I lean back and smile up at him.

His face goes soft, and he leans in and kisses my forehead.

"I can't get over how beautiful you have become," my mom whispers.

I turn towards her just as she engulfs me in a hug. Even though she said the same thing yesterday when we picked them up from the airport, my head soars from hearing her words. I hadn't realized just how much I missed them. They are the only parents I have ever known, and there was never a moment growing up that they didn't make me feel welcome and loved.

"I'm happy you're here," I whisper back honestly.

"You know, wherever you are in the world, if you needed me, honey, I would go through hell to make it to you."

A sob climbs up my throat. I know she is telling the truth, and that is why I have always tried to protect both my parents. The thought of something happening to them because of what their son has done has always made me fearful.

"Don't cry. We're here now." She holds me tighter then whispers in my ear, "Your husband looks like he's going to murder someone. I don't think he likes it when you cry."

I pull my face away from her chest, and my gaze collides with Kai's. "I'm okay." I wipe my face with a tissue my dad hands me.

Kai comes over to me and wraps an arm around my waist before kissing the side of my head. "I was telling your mom about our shark diving trip." He looks down at me and smiles.

"I told him about when you were little and you were fascinated with the ocean but how the closest you ever got to sea life was at the aquarium," Dad says.

"Dad used to tease me about him having to work more hours just to afford my obsession with the aquarium." I smile at the memory.

"I loved having that time with you," my dad says then looks at Kai. "My sons were always doing one sport or another, and life was always hectic. It was nice to spend a quiet afternoon once a month with a little girl who wanted nothing more than to sit in the observatory of the aquarium, watching the fish swim around."

"I loved that time with you too—just as much as I liked helping you in the bakery on Saturdays when I got older," I tell him.

"You were always a good kid." He looks at me with eyes full of sadness then takes my mom's hand. "I don't know what we did, but whatever it is, we're sorry. We tried to be good parents."

"Oh God," I choke out. "You didn't do anything," I get out around the lump in my throat. "You were amazing parents—the best. I just... I just..." I pause, not knowing what to say. There is no way to explain to them why I left home and never looked back without calling out their son, and I'm not willing to risk telling them what he did to me.

"I know there is much to talk about, but if we could put all of that off until another time, I would be grateful. Myla has been very stressed since we got married, and I really don't want my wife to spend the first few weeks of our marriage depressed," Kai says.

My face goes soft, and I lean deeper into his side.

"This should be a happy time for us, *makamae*," he adds, tilting his head down towards me.

I look up at him in wonder and know that this is one more reason why I could fall in love with him so easily. He has a way of reading me that no one has ever had before.

"I agree," my mom says quietly, and my eyes go to her. She is looking up at Kai with her eyes shining. "We have plenty of time to talk about everything. Let's just have a good time while we're here."

"Thanks, Mom," I whisper.

She smiles at me and reaches out to gently hold my cheek before dropping her hand to her side.

"I, for one, am starving," my dad chimes in, and the energy in the room becomes lighter.

Kai presses another kiss to the side of my head then leads me over to the table and pulls out a chair for me before taking a seat at my side.

"Thank you," I whisper, looking at him when the servers come in to take the breakfast orders.

"Any time."

He leans in and I tilt my head back without thinking, accepting his kiss. When our lips part, his eyes stay locked on mine and the look I have been trying to decipher appears on his face again before he turns away, not giving me a chance to figure it out.

"I'M GLAD YOU found a good man." My dad smiles at me as we walk down the beach.

After breakfast, we decided to take a walk while my mom went to lie out in the sun.

"You have always put everyone before you. I'm glad you found a man who makes sure you're taken care of."

"He's good to me," I say while taking in a lungful of ocean air.

"You can see it when he looks at you that he adores you."

"Really?" I question, then wonder if I should have said something different.

"When you picked us up at the airport yesterday, your mother and I paused the moment we saw you at the baggage claim. We were, quite frankly, in awe. Kai is...well, kind of intimidating."

"No, he's not." I shake my head. Kai is beautiful to me.

"He is, but he was looking at you with a softness in his eyes that I have only ever seen once before, and that was from you father when he looked at you or your mother," my dad whispers.

My head swings his way. I'm in shock because we have never, not even once, spoken about my father before.

"You were his star." He shakes his head before he looks out at the water and then back at me with a deep sadness in his eyes. "When he asked me to take you in, I knew how hard it was for him to do. Your mother and he loved you. You were the reason they were put on this Earth."

"I hate that I don't remember them," I say through tears.

"You do..." He pauses, takes my hand, and then places it over my heart. "In there, you remember them. They have always been with you, will always be with you."

"I know they loved me," I tell him after a moment, when I finally find my voice again.

"I know they did too," he says as his face softens.

"No, I know, because they gave you and Mom to me."

"Oh, Myla." He shakes his head and tugs me into a hug. "We miss our girl." I can hear tears in his voice, and it kills me that I have done this to him.

"I miss you guys too," I sob, wrapping my arms tighter around him.

"Let's make this the last time we wait so long between visits."

"Okay," I agree, holding on to him tighter.

We stay like this for a long moment. I have missed both of my parents, but my dad and I have always been close, so not having him in my life over the last few years has really hurt.

"Love you, Dad."

"Love you too." He pulls away then looks at my tear-stained face. "You need to stop crying before we get back to the house and your husband sees you."

"I'm done," I smile at him through watery eyes.

He wraps his arm around my shoulders, and we walk the rest of the way back to the house in silence. I feel like, over the last few weeks, I have been bombarded with things from my past—some good, and some bad. But I'm also grateful for the closure I'm getting from it.

Chapter 6

Tethered to Him

"**I** TOLD YOU the moment we got them together it was going to be bad," I growl at Kai, who has the nerve to smile at me.

After my dad and I got back from our walk on the beach, Kai's mom showed up and instantly began talking to my mom about weddings and how she believes we should have another ceremony where everyone can come to witness us exchange vows. Then my mother started telling her that they would only be able to stay until the weekend but she would love to have some kind of celebration before she went home. So now, my mother and Kai's have just told us what is going on and how we will be having a party with over one hundred and fifty people.

He shrugs. "It's just a party."

"Did you hear them?" I practically shout. "They said a hundred and fifty people. A hundred and fifty people is more than a party. That's like...a concert or something."

His eyebrow rises, and he shakes his head. "What kind of concerts have you gone to?"

"That doesn't matter." I roll my eyes, completely exasperated.

"I know you don't want to do this, but look at how happy our mothers are right now. And it will be good for everyone to meet my wife. I should have done something as soon as we got home, but with everything that happened, I didn't want to put to much pressure on you."

"I don't need to meet everyone, Kai," I tell him, feeling nervous from even thinking about it. "We don't even know what we're doing. Things between us are still up in the air."

"Stop," he growls, turning to face me. "Every time you talk about us, you make it seem like we have an expiration date. We agreed to try to make this work, but in order for that to happen, both of us have to be involved. You can't have one foot out the door already, Myla."

I swallow, close my eyes, and drop my forehead to his chest, realizing that he's right. I agreed to see where things go with him, while at the same time, I have been counting on us coming to an end.

"You're right." I open my eyes and look up at him. "I'm sorry. You're right."

His hands come up, and he gently holds my face between his palms. "Let's worry about one thing at a time." He kisses me softly then leans back just enough so he can look me in the eye. "Let's give our mothers this party. I know it will mean a lot to both of them."

I nod and lean into his touch.

"I'll be with you all night." He kisses me again, but this time, before he can pull away, I nip his bottom lip.

He growls deep in his throat and his hand tangles in my hair, forcing my head to the side. My mouth opens under his, and the moment his tongue touches mine, I whimper. I have never been with someone like him, and as much as it scares me, I still want him more than I have wanted anything in a very long time. He slows the kiss and pulls away, resting his forehead against mine.

"You're right."

"I'm right?" he asks, surprised.

"Well, it would mean a lot to my mom to be involved, even if it is just a party."

"And us?" he questions.

I debate for a moment how to answer him before pressing my chest against his. "I know you don't think I'm giving us a chance, but I am. I have never been with someone like you before. You scare me."

"Myl—"

"Oh, honey, I'm so excited!" my mom says, interrupting Kai. "Do you think we should have a photographer?"

"I don't think that's necessary," I mumble, gaining a squeeze to my waist from Kai.

"I'm sure your brothers would love to see some pictures of you."

My body freezes and I feel the blood drain out of my face as Kai's arms band around me.

"You don't look so well. Are you okay, honey?" my mom asks.

I nod, not able to speak.

"She's had a long day. I'm going to get her to bed. Tomorrow is going to be another busy day," Kai says.

"Of course," Mom mutters, looking me over.

I give her a shaky smile and a quick hug before Kai leads me back towards our room. Once we're inside and I hear the door close behind us, I walk to the bed, sit down, and then kick my shoes off before pulling my feet up onto the bed and tucking myself into a ball.

"Do you know that Rory was once my best friend?" I ask Kai as I watch him slip his shirt off over his head then pull his pants off, leaving him only in his boxers, which shows off the tattoo on his right hip that disappears into his underwear, the bottom of the ink ending just above his knee. I wish I could see the full extent of the artwork and get up close to the very detailed work.

"Thad's brother?" he questions, pulling me out of my thoughts as he walks towards me, holding a shirt in his hand.

I nod as I watch the muscles in his stomach flex.

"Do you still keep in touch with him?" he asks.

I shake my head. "No. When I moved away from Nevada, I just left everything behind," I say, sitting up on the side of the bed.

When he mutters a quiet, "Up," his hands go to my stomach. Then he pulls my shirt off over my head and then quickly tugs the new one down. I reach behind my back and unhook my bra, pulling it off then out one of the sleeves of the shirt.

"Why did you run after graduation?" he questions.

I look up at him, and he searches my face. Part of me wonders how he could know about that, but I'm starting to understand that Kai knows a lot more than I could even begin to realize. And I wonder if his question now is more of a test than him just asking out of curiosity.

"I got accepted into culinary school," I say softly, watching disappointment flash in his eyes.

I quickly slip my shorts off, watching as he walks around the bed and gets in behind me. I don't know why, but I expect him to ignore me, to just turn his back to me and go to sleep, but instead, he comes to me, pulling me down with my back to his front. Then he slides one arm under my neck and wraps the other around my stomach.

"So, you guys were friends?" he asks softly after a moment.

I feel his breath on my neck, so I close my eyes for a moment, memorizing the feeling.

"We had all the same friends, and when we were home, it was like living with my best friend. I think it was harder leaving him behind more than anything else."

"Huh," he grunts, and a small thrill fills me that perhaps he's jealous, but I squash it immediately, knowing he would never be jealous.

"I got an engagement announcement from him about a year ago, and I sent a congratulations card back in return, but I just couldn't find it in myself to even pick up the phone to call him."

"Something must have happened to make you cut off all ties with the people you considered family."

"I think I was just trying to find my own way in the world," I lie, gaining a squeeze from him.

"I wish you would talk to me," he says quietly.

I turn to face him and bury my face in his chest, wishing I had the courage to share what happened to me with him.

"I'm so tired," I tell him instead, breathing him in.

"Sleep, *makamae*," he says, wrapping his arms tighter around me.

Even though I try to talk myself out of it, and even though I know it's a huge mistake, I fall asleep feeling safe and wanted.

Kai's face is between my legs, his large arms holding me in place, his hands holding mine against my thighs, making it impossible to touch him. I cry out in frustration as I feel my clit pulse in his mouth.

I wake up breathing heavily, and I remember the dream I was having. I was begging him to make love to me, but he just kept me on the edge. I go to get up and realize Kai's hand his cupping me over my panties, and I can feel the hard length of him against my back.

"Oh, God," I moan quietly, squeezing my eyes closed. I know that all I need is the smallest brush against my clit and I will explode. I go to move again and his fingers press in. "Kai," I whisper, unintentionally rolling my hips forward into his hand.

"*TU Kai,*" he rumbles, pressing into my back.

My hand goes to his thigh and my nails dig into his skin as his fingers slide my panties to the side and his middle finger circles my clit.

"Drenched," he growls against my neck as his finger does another circle.

My hand on his thigh goes behind my back and down into his boxers, my fingers attempting to circle his width without coming close. From the feel of him in my hand, I can imagine how large and beautiful he is. I slide down then up, and he growls, his teeth nipping my neck.

He feels like steel covered in smooth silk. My thumb runs over the tip, catching the bead of pre-cum before doing another downward stroke.

"*Makamae,*" he says, and without warning, two fingers swiftly enter me.

"Kai!" I cry out and turn my head over my shoulder in time for his mouth to capture mine in a kiss that takes my breath away.

His fingers move in sync with the hand I'm pumping him with. I pull my mouth from his and cry out again as his thumb rolls over my clit, causing the orgasm that had been building since I woke up to explode through my body.

I squeeze my eyes closed as my pussy convulses around his fingers, and his teeth take hold of the skin of my neck as my hand fills with cum from his release. After a moment, I begin to come back to myself, and I can feel my face turn red from embarrassment. I never expected that to happen. It normally takes a while for me to feel okay with any kind of intimacy, but as with everything about Kai, he brings it out of me so easily.

"I could go again," he says.

I feel that his cock is still semi-hard. I let him go when I realize he is still in my palm. He flips me over to my back, and his fingers sink deeper inside me, causing me to moan loudly as aftershocks from my orgasm fill my lower belly.

"You're my wife, Myla."

"I know." I squeeze my eyes closed.

"This is natural."

"I'm not ready for this," I say then feel the bed begin to shake. "Are you laughing?" I ask in disbelief, popping one eye open.

"YOU MIGHT NOT think you're ready, but you were begging me for it...even in your sleep."

"No," I whisper, feeling my eyes get big and my face turn even redder.

"I haven't come from a hand job since I was thirteen. I'm just as surprised by what happened as you are. But I don't regret it. I don't regret anything that has happened between us."

I feel my face go soft, and I lean up, pressing a kiss to his mouth. Then I moan down his throat as his fingers begin to slide in and out of me again. He pulls his mouth from mine then looks down into my eyes.

"This time, I want to see you when you come. I've imagined it a hundred times, but now, I will have the memory of the way you look, the way you smell, and the way you taste," he says, lowering his face to my stomach, and then his teeth pull my shirt up, exposing my breasts. "I think I'm obsessed with your tan lines," he says, licking my breast and making me whimper. "One day, I'm going to strip you down and trace every inch of them with my tongue and teeth."

His mouth moves to my other breast, and I feel him lick it as well, his mouth avoiding my nipple with each stroke of his tongue.

"Kai!" I cry, my fingers threading through his hair when his lips lock on to my nipple.

His tongue flicks over the tip as his fingers stroke into me harder and faster, his thumb zeroing in on my clit. My head digs back into the pillow. My eyes squeeze closed, but then they fly open when he demands, "Open your eyes."

When our gazes lock, I fall apart in his hands, my insides becoming liquid as another orgasm explodes through my body. My eyes stay locked on his as I float off before slowly coming back to myself.

"I now understand what beauty really looks like," he says, pulling his hand out of my panties and curling himself around me.

"Thank you," I whisper, and he pulls away so he can look at me.

"I will do that for you any time you ask."

I feel my lips twitch, and I'm just about to say something when there is a loud bang on the bedroom door.

"Kai!" a woman yells. "Let Myla up! I have strict orders to take her from you, even by force. I need to get her ready for the party tonight."

"You're going to have to come back," Kai grunts, rolling us over so that I'm sprawled out on top of him.

"I'm telling Mom!" she yells dramatically.

I begin to laugh then quickly gasp when one of his hands slides up under my shirt then down into my panties before it cups one cheek of my ass.

"I should get up," I say quietly, looking down at him.

His hand goes to the side of my face then slides around as his fingers circle the back of my neck. He tugs gently, forcing my mouth down to his. His teeth nip at my bottom lip. Then he soothes it with a swipe of his tongue.

"You should spend the day in bed with me," he says, causing a tingle to shoot right to my core.

"Myla, if you can hear me, I really need you to come out here," Meka yells, and I begin to laugh against Kai's mouth.

"I'll see you later," I tell him.

His hand gives my ass a squeeze as his hips lift. I feel the hard length of him against my belly before I'm rolled again and he's over me, his hair like a curtain, making the moment seem even more intimate. His face lowers and he takes my mouth in a deep kiss then quickly pulls away. Then he hops off the bed. His eyes look me over before he walks over to the dresser, grabs a pair of sweats, pulls them on, and then opens the door to the bedroom, where Meka comes flying in.

"Oh, thank God. I thought I was interrupting," she says, and I bite the inside of my cheek, because she is obviously oblivious.

"You did interrupt us," Kai growls then looks at me on the bed again, and I can see the silent promise in his eyes.

"Are you leaving?" she questions, ignoring his last comment, coming to the bed, and flopping down next to me.

Kai grunts at her then looks at me, and his eyes change, appearing softer. "I'll see you at the party."

"See you at the party," I reply softly.

His eyes stay locked on mine for a moment then travel to his sister. "Take care of my wife."

"Will do," she tells him on a whisper.

I watch him leave and don't pull my eyes from the door until Meka pats my leg.

"It's going to take some time to get used to him being in love," she says.

My gaze goes to her. "Pardon?"

"I have never seen him look at anyone the way he looks at you."

I stare at her, unsure of what to say and not wanting to get my hopes up. But the feeling I have had in my gut since the moment I met Kai is causing a warm feeling to spread throughout my body.

"Anyways, you already know he's in love with you." She smiles then jumps off the bed. "Okay, go shower, We have a lot to do."

I get off the bed, stumble to the bathroom, and shower quickly. When I come out, the room has not only Meka waiting, but also my mom, Kai's mother, and a large woman wearing a very bright floral dress that accentuates her dark skin and fuller figure.

"You're here! Let's get started."

I begin to take a step back from the woman when she starts towards me holding a bag in her hands.

"Come on, child. We don't have all day." She rolls her eyes.

I look at Kai's mom, but she just smiles.

"Marcy is going to get you dressed and make sure your dress fits you. She can size it while we go out and get your hair and makeup done."

"Um…I thought we were just doing a small get-together."

"We are, but there will be a photographer and I would like to have some pictures of you and Kai," my mom says, making me feel guilty.

I swallow down my own personal feelings and walk towards the woman. "Where would you like me?"

"Here is just fine." She stops in front of me, sizes me up, and then opens the garment bag, pulling out a white dress. "You're much smaller than he normally likes," she mutters to herself.

I shake off the feeling I get from her words and look at my mom.

"You're going to look beautiful." My mom smiles then begins talking to Kai's mom and sister.

Even though I'm in a room full of people, I feel alone. I close my eyes and wish that I were back in bed with Kai again.

"MAKAMAE."

I lift my head and my eyes crash with Kai's. His eyes run over my hair and body then land on my feet before meeting my gaze again. When I looked in the mirror after his sister and Marcy finished with me, I was shocked. I looked like a model—nothing like myself at all.

My long, blond hair had been highlighted, with caramel lowlights added in too, and blown out completely straight so that it hangs down to the middle of my back. My skin, which has gotten darker from the Hawaiian sun, now glows from the lotion they used.

The dress I have on shows off my figure and does this crazy lift to my breasts that makes them look like they are fake, and the heels I have on make my legs look a mile long. His eyes look me over again, and when they meet mine again, I can feel the heat in his eyes.

I inhale a deep breath and take him in for the first time. His hair is back and his jaw is shadowed, making him look even more warrior-like than he normally does. His hands flex at his sides, and I notice he's not wearing his typical suit, but a pair of light dress pants and a white button-down shirt with the top two buttons undone. His eyebrows pull together, and he walks towards me when he realizes I'm not coming to him.

"What's wrong?" he asks, stepping up to me.

"I… Well…" I pause and look behind him at the closed door. When I decided to do this earlier, it seemed like an okay idea, but now that I'm in the moment, I'm not so sure.

"If you don't want to go, we can get undressed, put in a movie, lock the door, and put Aye and Pika on guard," he says, looking concerned.

I feel that feeling in my gut expanding further, making me warm all over. "You would do that, wouldn't you?" I lean into him, place my hands on his chest, and look into his eyes.

"Of course."

I swallow and let the feeling coursing through me settle in before I start to lean back.

"Where are you going?" he questions, snaking one arm around me while his other hand cups my cheek and his thumb runs over my bottom lip.

"You'll mess up my lip gloss," I complain.

He smirks then lowers his mouth, kissing me wet and deep before pulling back slowly, leaving me panting.

"Now, what were you going to say?" He leans back, and my fingers go to his mouth, where I wipe my lip gloss off his lips.

"I…" I clear my throat, feeling nervous all of a sudden. "I have something for you," I say, taking a step back, needing to have a little space between us. "I just want you to know you can always say no or that it's stupid—"

"Myla," he cuts me off, pulling me closer. "What is it?"

I bite my lip and step away from him again. This time, I go over to the dresser and open the top drawer, pulling out the small, black box I placed there earlier.

I realized this morning that the ring Kai had given me tethered me to him. I had a constant reminder of him with me, and the more I thought about it, the more I wanted him to be tied to me in a way that could be seen by anyone who happened to be in his presence. I could lie and say that I wouldn't be disappointed if he told me he wouldn't wear the ring I was about to give to him, but I knew deep down that this was going to be one of the moments that defined us and where we were going.

I turn towards him, and his eyes drop to the box in my hand. When his gaze comes back to mine, his eyes are filled with confusion. When I'm finally standing in front of him, I hand the box to him and he opens the lid.

"It's okay if you don't wear it," I whisper, unsure of what to say because I can't read his face as he removes the ring from the confines of the box.

"Put it on me," he says, lifting his eyes to meet mine.

I take a deep breath then take the ring from him, feeling the ridges from the design and the weight of the heavy metal between my fingers as I take his hand and slide the ring onto his finger.

When the idea about getting Kai a ring came to me, I wasn't sure what I was going to do. I went to the jewelry store and was escorted to the gold wedding bands most men wear, but none of them seemed like Kai. I gave up and was leaving the store when I noticed a ring in one of the display cases that held some pieces of traditional Hawaiian jewelry. The large, silver band with a black design engraved into the metal looked like the tattoo on his arm, and I knew it was something I could see on him.

I'm so caught up in my own head that I don't realize I'm moving until the backs of my knees hit the bed and I'm lying down with Kai covering me.

"You bought me a ring," he growls.

I can't read the look on his face, so I just nod.

"Thank you," he whispers, kissing me on my lips then down my neck to the tops of my breasts.

"Kai," I whimper.

"Yes, *makamae?*" He licks back up to my mouth, kissing me again.

"The party," I whisper as I feel myself falling deeper into the moment.

"I'm going to make love to my wife," he grunts, causing moisture to flood my center.

"Okay," I whisper then hear him chuckle as his hands go to the back of my dress.

"Come out here *right now!*" is yelled as someone bangs on the bedroom door.

"Fuck!" he roars.

I hear giggling outside, and then Kai's soft eyes look down at me.

"After this, you're mine," he says quietly, placing a soft kiss on my jaw.

"Yes," I agree immediately.

He smiles, gently kisses me, gets off the bed, and then pulls me up with him.

"So, is the ring okay?" I ask him, looking at the ground, feeling unsure.

His fingers go to my chin and he lifts my face towards his. "It's perfect." He kisses me again then searches my face. "You're perfect."

I bite the inside of my cheek to avoid saying something stupid or pushing him back over to the bed. "I just need to fix my lip gloss," I tell him, and a smile appears on his face.

"It won't last long." He kisses me again, making me laugh.

"Good thing I have a whole tube of it," I say, stepping away from him and into the bathroom.

I hear the door to our room open and his sister come in, and I smile and look at myself in the mirror, seeing a look of almost-blinding happiness in my eyes.

"Ready?" Kai asks, walking into the bathroom after a moment.

"Yep." I smile as he takes my hand and leads me out of the room.

When we make it down to the party, I'm astounded by the number of people who have shown up. One hundred and fifty people sounds like a lot, but seeing that many people is overwhelming.

"We were wondering if you guys were going to show up," my dad says, walking up to us, carrying a glass of wine in one hand and a beer in the other.

"I don't think Mom would let me skip this even if I wanted to." I smile, taking the glass of wine he holds out to me. Then I give him a hug.

"You look beautiful, honey."

"Thanks, Dad," I whisper and then lean against Kai when he pulls me back into his side.

"Kai." My dad smiles, shakes Kai's hand, and then hands him the beer. "You're going to need that," my dad tells him.

Kai's lips tilt up as he mutters, "Thanks."

"I'm going to go find your mom. I'll see you soon," Dad says and walks off into the crowd.

I take a sip of wine and look around then up at Kai. "It's going to be a long night."

"Tell me about it," he mumbles as his eyes drop to my breasts.

I can't help the laugh that escapes, and I lean up to kiss his cheek. It doesn't take long after that for everyone to notice that we have arrived, and they begin to come up and offer congratulations to us. It feels like we stand in the same spot forever, only having a moment's break when my mom brings the photographer over to snap a few pictures of us. When I notice a lull in the crowd and see that Kai is caught up talking with a group of people I don't know, I tell that I'll be back and make a quick escape to the bathroom. Inside the house, there are people everywhere, and there are long lines at both the bathrooms, so I make my way to our bedroom and quickly use the restroom there then head back outside.

"Would you like a glass of wine?" one of the servers asks, stepping in front of me.

I debate for a moment then decide yes and take the glass from his tray, giving him a quiet thank-you before I take a sip. I start back towards Kai then detour when I spot his mom, waiting until she is done talking to the person in front of her before telling her quietly, "Thank you for doing this for us."

She turns to face me and her eyes go soft as she runs her down my cheek. "I should be thanking you. As a mom, you always want what's best for your kids, and I've been worried for a few years that Kai was not going to find someone worthy of him. I'm glad he found you," she whispers, and I feel tears begin to fill my eyes. "No crying," she chides, leaning forward and giving me a hug while accidently knocking the drink out of my hand.

"It's fine." I smile as she apologizes.

"Thank God I didn't spill that on your dress." she mumbles, picking up the plastic glass and handing it to a passing waiter. "You go find your husband while I go and get you another glass of wine."

"Maybe that was a sign that I shouldn't have any more wine," I laugh, and her face goes soft again.

"You remind me so much of her," she says faintly then looks around.

I know this is making her uncomfortable, but I still have a lot of questions to ask her about my parents. Just…now isn't the time or the place.

"I'm going to go find Kai, but I would like for us to have lunch when my mom leaves. If that's okay?" I question, placing a hand on my stomach when it begins to turn.

"I would enjoy that. We'll work out the details later. Just go enjoy your night."

"Thank you."

She smiles then walks off as a wave of dizziness hits me. I brush it off and take a deep breath then head towards Kai.

When I reach his side, his eyes come to me and a small smile lights his face before he leans down and presses a kiss to my lips.

"Missed you," he mutters against my mouth.

As I start to reply, I feel like I might faint.

"What's wrong?"

I look up into his blurry face and everything tilts as I fall against his chest.

"What the fuck?" he growls, and I feel myself being lifted then carried.

I hear commotion going on around me, and I want to ask what happened, but everything goes black.

THE SOUND OF beeping off in the distance begins to grate on my nerves. When I finally get one eye open, I can tell I'm in Kai's and my room.

"Turn off the alarm," I croak, and my hand goes to my throat when I feel it burn. I try to sit up, and suddenly, strong arms are stopping me.

"Easy," Kai's rough voice commands.

I look at him, and there are dark circles under his eyes and he looks like he hasn't slept in days. My mind reels as I try to remember anything at all.

"What happened?" I ask as he helps me sit back against the headboard before reaching across me and grabbing a glass of water from the bedside table. When I lift my hands to take the glass from him, I notice an IV.

I look at Kai and try to understand what's going on, and he just shakes his head and lifts the cup closer to my mouth. I feel tears sting my nose as I take the glass from him and hold it between my shaky hands. I slowly take a sip of water and look around the room. Everything looks the same, except there is now an IV stand and a large machine next to the bed, which I instantly recognize as where the beeping is coming from.

"I'm sorry," Kai says, and my gaze goes back to him.

"What happened?" I repeat through the pain in my throat.

"You were poisoned." He rubs the back of his neck. "It was a small amount, but still enough to make you very sick."

"Oh, God," I breathe.

"They pumped your stomach. That's why your throat is so sore. The doctor assured me it would get better after a few days."

"How?" I whisper, still in shock.

"Mom said you had a glass of wine at the party, and it wasn't one that anyone recalls giving you." He rubs the bridge of his nose. "She said she accidently knocked it out of your hand when it was still full."

"I had a sip."

"That's what we figured. Do you remember anything about the waiter who gave it to you?"

"No." I shake my head, not recalling anything about him. "There were so many people there."

"I know." He sounds angry as he shakes his head.

"Are you okay?" I whisper when he doesn't look at me.

"Fine. Just glad you're awake." He leans in and places a kiss on my cheek. "Why don't you lie back down and I'll get your parents."

"My parents?" I ask.

"They've been worried they wouldn't get to see you awake before they left, and I wanted to be able to talk to you, tell you what was going on before you had visitors," he mutters, and I can tell from his demeanor and tone that he is exhausted.

"You should lie down here with me. You look tired. They can wait a little longer," I tell him, not liking the feeling in the pit of my stomach.

He shakes his head and takes the water from my hand, setting it on the table next to me before helping me lie back down.

"Kai," I whisper, noticing he's avoiding looking at me.

His eyes come to mine and I see pain flash through them before it disappears, when his face lowers and he mutters, "I'm sorry," against my mouth. He rests his forehead against mine for a moment. Then he gets up and leaves the room without looking back.

I watch him go, and tears fill my eyes because I know that was the end of us.

"Oh, honey, don't cry," my mom says when she finds me curled into a ball on my side, tears dripping onto the pillow, a few minutes later. She pushes my hair away from my face then hands me a tissue. "We're so relieved you're okay."

"Just a bad case of food poisoning." I spit out yet another lie, knowing there is no way I can possibly tell my parents that someone tried to kill me.

"Good thing your husband thinks fast on his toes," Dad says.

I tilt my head back to meet his eyes then nod in agreement.

"Do you feel okay?" Mom questions, looking at the machine next to the bed.

"Tired but fine," I assure her.

"We're glad you woke up before we left."

"You're leaving?"

"We wish we could stay, but the bakery's been busy and we don't have a lot of help right now," my dad mutters, looking guilty.

"Of course," I whisper, taking his hand. "I'll come see you guys soon," I promise him and actually mean it.

"Maybe we will be back before that. Perhaps for a baby shower." My mom smiles, and new tears begin to sting my nose, but I fight them back. "We love you, honey."

"Love you too, Mom," I whisper as a lump of emotion clogs my throat.

She moves out of the way, and my dad takes her place, leaning down and kissing my forehead.

"Remember you always have a safe place to fall," he tells me before kissing my forehead again and standing to his full height.

"We'll call as soon as we land in Nevada. Just make sure you rest and that your husband does as well."

"I will, Mom," I reply and then kiss her cheek when she leans down to give me another hug.

"Bye, honey," my dad says as he takes my mom's hand, and they leave the room.

I stare at the closed door for a moment before turning onto my side and carefully pulling the covers up over my shoulder.

I WAKE UP and the room is dark, but I feel the weight of Kai's arm around me and his warmth at my back, so I push myself deeper into him. He tightens his hold on me as he whispers something I can't understand. I try to pull myself out of my sleep-ridden state enough to ask what it means, but exhaustion takes me away before I ever get the chance.

I WAKE UP with the sun shining on me and the bed behind me completely cold. I lift my hand, and the IV that was there is gone, along with the machines. I roll over and look at the clock—it's after two in the afternoon. I almost think that yesterday was a bad dream, but then my eyes land on a folded piece of paper on the pillow next to me. I scoot up in bed, and with shaky hands, I unfold the note.

> *I was wrong. I couldn't keep you safe. My lawyer will be in touch with the divorce papers, and my men will take care of you until I know you're safe to go home.*
> *XX Kai*

My lungs compress and I fight to take a breath, as it feels like my heart is being ripped from my chest. Even though I knew it was coming, it still kills me. I carefully sit on the side of the bed, and the door opens.

I turn my head and my eyes collide with Pika's.

"Do you need help?" he asks softly.

I want to scream at him to go away, but instead, I shake my head and stand slowly.

"Let me help you," he says, ignoring me and walking into the room.

Tears begin to fall again and I swipe them away with the back of my hand.

"It will be okay," he consoles quietly.

The pity I hear in his tone causes a ball of anger to build in my stomach. He wraps his arm around my shoulders, and I push him away, stumbling slightly.

"Careful," he growls, sounding just like Kai, making fury explode through me.

"Go away!" I scream, pushing him away again. "Get out of my room!"

His arms come around me, and I pound against his chest with the back of my fist as tears stream down my cheeks.

"Shhhhh," he hushes me, forcing me closer to his body, where my fists wrap into his shirt and I bury my face in his chest to cry harder. "It will be okay." He rubs my back as my legs give out under me. He catches me before I fall to the floor, picks me up, and carries me to bed, laying me back down. "Do you want me to stay with you?" he asks, pulling the covers back over my shoulder.

"No. I just want to be alone," I breathe through my tears and attempt to pull myself together.

"I don't mind," he whispers.

I look at him and shake my head.

He nods, looking around and then back down at me. I can tell he wants to say something else, but instead, he kisses my forehead and stands. I hear the door close, but my eyes stay locked on the sky I can see out the window.

Myla, this is stupid. You weren't even in love with him. Stop acting like a lovesick fool, I lie to myself then bury my face in my pillow and cry harder.

Chapter 7

Limbo

"**N**OW WHAT ARE you baking?"

I look at the open kitchen doorway and narrow my eyes at Aye. "Nothing for you, and don't even think about coming in here." I wave the spoon at him, trying to sound firm. It never fails that he shows up when I'm in the middle of baking.

"You're really going to do that to Daddy?" he asks, and I can't help but smile at him.

"Fine. You can have one, but first, you have to promise you will take me somewhere."

"I'll take you," Pika says, joining us.

"You don't have to do that," I reply softly, watching as he comes over, dips his finger into the bowl of cookie dough, and swipes some off the edge before licking it off his finger.

"You know I don't mind." His eyes go soft, making me shift uncomfortably.

Since Kai left, Pika and Aye have constantly been at my side. I would honestly be lost without either of them, but over the last week, I have started seeing a change in the way Pika looks at me.

"I'll take her," Aye says, saving me.

"Thanks," I tell him, going back to placing some more dough in balls on the cookie sheet while ignoring the heat I feel coming of Pika, who is standing too close to me.

"Where are you guys going?" he asks after a moment.

I look over my shoulder at him and debate how to answer. "I have yet to receive divorce papers from Kai's lawyer, and you guys won't tell me anything, so I'm going to talk to a lawyer."

"Myla," Aye says.

I quickly swing my head towards him. "No." I shake my head. "I know you're his friend, and I totally get that this puts you guys in an awkward situation, but I have to do this. I will not be in limbo."

"I'll take you if Aye refuses," Pika says.

I look at him again then jerk my head up and down once.

"Pika." Aye throws his arms up in the air.

"I'm taking her," Pika replies evenly.

"Fuck this!" Aye shouts and leaves the kitchen.

"Come find me when you're ready," Pika rumbles.

I nod and let out a long breath as I listen to Pika and Aye fight somewhere in the house. I hate that I'm causing a rift between them, but I can't do this anymore. I moved out of Kai's room the day he left and haven't been back in there since then. I couldn't wake up in his bed again, with his smell surrounding me.

I hate that, every time I think about Kai, I still feel the pain in my chest that I felt when I read his note the first time. I hate that he did what he did, yet I can't bring myself to hate *him*. I didn't realize until it was too late that Kai had gotten under my skin. He came into my life, made me believe I was going to be given something beautiful, and then took it away from me without any warning.

I look down at the bowl of cookie dough and my eyes catch on the ring I haven't had the courage to take off. I let out a ragged breath and know exactly what I need to do. I just need to be strong enough to do it.

Kai

I LOOK OUT over the water for a moment and then turn my head back to face my computer. My eyes land on the picture that is now the screensaver on my personal laptop.

It's one of the photos taken the night of the party my mother threw for us. Myla was at my side, the front of her body plastered against me. My hand was on the top of her ass, her head was tilted back, and she was smiling up at me, with my face tilted down looking at her. You can't see it in the picture because of how the photo was taken, but I remember looking into her eyes, not understanding the look of wonder I saw there.

Myla has to be the most beautiful woman I've ever seen in my life. I now regret never telling her how beautiful she is every chance I got, but when I first met her, I assumed that, like with most women who look like she does, she knew it and knew how to get men to grovel at her feet.

I came to realize that she didn't understand the power she held over men with her looks alone. She didn't know that one smile from her could put a man on his ass. I look down at my hand and pull the ring off my finger, putting it back into my pocket. I only wear it when I know I'm going to be alone for a length of time.

I need everyone to believe Myla and I are done, even if I know within myself that it's not the case. When I left Myla behind, I knew it was going to be difficult, but I also knew that, if I stayed with her in Hawaii, I was putting her at risk of being harmed again.

I found out after she was poisoned that the culprit was an enemy of mine, and rumors were being spread that I now had a weakness. Before Myla, I had never been vulnerable. I never worried about my siblings because I knew they were under the radar and always protected. And I knew the same thing went for my parents. I didn't take into account that Myla would be seen as a way to push me off my throne until I was holding her in my arms as she fought to breathe.

In that moment, I knew I couldn't put her at risk. I wouldn't be able to live with myself if something happened to her, and although I had married her for my own selfish reasons, those reasons no longer applied, and the only thing that matters to me now is her safety and well-being. I also know that my leaving her is not enough to stop the threats against her, and in order to make sure she stays safe, I need to make an example out of the men who threatened her. As long as I am alive and breathing, no one will ever have the ability to harm her in any way.

I lift my head and look at the door when there is a knock on my office entrance. "Come in," I call while rolling my chair back. My brother informed me moments ago that Snider was on his way up with only one of his men. This pissed me off; he is basically saying that he doesn't believe I am a threat.

Since taking over for my father, I have lain low, staying out of all of the back-and-forth between families, and just concentrated on turning the family business into something my children could inherit. Because of this, my guess is some of the people I have done business with have begun to believe I'm weak. They seem to have forgotten that my family holds a power that goes back generations. In the past, there were not many people stupid enough to mess with us. The day Myla was poisoned, that all changed.

As soon as the door opens, Snider walks in with his bodyguard at his side. I stand and take him in, wondering how the fuck *he* has the ability to cause fear in people. Over the years, he has let himself go. No longer concerned about his appearance or health, he now carries around at least fifty extra pounds on his gut. He is balding on top, with long wisps that lie over his bald spot, a sad attempt at giving himself the appearance of hair. The navy-blue, velour tracksuit, gold jewelry, and sneakers make him look like he's watched too many episodes of The Sopranos.

"Nice digs," he says, taking a seat in front of my desk. "To what do I owe the pleasure of this meeting?" He sits back and laces his hands in front of him, looking like he doesn't have a care in the world.

I take a seat and slide the gun from its holder under my desk, flipping the safety off. "My wife was poisoned a month ago. I got word that you were the one to instigate that hit."

"Ex-wife, you mean?" he inquires, and the guy next to him laughs. "She went and spoke with a divorce attorney today." He smiles. "Oh, you didn't know that, did you? I knew you would think we are all idiots when you left her, but I had a feeling you were full of shit when you said you were done with her." He looks from me to the man next to him and begins speaking in Russian. *"A piece like her you could fuck for the rest of your life and still find new ways to fill her with your come."*

"I would tire of her quickly when she got fat from having my children," his man replies in Russian.

I see red, lift my gun, put a bullet through his head, and then turn the gun on Snider as his bodyguard's body crumples to the floor.

"Who do you have on her?" I growl, ready to put a bullet though his skull as well.

"You can't kill me, Kai, and you know it," he says, taking a Kleenex out of his pocket and wiping the blood splatter off his face.

"You must have forgotten who I am, who my family is." I shake my head in disgust.

"I've forgotten nothing. Just because you inherited the seat from your father doesn't make you as powerful as he was."

I smile and pull the trigger, putting a bullet through his shoulder. "You forget that, for years, I was my father's watcher."

His eyes get big and he cries out as he looks at his shoulder then back at me again. "You can't do this!" he groans.

"You think I fear you or them?" I shake my head and stand up. "I fear no one but the gods, and when my time comes, they are who I will answer to. Now, tell me. Who do you have watching my wife?"

"You kill me and you're as good as dead," he says pathetically, ignoring my question.

"Ah." I shake my head, stand, and walk around to sit on the front of my desk. "You're stupid, Snider. You have always been rash, and this situation is no different. You didn't think before you did what you did."

"If you kill me, there will be war."

"The moment you put Myla on radar, you started a war with me!" I roar, and fire a bullet through his other shoulder.

His body slumps lower in his chair, and he fights to lift his head to look at me.

"I will make sure pieces of you are divided evenly amongst your friends."

"Everyone knows who she is. Paulie Jr. wants her for himself," he wheezes out.

Ice-cold fear floods my veins, but I push that feeling aside and growl, "He's going to have to get through me." I pull the trigger and the bullet hits him between the eyes.

A moment later, the door to my office opens and my brother walks in.

"Did Myla go and file for divorce today?" I ask him.

He looks at the guys on the ground then at me. "She did. Aye told Pika not to take her, but he wouldn't listen. He thinks Pika has feelings for her," he replies.

"She's my wife!" I roar and push everything off my desk with a sweep of my hand.

"Not for long," he says calmly, shaking his head.

When I left Hawaii, I left all of my men with Myla and brought my brother with me. I also told him what had happened with Myla and that, although things between us had begun on a lie, that was no longer the case now.

"What attorney did she go to?"

When he looks at me, I can tell he doesn't want to answer, and I know exactly why.

"Fuck," I growl.

There are only two divorce attorneys I know who would be around this time of year, and one of them would be more than willing to help Myla divorce my ass. The lawyer would also do it quickly and enjoy every moment of it.

"Are we going home?" he asks, pulling his phone out of his pocket.

"Yes, and call the cleaners," I tell him while pulling Snider's phone out his jacket pocket and looking through his call log until I find the number I'm looking for. I press send on Paulie Jr.'s number and then hold the phone to my ear.

"What?" Paulie answers after a moment.

"I hear you're interested in my wife."

"Fuck," he breathes, and I can hear shuffling coming down the line.

"Let me give you the message Snider will unfortunately be unable to deliver. You so much as even think about my wife and I'm coming for you."

"Kai," he says, and I can hear fear in his voice.

I have known Paulie Jr. since we were both ten and our fathers began molding us to take over the family businesses. It was during our first meeting that I learned the difference in ways our fathers were raising each of us. Where my father had raised me with a firm hand and a large amount of respect, Paulie Sr. had been raising his son to fear him, and over the years, that fear has slowly caused his son to resent him and crave the power he held over his head. But just because he wanted to dethrone his father doesn't mean he wants his father to know he is after his seat. If his dad ever caught wind of what his son was up to, Paulie Sr. would take his own son out without a second thought.

"Be smart. Forget you know anything about my wife." I hang up then look at my brother, who is just getting off the phone as well.

"Sweepers are on the way, and the plane is ready when we are."

"Thanks," I mutter, walking over to my laptop, shutting it down, and watching the picture of Myla and me disappear. Even with the war that is brewing, I know the most important fight I will ever be in is waiting for me at home.

Chapter 8

Honey I'm Home

Myla

I WALK THROUGH the house looking for Pika and Aye. Since I woke up this morning, they have been incognito.

Yesterday, Pika took me to begin the process of filing for divorce. When we arrived at the lawyer's office, I was a nervous wreck. The old brick building looked like all the others in the area, but there was something about it that put fear in me.

"Are you sure you want to do this?" Pika asked.

I looked over at him and then back to the building. "I'm sure." I opened the car door and climbed out. "I'll be back."

"I'll be here."

"Thanks," I murmured before slamming the door closed and heading for the building.

When I was halfway there, I stopped myself from turning around, heading back to the car, and telling Pika to take me home. I knew I couldn't do that. I knew I couldn't let Kai be the decider of my future, and waiting for him to get me the divorce papers was doing exactly that.

As soon as I opened the door to the building, the bell over the door rang and a beautiful woman wearing a business suit walked out of the back office and greeted me in the lobby.

"Myla?" she questioned, giving me a small smile and sticking out her hand.

"Hi," I replied, placing my hand in hers, surprised by the firmness of her shake.

"I'm Tammy. My receptionist took the afternoon off, so I hope you don't mind if we just get down to business?" she asked.

"No, that's fine."

"Would you like a bottle of water or a soda?" she asked.

I shook my head and wrung my hands together.

"It will be okay." She smiled again. "Just follow me and we can get started."

"Sure," I agreed and followed her into a large office, where she nodded at me to sit down in a chair in front of her desk.

"When we spoke yesterday, you said that you were wanting to file for divorce. Is that right?"

"Yes," I whispered, and then I looked at the door, wanting to make a run for it.

"Can I ask you why?" she probed.

I looked at her then back at the door. "I think I made a mistake," I whispered.

"I think a lot of women feel like that," she muttered.

I started to laugh hysterically until tears were falling down my cheeks. It took a minute to get myself under control, but when I did, I looked at her and found a smile on her face.

"I needed that," I told her, wiping under my eyes and relaxing into my seat. After that, the rest of the meeting went by quickly, and when I left, I felt like I had not only made the right decision by filing, but that I had done the right thing as far as stopping all the lies.

Tammy had told me that she would get the papers prepared and have Kai served. She'd also explained that, if Kai didn't agree to sign them, we could proceed without him because I wasn't requesting any of his assets that had rightfully become half mine when we'd married without a prenup.

I come out of my thoughts when I hear voices coming from Kai's office. Since he's been gone, no one has been in this part of the house, so I'm surprised to hear the hushed tones of men speaking behind the closed door. I tiptoe across the hall, careful not to make any noise. I slowly put my ear to the door and my hands around my ear so that I can zero in on the sound.

Weight and warmth press me harder into the door.

"What are we listening for?" is whispered in my ear.

I scream as strong arms wrap around me.

"Easy," says an all-too-familiar voice, causing my body to instantly react and pain to compress my chest.

"No," I whisper as Kai's office door is opened and Pika's and Aye's eyes land on me. I tilt my head back, praying I'm wrong—that Kai isn't home—but my eyes collide with his.

"Let me go," I whisper, bucking against his hold.

His eyes go soft as he whispers, "*Makamae*," tightening his arms around me almost as if he doesn't want to release me.

"Let me go," I repeat a little louder this time.

"We must talk," he says calmly.

"Ha!" I lean my head back and scream at the top of my lungs. "Well, then, if you say we must talk, Kai, by all means, let's talk."

"I know you're upset."

"No, Kai, I'm not upset." I franticly shake my head back and forth, knowing I probably look insane.

"If you'll just listen for a moment, I can explain everything."

My body stills and I force myself to relax as his hold on me tightens almost painfully. "Okay," I breathe, wanting to hear what he's going to say. I so badly want him to make this right, to make me understand so the pain in my chest will go away.

"I needed the people who were trying to harm you to believe we were no longer together."

My gut twists, and I know that, even if that were the case, even if he was doing it as a way to protect me, no one would have known he'd left me a note. No one would have known he told me that his lawyer would be in touch. No one would have known I cried for hours, alone, in our bed, surrounded by his smell. He could have spoken to me, could have told me what he wanted to do, but he didn't even give me a choice in the matter. He left me without so much as a "fuck you."

"You did a good job," I say snidely.

"You have to understand," he says quietly, giving my waist a squeeze.

I jerk away and turn to face him. "I understand I told you before that I needed you to be up-front with me about *everything*." I accentuate the last word. "I understand that you could have talked to me, but you chose not to. And I also understand that what we had was never real, so the fact that it ended shouldn't really hurt." I shove past him and head towards the kitchen.

"Myla, I'm not going anywhere!" he shouts down the hall.

I turn to look at him. Words get stuck in my throat, so without another word, I turn away and head towards the kitchen. There, I grab a glass of water before making my way down to the beach, where I sit staring off into the ocean until a chill fills the air and I'm forced to go inside.

I GET OUT of bed, pulling on a pair of shorts and a hoodie before heading to the kitchen, finally giving up on getting any sleep. I have tossed and turned for the last hour, unable to turn my brain off. I finally decided I would just get up and bake something.

Since I was young, baking has been an escape for me, and I know it's the one thing I can do right now that will help me clear my head. I make it to the kitchen and turn on the light. Then I pull out all the ingredients I need to make pineapple cupcakes with rum cream frosting. Just as I begin to crack eggs into the bowl, I see movement out of the corner of my eye. My belly does a flip, expecting to see Kai, but instead, my eyes connect with Pika's.

"I see you," I tell him, going back to putting the ingredients into the bowl.

"How are you feeling?" he asks, coming to sit on the counter next to me.

I think about his question for a moment then think about the way my stomach felt every time I thought about Kai, and I honestly didn't know how to answer.

"I don't know." I shrug, pull out a baking pan, and fill the holes with cupcake liners.

"I have known Kai for a long time."

I swallow but don't look at him.

"I know you don't want to hear this right now, but he was right in his actions."

My head lifts and my eyes meet his. "You don't think he should have told me something? Anything? At least given me some kind of clue he was coming home and we were *not* over?" I feel the pain in my chest expand. "I'm sorry, but I cannot imagine being with someone, caring about them, and then leaving them without a backward glance...without even a proper goodbye."

"Myla, think about where he's coming from. You meet this girl, and out of nowhere, your life changes and she becomes someone worth fighting for, worth protecting. Think about the kind of guy you know him to be, and *then* tell me he wasn't doing the right thing."

"He didn't do that, Pika. He didn't fight. Not for me," I whisper and then look down at the bowl in my hands. "So if youre going to stay in here and try to convince me that what he did was okay, you might as well just go."

"I'm here for you as your friend," he says then tugs on my arm until I go to him.

My waist goes between his legs, my head leans on his chest, my arms wrap around him, and I feel his lips on the top of my head.

"One day, Myla, you will see he was right."

I LOOK OUT the window, down at the rain falling into the ocean, which makes it look as turbulent as my emotions. Kai came to my room an hour ago and knocked on the door, yelling through that his mom would be here at noon. I ignored him and the feeling I got when he didn't say anything else or try to and kick down the door to get to me.

I hate that I am feeling so confused. I can't figure out what I want him to do. Do I want him to fight for me, or do I want him to just leave me alone?

I shake my head at my own stupid thoughts and turn towards the mirror to look at myself. I want to look decent for Kai's mom. I don't think she would understand my showing up in a pair of sweats with dark bags under my eyes from not being able to sleep properly over the last month. Actually, I know that, if I showed up like that, she would have a million questions I'm just not ready to answer.

So, instead of sweats, I pull out my favorite jeans. They have seen better days, and those days were about ten years ago. They are a pair of medium-washed jeans with holes along the front. I bought them that way, but over the years, those holes have gotten bigger and bigger— some from normal wear and tear, and others from me and my constant picking at the material when I have them on.

I put on a plain, white tank top, and since it is raining, I put on my favorite orange sweater that has bell sleeves and little white polka dots on it. Then I put my hair in a bun on top of my head and dab on some concealer, a little blush, and some mascara. I sigh, slip on my flip-flops, and head for the door.

If you would have asked me a month ago to sit down with my real mom's best friend and talk to her about the kind of person she was when she was alive, I would have jumped at the chance, but today, I don't feel like doing that. I don't want to talk about my past. I don't want to talk about anything. I want to lie in bed and feel sorry for myself. Or maybe lie in bed, turn the air conditioner on high, bury myself under a million blankets, watch movies, and eat ice cream.

I open the door, and my eyebrows pull together when I come face-to-face with a man I have never seen before. He is large—at least three hundred pounds and six two. I would guess he's in his early forties. His skin is the same color as Kai's, and his hair is long and slicked back from his face. He is wearing a bright floral shirt with the top two buttons undone, showing off the mass of hair on his chest and a thick, Cuban-link, gold chain. My eyes travel farther down and take in his beige khaki pants and a pair of leather sandals on his feet, which have thick black soles and large straps that wrap across his feet then around his ankles.

"Who are you?" I ask, taking a step back.

"Frank." He smiles, showing off a set of perfectly straight, white teeth with one of the front two outlined in gold.

"Um…" I look at him, confused, and his smile gets bigger.

"Uncle Frank," he says like I should know exactly who he is. "Aww, come on!" He throws his hands up in the air, and I notice that every one of his fingers has a gold ring on it. "That damn boy never gives me any credit." He shakes his head. "Kai's my nephew. His mom is my sister."

"Oh," I mutter, still confused on why he is standing outside my bedroom door.

"He sent me to look after you."

"What? Where's Aye or Pika?" I question, and his face changes slightly.

"They were needed elsewhere."

"Where's Kai?"

"Don't know." He shrugs then smiles again. "You ready to do this thing?"

"What thing would that be?"

"Go down to the library," he explains like we are going to be doing something much more exciting than just going to the library.

"Sure," I mumble, still confused.

He smiles bigger then pulls a gun out from behind his back. When I see it in his hand, I scream then back up into the room and quickly shut the door. My heart is pounding hard as I get down on the ground and crawl over to the window, not wanting to be shot if he decides to shoot through the door.

"Aw, geez. I'm not going to shoot you, girl! I'm here to protect you!" he yells through the closed door.

"Go away! I have a gun and I'm not afraid to use it!" I yell back, knowing damn well I don't have a gun. I don't even know how to shoot a gun, and God forbid I ever be given a gun. I would likely shoot myself by accident.

"Fucking great," he mumbles, and then he lightly knocks on the door. "Please come out. I put the gun away."

"Go away!" I yell then open the window and look down to the ground below, realizing I'm stuck. If I jump out the window, I would likely fall to my death, but if I go to the door, I might be shot by a crazy man.

"I'm going to get my sister," he says, knocking on the door again. "Could you please not tell her or Kai about the whole gun thing?" he asks, and I begin to wonder if he is fricking crazy. "I'm going to take that as a yes," he says, and then there is silence.

I look around the room. It's huge, with a king-size bed, two nightstands, two dressers, a large closet, and its own bath. But what it doesn't have is someplace to hide. I look at the door again and know that "Frank" could be trying to trick me and still be standing outside the door, waiting for me to be like all the dumb chicks in every scary movie ever made and walk out into the hall, right into his grasp.

"Myla," the familiar voice of Kai's mom, Leia, calls though the door, and my stomach pitches, because now, she's in danger. "Myla, honey, please open the door. My brother is an idiot. He didn't mean to scare you," she says, and I swear I can hear the smile in her voice.

"I told you, girl. I'm here to protect you," Frank says, and I hear a loud *thwack!*

"Can you please stop until I get her to come out here?"

"I just want her to know that I'm her bodyguard," he whines.

"You already said that, Frank, and you obviously scared the poor girl to death. So why don't you let me take it from here?"

"Fine, fine."

"Myla, honey, please come out."

I look around the room for some kind of weapon, and the only thing

I can find is one of the lamps from the bedside table. I pick it up, take off the shade, unplug it, and carry it to the door. If I needed to, I can try to at least save Kai's mom. I slowly open the door, and my eyes lock on Leia's.

"Ah, thank fuck," Frank mutters, throwing his hands in the air and looking up at the celling.

"You will have to forgive my brother. He can be a little"—she pauses, searching for the right word—"excitable."

I look at her then Frank and shake my head, thinking "a little excitable" is a giant understatement.

"Sorry, girl," Frank says then smiles, throwing his arm around his sister's shoulders. "She's cute," he tells her, and then his face goes serious. "Don't tell Kai about this."

"Ugh...sure." I bite my lip to keep from laughing at the look on Leia's face. I can't believe that someone as elegant as she is is related to this guy.

"You'll learn to love him," she mutters, taking the lamp out of my hand and setting it inside the room. Then she takes my hand and leads me down the hall.

"Hold up," Frank says, and we stop in our tracks.

He gets in front of us and begins walking down the hall, looking right and left like he is making sure the coast is clear. Kai's mom wraps her arm around mine and leans into my side, and I feel her silent laughter as we watch her brother the whole way to the library.

I LOOK AT the picture that was just handed to me, and I can't believe how absolutely stunning my mom was. She looked like she could have graced the cover of *Vogue*. Her hourglass figure, beautiful, porcelain skin, and long, thick, blond hair were all perfect in a way that people today pay loads of money for.

"You look just like her."

I look up from the picture and into the smiling face of Kai's mom and shake my head.

"You do. You have your dad's nose, but everything else is all your mom."

I look down at the picture again and notice that my lips are the same as hers, the bottom one full and the top one slightly thinner. Her cheekbones were pronounced, just like mine, and her eyes were almond-shaped, also like mine.

"See? Your nose is all your father's." She smiles, handing me another picture, this one of a handsome man wearing a suit that fit him well, showing off his toned physique.

I can tell, even through the photo, that he took care of himself. His hair was dark brown and styled in a way that said that he took his time to tame it, and his skin was naturally tan. I look at his face, my eyes zeroing in on his nose, and I can see we do have the same one.

"How old were they in these pictures?" I ask, still staring at the photos.

"This was right after they were married, so I would guess early twenties. Your mom was about a month pregnant with you when this picture was taken. She had griped that she looked terrible because she had been having horrible morning sickness. I told her she was crazy. I had never once seen your mother look anything but perfect," she says with a giggle.

"She was really beautiful," I whisper, taking another picture when it's handed to me, this one of my mom and dad together, my mom with a large, round belly that looks like a perfectly shaped basketball under her form-fitting dress.

"She *was* beautiful."

I look up from my position on the floor and see a sadness in her eyes that makes my heart hurt. "We don't have to do this," I whisper, not wanting to cause her any more pain.

"Oh, honey." She shakes her head, her hand coming down, running over my hair. "Even though this hurts, it feels good. Your mom was my best friend. She was someone who could walk into a room and everyone would stop to take notice that she was there. It wasn't her beauty that did that, either. Her spirit called to you, made you want to be around her. I'm sad that you will never know what it was like to be in her presence, to have her shine her light on you. So if this is the only part of her you will be able to experience, then I'm so happy to be the one to share it with you."

Wow, I think, loving Leia just a little more than I already did.

"Thank you." I clear my throat as tears begin to clog it.

She smiles then hands me another picture, this one of my mom sitting on a bed with my dad next to her, one arm holding her close, the other wrapped around a tiny baby.

"You see what I mean? Your mom had just given birth, yet she looked absolutely perfect," she says, and she is not wrong.

My mom's hair was on top of her head in a tight bun, and her makeup was still perfectly in place. She looked like she had just gotten through with a day at the spa, not just given birth.

"They look like the perfect couple," I say wistfully.

She laughs and her face lights up. "They were crazy about each other. Your mom told me she was going to marry him the first night they met."

"Really?" I ask, looking at the picture again.

"Oh, yeah. We were both in our freshmen year of college and had just passed our first semester exams, so we decided to go out to dinner to celebrate. The moment we walked into the restaurant, your mom stopped dead in her tracks, causing me to plow into her. I looked around to see why she was stopping, but then I noticed a tableful of men. All of them were handsome. I told her she was staring, and she whispered that she couldn't help it—her future was sitting right in front of her. At this point, I swore she was crazy. Honestly, who sees a man and says something like that? But then your dad's head turned our way and his eyes locked on your mom, and without another word to the men at the table, he came over to us, stopped in front of your mom, took her hand, and led her to the bar."

"No way." I smile. My dad had balls.

She laughs hard and her eyes go soft. "Yes way. I stood there for a few minutes, wondering if I was seeing things, but I wasn't. A few minutes later, your dad brought your mother back to me, introduced himself, and then went back to his table."

"What happened next?"

"It's like you say—the rest is history. Your dad made plans with your mom for the next night, and from that moment on, they were inseparable."

"That quickly?" I ask, running my finger over another picture of my parents, this one of them laughing while looking at each other.

"That quickly. Sometimes, you just know, and your mom and dad both knew. It was almost as if, the moment they saw each other, their souls had recognized the other as their perfect match."

"That really sounds crazy," I murmur, but an image of Kai flashes through my head and how something deep in me knows him and went to him without a fight the moment I saw him. I think about how, every time I have been with him, it has been easy, about how he makes me feel. I shake off that thought, not wanting to feel the pain I feel every time I think about him now. Not right now, when I have the opportunity to learn about my parents.

"Sometimes, you just know," she repeats. She smiles then pulls out another stack of pictures.

For the rest of the day, I sit on the floor while she sits on the couch, and she shares pictures and stories of my parents with me. By the time she leaves, I feel like a weight has been lifted off my shoulders. She unconsciously helped mend some of the pieces of my heart back together again.

Chapter 9

One Day at a Time

"WHERE'S PIKA?" I ask Aye.

He looks at me, presses his lips tighter together, and then looks back to the TV.

"What does that mean?" I question, confused by that response.

"He's not here."

"I obviously know that. He hasn't been here in two days, but I'm asking you where he is."

"You're going to have to speak with Kai about that," he mutters, not taking his eyes off the TV, knowing damn well there is no way in hell I will be speaking to Kai about anything, let alone where Pika is.

I haven't talked to Kai since the day he arrived home, and at this point, I'm not sure who has been avoiding whom.

"Guess you don't want to know that badly," he mumbles.

I feel my pulse start to pick up when I remember how I met Pika for the first time.

"Is he okay?" I whisper. Pika has become a friend, and the idea of him being hurt doesn't sit well with me at all.

"He's fine," I hear growled, making me jump, turn my head, and look over the back of the couch at Kai.

I feel my stomach drop. I've seen Kai angry before, but I have never had that anger directed at me. I shrink down into the couch but can't break eye contact.

"Aye, go. Myla will be with me for the rest of the day. I'll call you if you're needed," he says, and his eyes never leave mine as his energy pulses against my skin.

"Sure," Aye says.

I want to tell him not to leave me, but I can't do anything but stare into the cold eyes that are boring into mine.

As soon as Aye's gone, Kai runs his hand over his hair then looks at me and shakes his head. Then he looks at me again and growls deep in his throat, "We're going out."

"Um…" I mutter under my breath as I watch his chest expand with a deep inhale.

"Be ready in ten minutes."

"I…" I shake my head. There is no way I will be able to get ready in ten minutes. I'm still wearing my pajamas. It takes me longer than that just to shower.

"Ten minutes," he repeats then turns around and leaves the room.

I look at the doorway, shake my head, get off the couch, and head to my room. I doubt I can get ready so quickly, but I sure as hell am going to try. Kai has never scared me before, not even a little bit. Even when I'd watched him kill someone, he had never appeared as angry as he did a few moments ago.

Kai

I LEAVE THE living room and prowl straight to my office, slamming the door behind me. I try to breathe, but it doesn't cut through the madness that has been building and expanding since our fight, and then seeing her in the kitchen in the middle of the night, with her arms wrapped around another man while he kissed her, even if it was not an intimate kiss, was too much for me to handle.

Every day has been an internal battle of self-control, and the constant weight in my gut and fucking irritant under my skin has not been helping. When I married Myla, I had no idea this was going to happen to me. I didn't understand what I was feeling when I looked into her eyes when we said our vows to one another. I might not have expected these feelings when I married her, but I have them now, so there is no fucking way I'm going to sit on the sidelines and let someone—who I have known since I was a kid—come in and steal away the woman who belongs to me, a woman I know, if I admitted it to myself, I am falling in love with.

A woman who I know was feeling the same thing I am right now before I left.

I take another breath, and then another. Pika is lucky he is still alive. After what I had seen, I wanted to fucking slaughter him, but I knew that, if I walked into the kitchen and did that, it would only make her believe she was right about me.

It wasn't like me to sit and wait, but I had to do it. But that didn't mean I had to let Pika stick around. I sent him away two days ago. He was back on the mainland, helping my other men keep track of Thad and Paulie Jr. When I confronted him about his relationship with Myla, he told me that he had feelings for her. I decked him and he didn't back down. He even told me that I was a moron for having left her without telling her anything. Then he told me that it didn't matter how he was feeling about her because she couldn't see past me, and he didn't suspect she ever would.

His words gave me a margin of hope of winning Myla back, but I'm not a stupid man. I know that it is going to take work. I know I'm going to have to take it slow. But slow with her feels impossible.

Fuck. The moment I brought her into my home, I had her in my bed, even if I wasn't sleeping in there with her. I just knew that I wanted her in my space, wanted to know she was in a bed I would share with her eventually. Sleeping with her those few nights her parents were in town also changed things. I have slept with my share of women, but I never felt a connection to any of them. Even just holding Myla eased something within me, brought peace I thought was long gone to my soul.

She was my peace in a world I knew was fucked up beyond most people's understanding.

I look at the door and let out one last breath. I probably just scared the shit out of her. She is probably running for the hills, but Pika's name leaving her mouth, the soft tone in her voice from worry over him, had set me off. Even if I know she doesn't see him as anything more than a friend, I know he doesn't feel the same.

I also know that Pika is a player. He has a girl in every town he visits, and often two if he is in the mood for that kind of play. Women throw themselves at him, and having Myla around him right now is not a risk I am willing to take.

I move to the door, opening it then moving down the hall to the room Myla has been staying in before knocking once.

"Yes?" her quiet voice asks through the door.

"Can I come in?"

She doesn't reply for a moment, but when she does, it's soft and unsure. I push the door open and see that she's sitting on the side of the bed with a pair of sandals in her hand.

"I'm just about ready," she mutters, ducking her head to look at her feet as she slips the sandals on one at a time.

"I wanted to tell you that you can have more time if you need it."

"I'm ready now. I hurried," she whispers, and my gut clenches when I hear the fear in her voice.

I live off power.

I have my whole life.

In my business, fear is power.

You can control most people by using fear.

With Myla, I do not want that. I do not want to think she is with me out of fear of repercussion.

"Take your time," I tell her.

Her head lifts, her gaze meets mine, and she looks confused. "I thought you said we were going somewhere."

"We are, but it can wait. Take your time."

"I'm ready now." She stands.

My eyes travel over her the plain, black dress, which is loose with thin straps that show off the fact that she isn't wearing a bra. Then it billows out down to her feet.

"I didn't know what I should wear," she mumbles, looking uncomfortable.

I shake my head then tell her what I should have told her a million times before. "You look beautiful."

Her head lifts and her gaze meets mine. "I…" She pauses, and her eyebrows pull together. "What?" she questions, looking completely confused and cute as fuck.

"You look beautiful."

"Okay." She looks at me again then straightens her shoulders almost like she's preparing for war. "Are we going?" She tosses a hand out towards the door.

"We are." I smile, take her hand, and hold it tighter when she tries to pull away.

I lead her out of the house to my Jeep, helping her in before jogging around and getting in behind the wheel. I have absolutely no plans set for today, so I'm going to have to make some shit up.

Myla

I LOOK AT Kai out of the corner of my eye and feel my eyebrows pull tighter together in confusion. I have no idea what he's up to, but I know it's something.

"Where are we going?" I ask after a few minutes of silence.

"Dinner." His hands tighten on the steering wheel, and I wonder if this is some kind of business dinner.

Then, butterflies erupt in my stomach once again. Chances are, if we are having dinner, I will have to play the role of his wife, and as much as it pisses me off, I'm secretly excited about it.

We only drive for about ten minutes, and when we reach our destination, I'm even more confused. I look out the front window and double-blink. It's not a restaurant he would usually have a dinner meeting at. It's not even really a restaurant. It's a small trailer with a few tables set up outside of it. The sign out front says *Tides* in large lettering, the small sign under it claims that restaurant has the best fish tacos in Hawaii.

"I thought we were having dinner."

"We are." He shuts the Jeep off, opens his door, and hops out, and I watch him jog around to my side. When he opens my door, I turn to get out, but he mumbles a quiet, "Just a moment." He slips his jacket off and then his tie and cuff links before unbuttoning the top two buttons of his shirt and rolling up his sleeves. Once his appearance is more casual, he takes ahold of my waist and helps me out of the Jeep. Then he turns with me in his arms and shuts the door before taking my hand again and leading me towards the trailer.

"Aloha, brother."

"Aloha, friend," Kai returns to the large guy whose head is sticking out of the small window.

"Who do we have here?" he asks, looking me over.

"My wife, Myla. Myla, this guy here is Derek. He and his wife are the owners of Tides."

"Wife?" the guy says, seeming shocked.

"Nice to meet you." I smile through the anxiety I'm feeling.

"I didn't know you got married. Babe, did you know Kai got married?" he shouts, and a petite woman comes to the window and smiles at Kai and me.

"I had no idea. It's about time." She smiles bigger while wrapping her small hand around her husband's large bicep.

"Got that right. Been waiting years for you to settle down," Derek says.

His wife comes to stand in front of him. "Do you want the usual?" she asks, leaning slightly out the window, looking down at us.

"Do you like fish?" Kai asks softly.

I look up at him and feel the weight of Derek and his wife watching us. "I do," I reply just as softly.

"Make the order double, Derek, and do you have any fresh pineapple juice? Myla loves it," Kai adds, wrapping his arm around my shoulders.

I unconsciously lean against his side and then try to lean away when I realize what I'm doing, but his hold tightens, preventing me from moving.

"That I do. Take a seat, and we'll bring you your order when it's up." He waves us off.

Kai turns us around, leading me over to one of the picnic tables that are set up. I sit and look around, avoiding looking at Kai. Once again, my emotions are in turmoil, and it is all his fault—or at least I'm going to blame him for it.

"What are you thinking, *makamae?*" His hand takes mine.

Part of me wants to pull away, but the other part of me, the part that is tethered to him, wants to grab him and never let go.

"I'm so confused." I shake my head then turn to look at him. "I really hate that you make me feel like I'm two completely different people."

"What do you mean?"

I let out an irritated huff before answering him. "There is this side of me that really dislikes you and the things you do. Then there's this other side of me that doesn't care about the part that dislikes you. She just likes you, all of you." I let out a breath then glare when I see his smile. "You should know I think the part of me that likes you is an idiot."

He presses his lips together then lets his head fall back, and roaring laughter comes out of his mouth. I have seen him laugh before, and like all of those times, my stomach flutters.

"It's not funny." I roll my eyes.

"Yes, it's funny." He continues laughing.

A smile forms on my lips from watching him. His eyes drop to my mouth and his expression goes soft.

"All the parts of me like you, *lakamae,*" he tells me with such sincerity that the warm feeling begins to seep back into my belly.

"What does *makamae* mean?"

His hand comes up and he cups my cheek, his thumb running over my bottom lip. I don't expect him to answer me, but unlike all the other times, his face comes closer to mine so close that I can feel his lips brush mine as he whispers, "Precious."

Holy shit! I jerk my head back in shock and search his face.

"Grub's up!" is yelled, breaking the moment, and I face forward just as Derek sets a plate in front of me and another in front of Kai.

"Thanks," I tell Derek while my insides churn.

Kai calls me precious? I look over at him, and his gaze is still on me.

"Let us know if you need anything else," Derek mutters, and I'm sure he can feel the strange energy that is floating around between Kai and me.

"Will do," Kai assures him, his stare never leaving mine.

As soon as Derek is out of earshot, Kai speaks again. This time, his voice is soft in a way that wraps around and inside me.

"I know this is difficult for you, Myla. I know I've done wrong, but I want you to understand something. I'm a man who was raised to do what needs to be done, never taking into consideration anyone else. I know the results of that have hurt you, but as I've told you from the beginning, I will tell you again. I will do *whatever* I have to in order to protect you. So, at the end of the day, even if you're pissed at me, that works, 'cause that means you're still breathing."

He looks over my shoulder then back at me again, letting out a long breath before continuing, "I will not give up on there being an us because I know we are worth fighting for. So you can be pissed and hold your ground, but I'm going to do the same, and while I'm doing it, I hope you will give us another chance."

"You're really good at this apology stuff...when you're not being a jerk," I mutter.

He smiles then takes my hand, placing a kiss over the ring I still haven't taken off. It's almost like he's telling me that he sees it and knows that, as upset as I am, I still haven't given up on us either. I look at his hand and notice that the ring I gave him is still sitting on his finger.

"One day at a time, Kai. That's all I can offer you," I whisper.

"I'll take it, *makamae*." He places another kiss on my hand then nods down at my plate. "Eat. They really are the best fish tacos in Hawaii," he divulges to me.

He isn't wrong—though I'm not sure if it is the tacos or the feeling of warmth I have back that makes them taste so good.

I WATCH THE sunrise and take in the beauty of the moment. From the sound of the ocean to the smell that's surrounding us, I can't quite figure out what it is, but I know that it's perfect. I lean back against Kai, and his arms wrap tighter around me, his thighs tightening against my sides. Since our dinner of delicious fish tacos two weeks ago, we have been working on us, and this *us* is way better than the previous one. I have let down my guard slightly, and I'm just enjoying the day-by-day time we spend together.

It isn't so much that I have forgiven him for leaving me the way he did, but I'm trying to be understanding of the man he is, and like he told me, he is a man who is not used to answering to anyone. He is a man used to doing what needs to be done—damn the consequences. I can't say I completely agree with this way of thinking, but I've been trying, and I can tell he is also trying to care when it comes to me and what I need from him.

"This is my favorite time of day," he whispers, placing a gentle kiss on the side of my neck.

I have also learned something else about Kai; he is seriously romantic, even if he isn't trying to be. Just this morning, when he woke me up, he handed me a sweater and led me out to the beach so I could experience my first Hawaiian sunrise. He often does small things that let me know he is thinking of me.

"It's so quiet," I tell him, rolling slightly to my side, letting my face rest on his bare chest while wrapping my arms around him.

"That's why it's my favorite. I have a moment to think. No phone, no one telling me that I'm needed—just me and nature." He kisses the top of my head. "And now, you."

Okay, that was sweet...really sweet. See what I mean when I said he is seriously romantic?

I tilt my head and place a kiss to his skin, wordlessly letting him know how much that means to me. We sit here for a long while, watching as the sun rises into the sky. I'm not sure what he's thinking about, but I know I'm silently hoping that we have hundreds more moments just like this one.

Chapter 10

Consummation

I WALK INTO Kai's office when I hear him calling me. I have no idea what could have set him off now, but judging by the bellowing of my name, I'm assuming it's not a good thing.

"What's going on?" I ask as soon as I walk over the threshold.

"What the fuck is this?" he roars, shoving a stack of papers at me.

I take them from him and instantly feel guilty. I haven't had a chance to talk to Tammy about the divorce. I've been so caught up with Kai and us spending time together, getting to know each other, that it didn't cross my mind. *Not even once.*

"Divorce papers," I whisper when I read the first page.

"I see that, Myla. Why the fuck did I just get served with divorce papers?"

Oh, shit.

"I wanted a divorce?" I whisper then look up in time to see him plowing towards me.

I naturally back up until I feel the wall behind me. His face comes within inches from mine, and my pulse picks up.

"I told you I'm not going anywhere," he growls, caging me in.

"I know." I close my eyes and turn my head to the side.

"I told you that we are going to work this out," he snarls, and I feel his hand on my side. "I told you we will *never* be over." His hand comes up and he cups my breast through the material of my top as his teeth nip into my earlobe.

"Kai," I breathe, and then I'm turned around and moving backwards. My ass hits his desk, and he leans over me slightly as he pushes all the papers and items off the top of his desk and onto the floor. "Kai," I repeat nervously as his hands go to my shorts.

He quickly unbuttons them, sliding them down over my hips along with my panties. He takes the papers I didn't realize I was still holding out of my hand, setting them on the desk. Then he lifts me to sit on top of them, spreads my legs wide, lowers his head, and buries his face between my wide-open thighs.

"Oh, God," I moan, holding on to his hair.

"Not God, Myla," he growls against my pussy, his teeth and tongue bringing me closer to orgasm.

"Kai!" I cry out, squeezing my eyes closed.

"Who's your husband, Myla?" he growls, burying two fingers inside me.

"Oh, God."

A loud slap sounds in the room as a sting tingles the skin of my thigh. My eyes fly open and I look down at him.

"Not God. Who's your husband?"

"You are."

"What's my name?" he demands.

"Kai," I whimper as his fingers move more quickly, curling up to hit my G-spot.

"Oh yeah." His mouth latches on to my clit, and I feel my body light up as my orgasm rocks through me.

My clit pulses in beat with my rapid heart rate. I squeeze my legs together as my thighs begin to shake with the intensity of every feeling coursing through my body. I look down at him as he lifts his mouth away. Then he wipes his chin on the inside of my thigh. I take a trembling breath, and my body relaxes back onto the desk, unable to hold myself up any longer.

"You okay?" he asks, leaning over me, taking my mouth in a deep kiss before I have a chance to answer.

"Awesome," I whisper when he pulls away.

He helps me sit forward, pulls my shirt off over my head, and then unhooks my bra, tossing them both to the floor. He then chuckles, leaning me back against the desk when he realizes that my body is of no use to me right now. I hear the soft whoosh of material and open my eyes just in time to see his shirt hit the floor. I look back up at him, and his hand lowers to his pants, undoing his belt and button then sliding them down. For the first time, I see how truly beautiful all of him is as his cock springs free then bounces against his lower belly.

He wraps his hand around his girth and pumps up and down, with his eyes locked on me. "Open up," he grunts as his hand runs up the back of my calf then up over my knee, pulling my legs apart.

I spread my legs, and he hooks his arms under my knees, pulling my ass to the edge of the desk. My legs wrap around his hips as my thumb runs over my oversensitive clit, making me jump.

"Easy, love," he whispers as I feel the head of his cock sliding over my clit then down, and I feel the crown press in as his head lifts and his eyes lock on mine. He slowly slides inside me. "*TU Kai*," he rumbles, sliding out then back in. My thighs wrap tighter around him, and my hips lift off the desk so I can take him deeper.

"Yes," I hiss as his hands go under my ass and lift me into each of his thrusts.

I move my hands up over his abs, feeling the strength under my palms then sliding them farther up over his chest and around his neck. His hands wrap around my waist, holding me in place as his thrusts speed up.

"I'm going to come again," I whimper.

His mouth comes down on mine, his tongue sliding into my mouth. I kiss him back then feel the waves of another orgasm close in, so I turn my head and, without thinking, sink my teeth into his shoulder. He roars as his hips jerk before planting himself deep inside me. I wrap my legs and arms tighter around him, not wanting to lose the connection. *Not yet.*

"Are you okay?" I whisper after a moment.

His head comes away from my neck, and his eyes lock on mine. "I had no idea," he says after another moment of silence.

"No idea what?"

"No idea that, when I married you, I would end up with this." He presses deeper into me. "I knew when I told you we should try to make this work that I wanted it to, but I didn't realize how important it was going to become to me. The idea of being without you is almost unbearable."

His soft-spoken confession causes warmth to spread deeper, but then I realize what set him off.

"I forgot all about you being served. I've been so caught up with us that I haven't even thought about anything," I confess, watching as understanding fills his eyes.

"They're ruined now," he smiles, and I realize that the papers are still under me and covered in us.

"Ewww." I frown.

"We just consummated our marriage on our divorce papers."

"That's very caveman-ish." I shake my head.

His smile softens, and his eyes search mine. "How are you feeling?"

"Happy." I run my fingers through his hair, and his eyes turn lazy.

"We need to get just enough clothes on to make it to our bedroom."

"Why?" I ask, feeling my eyebrows pull together.

"Because we're going to spend the rest of the day in it making up for lost time." His head dips and he licks up my neck. "I really need to be better acquainted with my wife's body."

"Okay," I breathe, pressing my thighs tighter around his hips.

"Hold on, love." He nips my neck and leans back, watching my face as he slides out. The endearment causes those ribbons of warmth to wrap tighter around me.

"Oh *no*." I close my eyes and cover my face. "No, no, no..." I shake my head. I can't believe how stupid we were.

"Myla, what is it?" He pulls my hands away from my face and looks down at me, frowning.

"We didn't use protection, and my birth control ran out."

"We did use protection." He smiles before pulling out completely.

I watch him pull the condom off, tie the end, wrap it in a tissue, and throw it away. I let out a silent, *Thank God*. This situation between us is complicated enough, and I cannot imagine adding kids as a factor.

I let out a breath and sit up, watching as he fixes his pants before coming back to me with his shirt. He opens it up, helping me put it on. He leans in, and his fingers go under my chin, tilting my head back and locking his gaze with mine.

"I would like you to get back on birth control. I almost didn't remember to use a condom, and I have a feeling it's going to be difficult to stay prepared." His hands run up my inner thighs before curling around my waist.

I think about how amazing it felt having him in me and how much better it would be if we didn't have anything between us, and my legs tighten.

"Oh yeah," he breathes. "I can imagine it too, sliding into you, feeling your hot, wet heat strangling my cock while your nails dig into my back."

"Kai," I whimper at the image then squeak when he lifts me. My arms go around his neck, my legs wrap around his hips, and his hands go to my ass.

"Hold tight." He opens the door to his office then quickly walks to his room, taking me into the bathroom. "Let's get cleaned up, and then I'm going to have a closer look at your tan lines." He sets me on the vanity.

"YOU'RE OBSESSED." I laugh, remembering all the times he has brought them up before and how strange I thought it was at the time.

He walks over to the shower then looks at me over his shoulder. "For months, I've had to look at them from afar, watch your skin darken, knowing that parts of you would forever be creamy white, and those parts are the best ones. So, yes, I'm fucking obsessed with your tan lines because I know that no one else will ever be able to see them but me."

He starts the shower then comes back to me, his hips going between my legs. My breath is still paused from his words, and I let out a harsh exhale as his hand comes up and his fingers run along the underside of my jaw. Then they move down to trace my collarbone and farther down between my breast before undoing the buttons of his shirt to spread it open.

I look down at myself, seeing what he's seeing. My breasts are pale, along with my lower stomach and hips. His finger traces the outline where dark meets light before going lower and doing the same along my stomach, making my muscles contract as his fingers run over my skin.

I take my hand and place it over his, admiring the contrast in our colors. He grunts, pulling me from the counter with his hands under my ass, carrying me into the glass-enclosed shower. As soon as we enter, the spray of warm water engulfs us, causing a moan of pleasure to leave my mouth.

"You can't make those noises right now—not when I don't have a condom in here and my cock is so close to the heat I can feel coming off your pussy." He slides me down his body, his cock hard against my belly as my feet touch the floor. "Step back."

I do and tilt my head back under the spray, wetting my hair as his fingers work through it. Then I lean my face forward, my gaze colliding with his as he pulls a bottle of shampoo off the shelf. He runs some through my hair before he tilts my head back again, rinsing the suds clean. When I step forward this time, he smears some conditioner in my hair and starts to lean me back again, but I stop him.

"My turn." I turn us and step up in front of him, grabbing the bottle of shampoo. I look at him, wondering how I will be able to reach the top of his head.

He smiles then mutters, "Hop up."

I put my hands on his shoulders and hop, wrapping my legs tight around him, the slickness of our bodies making him hold me tighter to him so I don't slide down. I reach over and grab the bottle I set down moments ago, squirting some in my hand then massaging it through his hair, using my nails to scrape over his scalp.

"Hell," he mumbles, closing his eyes.

I smile and press a quick kiss to his lips, whispering there, "Lean back."

He does, and I rinse the soap from his hair then grab the conditioner, following the same steps, only this time, his eyes are locked on mine as my fingers move through his hair, making the moment feel even more intimate.

When I'm done with his hair, his hands squeeze my ass once, signaling for me to hop down. When my feet hit the ground, he turns me in his arms and grabs a bar of black soap off the shelf. Holding it in his hand, he starts at my arms and slowly moves to my chest. Then he works it down over my stomach and lower to slide between my legs, where he carefully washes me. When he's done, my body is on fire.

I take the soap from him and lather my hands up before running them up his chest, over his smooth skin, which is warm and hard to the touch. As my hands travel over his abs, I become fascinated as his muscles twitch under my touch. My eyes travel lower, noticing the bead of pre-cum on the tip of his cock. Without thinking, I lean lower and lick the head, the salty taste of him exploding on the tip of my tongue.

"*TU Kai*," he groans, taking hold of my chin, forcing my face up to his. "Don't test my willpower right now, *makamae*. I'm hanging on by a thin thread."

The thrill of his words causes my eyes to go half-mast. I love that I can do that to him. I swear I feel my body feeding off the power I have over him, knowing he wants me so badly that he might snap. It causes me to sink to my knees, place my lips over the head of his cock, and swirl my tongue around it once. Then I wrap my hand lower, using my fist and mouth at the same time. My head tilts back as his hand tugs on my hair.

"I'm going to punish you for this," he growls, causing my pussy to convulse and a whimper to climb up my throat.

I take him as deep as I can as he thrusts into my mouth. Without warning, he pulls me up, the sound of me releasing him from my mouth echoing through the glass-enclosed space.

"I—" I start to tell him that I wasn't done, but his mouth crashes down on mine and he lifts me up, spreading my legs and impaling me on him. I cry out, my hands go to his shoulders, and my nails dig into his skin as he fucks into me hard and fast, my body gliding easily against his with the wet sheen of soapy water that is coating our skin.

"Come!" he roars.

My body takes over, listening to his command, my pussy convulsing as his hips jerk then still.

His forehead lowers to mine. "Yes, you're going to be punished. That time, I didn't use a condom," he says, but I hear no anger.

My eyes slowly open, my orgasm still floating through my system, making it hard to focus. His hand comes up, running from my temple down along the underside of my jaw. I lean in towards his touch and sigh when he pulls me away from the wall and back under the water.

"I'm clean," I mumble as the haze clears.

His hold tightens, and my arms slide farther around his shoulders as my ankles lock behind him.

"Not worried about that."

"We will be more careful."

He shakes his head, pulling out of me and setting me gently on the floor once again.

"The first chance I get, I'll get on birth control."

"We have a lot to learn about each other." His hand cups my cheek. Then he lowers his head, placing a kiss on my lips. "And if the gods are in our favor, a lifetime to do it in."

I like that a lot. I like that he wants this thing between us to work. "You're pretty amazing," I tell him honestly, feeling the warmth that is always in my stomach engulf me.

"It means a lot that you believe that."

His words catch me off guard, and I search his eyes for understanding. He carries himself with an air of confidence that is almost intimidating. Since I met him, he has seemed so sure of every single thing he has done, even things that have put a strain on our relationship.

"You don't believe that?" I question as he begins washing me up again.

His hands pause, and I can see that he's really thinking about how to respond. "Like I have told you before, I have never taken anyone else's opinion into consideration, good, bad, or indifferent. In my business, it's about how you respond to each and every situation. There has never been a time that I have considered someone's opinion of me."

"What about when you have dated?" I ask even though the thought of him with anyone else makes me feel uncomfortable.

"You're the first woman whose opinion of me I've cared about. I was never concerned with an assessment of the kind of man I am from the women I have been with before you."

"It seems like you've closed yourself off from everyone," I whisper sadly.

"It comes with the territory. I'm not talking about my family or even some of my men, but with others, you never know who could turn on you. You never know if the man who is laughing, showing you pictures of his children, is poisoning your drink behind your back."

His words cause a wave of sadness to crash over me. I can't imagine living my life in a constant state of worry, having to be on guard at all times. Without even thinking, I wrap my arms around him and burrow my face into his chest.

"I'm so sorry," I tell him, and his arms, which have wrapped around me, tighten.

"It's not going to be forever, Myla. I have been working to make sure that I will not have *years* of this left. When my kids come into this world, they will be able to live normal lives, never knowing about the life their father led before them. It's important for me that you understand that as well. This is not going to be forever. There will come a time when the house is just ours and there are not going to be others around on a constant basis. I hated having guards when I was growing up. It wasn't a good feeling when I went to speak with my father only to have one of his men stop me. I don't want that for my children, and I don't want that for you."

"I never thought about that."

Since I have been with Kai, there has always been someone around, and I have known since day one what they were here for, but I honestly never really thought about what their roles were in being around, never put much thought into why exactly they were here. And now that he has me thinking of it, I wouldn't want my kids to grow up with constant guards either.

I kiss his chest then step back. He turns off the water and opens the shower door. Then I follow him out, and he wraps a towel around me. I watch as he dries himself off and turns his head to look at me.

"I normally find it annoying that there are people around all the time. But I think I might find them useful tonight," he mutters.

"Pardon?"

"I only have a few condoms, and they can run to the pharmacy."

"You wouldn't," I gasp.

He kisses the frown off my face then swoops me up into his arms, making me scream out and clutch his shoulders. "I would." He smiles, tossing me onto the bed before following me down.

"You won't," I tell him as he spreads my towel open.

"I will."

And he does.

It's after midnight, I am starving, we only have one condom left, and I know that, at the rate we were going, we are going to need to stock up. At this point, I am thankful for having people around. That means I get to ride Kai to completion right before Chinese food and condoms are delivered to the door by one of his men.

Chapter 11
New Dreams

I WALK OUT to the water and dive under, needing to forget the last two hours. My mind is reeling over the information Kai has just shared with me. I do not want to be angry with him about keeping yet another piece of information from me, but I feel like I'm repeating myself over and over.

"Talk to me."

"Be honest with me."

"Tell me what's going on and don't surprise me with stuff."

Why is that so hard to understand?! I scream in my head, diving down deeper.

Kai and I had the perfect morning. He woke me up with his mouth between my legs. I love waking up with Kai, but I love even more the way he wakes me up most mornings—like I'm his breakfast and he's starving.

I have learned over the last week that Kai likes me on my hands and knees in front of him, and normally, after he has his fill of me, he flips me onto my stomach and pounds into me until his own orgasm takes him over. But this morning, he didn't do that. He took me slowly, his face close to mine while he rocked gently into me. I loved it, every moment of it, and when I was looking into his eyes as the waves of my orgasm hit me, I could have sworn I saw love there as he looked down at me.

When we finally got out of bed and showered, we had a small breakfast out on one of the balconies before heading into his office. I hadn't had a job and had gotten to the point that I was ready to jump out the window if I didn't find something to do with my days, so Kai had told me that I could help him out and get him organized. His office was a mess. There were papers and folders everywhere, and he didn't even seem to have a system.

So, a few days ago, I started getting things separated and put away into a filing cabinet I found, and then I scanned others things that could go straight into the computer. Today, I found a paper with my name on it. I was confused by the wording and didn't really understand what I was looking at, so I took it over to Kai, who had just gotten off the phone. When he saw the paper in my hand, his face had closed off and my stomach had dropped.

He sat me down on the desk in front of him to explain. My father had left real estate in my name before he passed away, and Kai's father—and now Kai himself—held the deeds to those properties. Not only was the land left to me worth millions of dollars, but the casinos that now sit on the land that was once owned by my father produced extra income.

I swim harder, cutting through the water, and then come up for air, inhaling deeply.

This whole thing wouldn't be so bad if I weren't falling in love with Kai.

He has done everything within his power to make me feel like he needs me as much as I need him, but this has me doubting his real reasons. Millions of dollars are attached to me, giving me the knowledge of why Thad was attempting to kidnap me. Whoever I married would have access to that property and, in turn, have access to all the money that was now mine.

And that is why my heart hurts. I married Kai without really questioning his motives. I didn't question why he would insist that it was the only way for him to keep me safe.

You're an idiot, Myla, and your self-preservation is basically nonexistent, I reprimand myself, looking at the horizon. It's so beautiful, almost as beautiful as the man I just ran out on. The life he has given me has all the makings of the perfect fairytale—a handsome knight saving the day, living in a beautiful castle, and falling in love.

"Fairytales don't exist," I whisper into the salty air then turn around and swim back to shore.

As I come out of the water, I see Kai sitting on one of the chairs that are closest to the beach. His eyes are covered with his sunglasses, but even through them, I can feel the burn of his gaze on my skin.

"We're not done talking, Myla," he growls, standing up and walking towards me.

I ignore him and walk into the house, not caring that the clothes I have on are the ones I just dove into the ocean wearing, dripping water everywhere.

"We need to talk."

I round on him and know that, if he would just give me a little bit of time, I would be better adept at understanding how I'm feeling, but like always, when he wants to talk, we must talk, and now isn't any different. All that does is serve to piss me off further.

"Stop." I hold up my hand when he starts towards me.

He pulls his sunglasses off and his gaze drops to my hand then lifts to meet my eyes again.

"I never wanted this—any of this." I wave my hand around. "I didn't want my parents to die, I didn't want my childhood to be blackened by someone I had trusted, and I didn't ask to fall in love with a man I'm not even sure I really know. So if you could just give me five fucking minutes to deal with how I feel, I will get back to you!" I scream and start to storm off again, but this time, I'm stopped when I'm suddenly pinned to the wall by Kai, who is breathing heavily, his face inches from mine.

"What did you just say to me?" he growls.

I push against his chest, wanting to get away.

"What did you just say?!" he roars.

My body stills, and I lean away from him. "I said I didn't want any of this," I whisper, closing my eyes.

"No, Myla. You said you didn't ask to fall in love."

"I never said that." I open my eyes and then close them when I realize he is right—I did say that.

Shit, that was not good. Not good at all.

"Do you think you're the only one with shit on the line here? Do you think it's easy for me to know that the woman I married—the woman I *love*—has a fucking target on her back? One that gets bigger every fucking day I spend with her? I make that shit worse. Knowing I could be the reason she's hurt—or worse—but not having the fucking balls to stay away from her because I knew she was meant to be mine from the moment I met her when I was ten years old..." He pauses, taking a breath. "This isn't fucking easy, Myla, but nothing good ever is."

HIS HAND COMES to wrap around the back of my neck, and his face dips closer to mine. "I understand that you need me to be honest with you, but I know—I fucking *know*—there is shit you're keeping from me as well. Shit that is big. So big that it forced you away from your family."

I inhale, feeling my pulse spike.

"I have let you have that, been waiting for you to figure out when you would be ready to talk to me about it, not wanting to push you too hard." He pauses again.

My insides feel like they are going to collapse in on me with the weight of his words.

"I should have told you about the shit your dad left you, but I didn't really see the point in doing that. You will never touch the money that comes from that land, even if we're not together. I won't allow you to touch it because it's fucking dirty. The men who want it are not good men, and I mean they are *not good men* in a way that they will kill you without even thinking twice about it. That is not what I want for you, and that sure as fuck is not what I want for any children we bring into this world."

His hand lets me go and he takes a step back. "So you can be mad that we didn't talk about it, but you need to get over it and trust me."

His jaw ticks and his hands fist before his voice softens to a tone I have never heard from him before. One that makes my insides feel like they have withered up and died. "This is what I was raised to do, and no one—not even you—will stop me from doing that." He snarls the last words then storms off down the hall.

I STAND THERE stunned for a moment as tears fall down my cheeks before walking to our room, where I start the shower, pull my wet clothes off, and get in. Then I slide to the floor, letting all of his words sink in. He loves me. He said that he loves me in a way that I know he really meant it, and I have no doubt that it is true.

I also believe him. He wouldn't want me to deal with anything that came from the money from the casino, and if I were honest with myself, I wouldn't want anything to do with that money either. My parents died, and before they did that, they'd sent me away, never wanting what was happening to *them* to touch *me*. I hate that I didn't have them, but for me, the idea of growing up knowing that the things I had around me had been purchased with dirty money didn't sit well with me.

I would never want that. And I understand why Kai has been working so hard to get his family out of the business they are in. I wrap my arms around my legs, put my forehead on my arms, and let the tears fall. I don't know how long I sit on the shower floor, but when I sit up, my body is stiff and the tears have finally started to lessen. I get up and take my time washing myself, not wanting to face the consequences of my actions.

It's so hard to trust anyone. And even though Kai has never given me a reason to doubt him, I have. I get out of the shower, go to the bedroom, and crawl under the covers without even drying off. I know I need to go find Kai and apologize for running out on him without giving him a chance to explain, and then I need to apologize for acting like a crazy women. Then I need to tell him that I love him and hope he forgives me.

More tears begin to fall as I think about the look in his eyes as he spoke his last words to me. I hate that I did that to him. I hate that I'm so screwed up that I didn't even take a moment to think about what I have learned about Kai over the last few months. I just jumped to the conclusion that he was out to hurt me and road that train all the way to Crazyville. I press my face deeper into the pillow, just wanting to forget everything that has happened.

I WAKE UP and the room is dark except for the moonlight that is glowing through the window. I roll over and realize that the bed is empty, and my pulse skids at the thought that Kai didn't come to bed. Sitting up, I push my hair out of my face. I gather my courage and get out of bed, walking to the dresser and finding a pair of panties and a top to wear before pulling my hoodie on over my head. I don a pair of sweats and head out of the room.

"Do you know where Kai is?" I ask Aye as soon as I open the door and step out into the hall.

"No. He hasn't been this way yet." He moves to my side. "What's up? You feeling okay?" he asks softly.

I'm sure that I look horrible. I don't even have to look in the mirror to know that my eyes are red and swollen from crying.

"I'm fine. I just need to find Kai," I mumble.

He starts to say something, but I shake my head and begin walking. I go to Kai's office first. The door is wide open, and the dark room is empty.

I continue on my way, and with every empty room, my anxiety begins to grow. Pausing in the main hallway and look out over the ocean at the moonlight that has cast a glow on the water. Inhale a frustrated breath then see Kai standing on the beach with his hands in his pockets. I swear I can feel his pain even from so far away.

I run down the stairs, out of the house, and onto the beach. I hear Aye yell behind me, but I ignore him and head straight for Kai, whose body has turned to face me. His arms open, and I jump into his embrace, but unlike the movies, where he should have caught me in flight, I knock him down, his body hitting the ground in a *harrumph* as the air is knocked out of his lungs.

"I'm sorry," I tell him, straddling his waist and kissing his face. "I'm *so* sorry," I whisper, looking into his eyes. "I promise, from now on, I will try to give you a chance to explain yourself instead of going off half-cocked. I didn't mean to hurt you. I would never want to hurt you."

"I know, love," he says gruffly, pushing my hair out of my face.

I close my eyes then open them up slowly, looking down at him. "I love you. I know I haven't done a good job of showing that, but I do love you."

His eyes close and he pulls my head down to his chest. "We both have a lot to learn," he repeats, something he has said to me a few times in the past.

"If the gods are smiling down on us, we will have a lifetime to do it in, right?" I question quietly.

"The gods have been smiling on me since I was ten years old and found a beautiful little girl crying in her tree house."

Tears begin to fill my eyes, and I place my chin on his chest so that I can look at him. "You saved me," I whisper. "I don't just mean what happened in Seattle. You saved me from myself. You have shown me that sometimes things that are a little scary and new can be the best possible things for you. You have shown me that I can trust again, and you have given me my family back. You saved me from me, and I would be lost without you." I sob, burying my face in his chest.

He holds me tighter to him, my tears continuing to fall. I cry until I can't cry anymore, until Kai shifts me in his arms and carries me inside. Then he lies with me in bed, holding me close to him, letting his warmth and love seep through the years of heartache.

I ROLL OVER, and Kai tightens his arms around me as I turn to face him. Once I'm comfortable, I study his face as he sleeps. It almost seems like all the power he normally has buzzing around him is shut off. I never would have believed I'd end up falling in love with a man like him. I lift my hand and run my finger along the scruff that has taken up residence on his chin.

"Why are you awake?" his sleepy, rough voice asks as his head tilts down and his eyes meet mine.

"I just couldn't sleep." I snuggle closer to him.

"Do you miss Seattle?"

He catches me off guard with his question, and I think for a moment about what I left behind. I miss the few friends I have, and I miss my bakery, but I don't miss Seattle.

"I don't miss it. I miss my bakery and some of my friends, but that's it," I say.

"When things settle, you could open a bakery here," he says quietly.

"I could call it 'Sunshine and Sprinkles.'" I smile at the thought. I have been so caught up in everything that has happened that I haven't really thought about what I want to do when life goes back to normal.

"You could. I want you to make a life here with me. I want you to be happy."

"I'm happy." I frown at him.

"You're happy now, but I've seen you bake. You smile when you're baking."

"My real mom used to bake. I don't remember much about it, but I know it was something she loved doing, and when I moved, my adoptive dad taught me how to bake. I used to love that quiet time with him. Then, when I left home, it was something that made me feel connected with a time when I felt loved," I say, whispering the last part.

"You wanna talk to me yet?" he asks cautiously.

"Not yet," I reply just as carefully, hoping that, one day, I will have the courage to open up to him. He's right. It's not fair for me to expect so much from him when I haven't fully been honest.

He rolls to his side and places his face near mine. "When you're ready, love, I'm here."

"I know." And I do know that I need to talk to him about it, but I hate myself a little for what was done to me. Even with the counseling I received and knowing that it wasn't my fault, I still hate that I wasn't stronger, that I didn't fight harder.

His arm slides around my waist, and his hand goes under my neck then up to thread through my hair at the back of my head, pulling my face closer to his chest. I wrap an arm around him in return then drift back to sleep.

When I wake a couple of hours later, I hear Kai talking to Aye at the door, and when Pika's name comes up, my ears perk up.

I have been worried about my friend, and Aye seems to be keeping his lips sealed on where he is, so the only thing I can imagine is that wherever he has gone to is not safe. Kai turns around to face me then says something out the door before walking over to where I'm still lying.

"What's going on?" I murmur as he comes to sit down on the side of the bed.

"Nothing." He leans over and kisses me, but I can tell that something's wrong.

"Please talk to me," I beg him.

"I have to go away for a few days."

"Why?" I sit up, pulling the blankets up with me, and scoot back to the headboard. I don't know what I will do if he tells me that we're over now.

"There's some business I need to attend to in Vegas."

"Okay," I say slowly, hoping he will continue. But instead, he looks around the room, anywhere but at me. "What is it?"

He stretches out his neck then looks at me again. "Pika's in jail."

"He's in jail?" I feel my eyes get wide. "What did he do?"

"Don't know. No one knows. The cops aren't letting him speak to anyone."

"That's illegal," I tell him.

He smiles then frowns. "I really don't want to leave you."

"I can come with you if you want," I suggest.

"You're not coming with me. You're safest here."

He's right. Here, all the flights and boats that come to the island are monitored, so Kai's men know if someone shows up. Plus, the house is completely secure. I feel safe here, and I know I wouldn't be able to say the same thing if I went to Vegas, even with Kai.

"I'm not sure how long I will be gone, but I need to go and make sure he's okay."

"I understand. I'll be fine. Is Aye staying with me?"

"Aye and Frank," he replies.

"So, basically, Aye is going to have to watch over Frank and me while you're gone?"

"Basically." He smiles and I giggle. "It makes my uncle feel useful."

"I like him a lot, and, your mom's right. He's funny, even if he is crazy."

"He likes you too. All of my family does," he says in a tone I have come to crave from him. Something about the way his voice goes soft makes that warmth seep into every cell in my body.

"Who are you taking with you?"

"My brother. I have my cousin and some men in Vegas, so I know that, once I get there, we'll be good.

"I hope Pika's okay. He didn't even say goodbye to me before he left," I whisper.

"He'll be fine," he says gruffly, and I nod.

I know Kai will make sure Pika is okay. I just wonder why the police are keeping him quiet.

"When do you need to leave?" I ask.

"After I get ready. The plane is being prepared as we speak."

"Do you want me to do anything? I can pack you up some clothes while you shower if you want."

"I have a place in Vegas. I keep clothes there."

Of course he has a place in Vegas, I think, and then I gasp as his finger runs over my nipple.

"There is *something* you can do though."

"What's that?" I ask.

"I need you to come shower with me."

A smile forms on my mouth and grows wider as his eyes heat. "You *want* me to come shower with you?" I scoot to my knees on the bed so I can get closer to him.

"Need," he rumbles as his hand wraps around the back of my neck, pulling my mouth to his.

His hands go to my waist and travel up my sides, pushing my tank top up and over my head, his mouth only leaving mine for a brief moment. His hands tug at my pants and he quickly pulls them off, placing his hand between my legs, his fingers zeroing in on my clit.

"Oh," I moan, and he pulls me onto his lap.

My hands go to his shoulders and my head falls back as his mouth leaves mine to trail down my neck. He widens his thighs and opens me up to his touch. His lips lock around my nipple as one finger enters me for a moment before trailing up and over my clit, circling it again. I grab his hair as his mouth trails over to my other nipple and tugs hard.

"Kai," I whimper as my nails scrape across his scalp and my hips buck against his hand. I trail my hands down over his chest to claw over his abs then run my fingers under the edge of his boxers, over the head of his cock.

"You want it?" he growls.

My head comes up and my eyes meet his. "I want it."

"Yeah?"

"Yes."

My head flies back as he enters me with two fingers. His other hand holds on to my ass, helping me to rock against his hand. I come on a moan, my face going to his neck. I come back to myself as his fingers leave me. I pull my face away from his skin and lean back enough to look into his eyes.

"Lift."

I lift my hips at the same time he works his cock out of his sleep plants. He reaches over to the bedside table and pulls out a condom. Then he uses his teeth to rip open the gold foil packet, making quick work of sliding the condom down his length.

"Com'ere." His hand wraps around my hip and he pulls me closer while he holds himself in place.

I slowly slide down, feeling every inch of him stretching and filling me. I still my movements when I have taken him in fully. His hands come up to frame my face, and no words need to be said. I can see everything he wants to say right there in his eyes. I hold on to his shoulders, using them as leverage as I lift and roll my hips. Our eyes stay locked on each other, just our hands moving. His cups my breast and rolls my nipples then slides down my waist, his thumb running over my clit. My hand drops and goes to our connection, feeling his cock entering me.

"You feel that?"

"Yes," I breathe as his thumb rolls over my clit. "So full."

"*TU Kai.*" His eyes close, and when they open, he takes his bottom lip between his teeth and starts pulling me up and down on him hard.

I whimper when he reaches a place deep inside me that has never been touched before. The pain mixed with pleasure brings me closer to orgasm. I lean forward and bite his chin then pull his lip between my teeth, nipping it before licking his mouth until his tongue tangles with mine and the taste of him I love so much seeps into my pores.

His hips begin to buck, and I grind myself down, crying out into his mouth as my orgasm erupts through me, causing a wave of pleasure to roll along every cell in my body. I distantly hear Kai roar my name as I slowly come back to myself. I feel his arms wrap around me and his face bury in my shoulder. Our breathing is labored, and my body feels like it weighs a million pounds as I slump against his chest.

"Are you going to be okay while I'm gone?"

I lazily lift my head and look into his eyes. "If I say no, would you stay with me?"

"Absolutely."

I blink at the absolution in his tone and swallow back my emotions. "I'll be fine." I don't want him to worry about me. I know he has his friend to think about. And I hope he can get things sorted out with Pika so that he can come home quickly, but I really don't want him to worry about me when he's away.

"While I'm gone, Mom's going to come over and go with you to look at some real estate."

"Real estate?"

"Just a few spots that you could open up a bakery at."

I take in his words and lean forward, kissing him again. "I should be receiving the money from the fire in the next few weeks."

"Then it's perfect timing." He smiles and my heart soars. "Though I will be paying."

"Paying for what?"

"Your new bakery."

"No." I shake my head. "You've already done too much for me."

He studies my face for a moment before looking away, and I have a feeling he just mentally erased everything I just said.

"Let's go shower so I can get to the airport." He lifts me off him and sets me to my feet before taking care of the condom, wrapping it in a tissue, and then throwing it in the trash.

I PUT MY hands on my hips. "I'm serious, Kai."

His eyes take in my posture before he mutters, "We'll talk about it when I get home."

I bite my bottom lip to try to keep quiet. I really don't want to fight with him right before he leaves, but I know we'll be talking when he gets home. When I first arrived in Hawaii, I tried to give him money for some stuff I needed from the store, but Kai turned me down and absolutely refused to even discuss my giving money for the things I needed. At the time, I was in such a bad place in my head that I didn't fight him harder on letting me pay my way.

He places his hand on my lower back, leading me to the shower and pushing me inside before following me. After the shower, we both get dressed—Kai in his usual suit and me in a pair of sweats and a tank top.

"I know you want to stop working how you work now, but does that mean you will stop wearing suits?" I question, taking him in. The dark-blue suit with the white dress shirt and tie all fit him like a second skin, showing off the taper of his hips and the wide expanse of his chest. I have never put much thought into men's clothing, but he seriously knows how to dress and does it well, so the thought of never seeing him dressed like he is now is slightly disappointing.

"Don't look at me like that when you know I have to leave," he growls, wrapping an arm around my waist, pulling my body flush with his.

"I was just asking a question," I mutter against his lips when his mouth connects with mine.

"Be good for me while I'm gone."

"You be careful," I whisper gently, trailing my fingers down his neck.

His eyes go soft as he shakes his head, kisses me once more, and then pulls me out of the room. I walk hand in hand with him to the front door, where he kisses me one last time before stepping outside and heading to his car, which someone has pulled up in front of the house for him. Once he's behind the wheel, he gives me a chin lift and I blow kisses at him.

Chapter 12

A Bullet and a Band-Aid

"**S**O, WHAT DO you want to do?"

I turn, come face-to-face with Frank, and smile. "Go to the beach."

"Oh," he says, sounding disappointed.

"What did you have in mind?" I ask him, and his face transforms and he gets a glint in his eyes.

"Have you ever shot a gun?" he asks.

I shake my head before replying, "I took self-defense classes and have done some martial arts training, but I have never shot a gun."

"Well, there is no better day than today." His smile widens, and he puts his arm around my shoulders.

"What's going on?" Aye asks when we walk into the kitchen.

"I'm taking Myla to learn how to shoot," Frank says.

Aye looks at me then to Frank and frowns. "Myla is not going to be anywhere near a gun. She would end up killing herself...or one of us."

"Hey!" I pout.

He looks at me and shrugs. "You know it's true." He raises a brow.

I roll my eyes.

"What if we get in a shootout?" Frank asks.

I look at him like he's crazy.

"It could happen," Frank adds.

I feel the blood drain out of my face, because I know he's right. It *could* happen.

"It won't," Aye assures me when he takes in my ashen appearance.

I swallow and think about what Frank just said. As nervous as it makes me, I know that he's right. I need to learn how to shoot.

"I want to learn," I say.

Frank's, "Really?" and Aye's, "Not happening," come at the same moment.

I ignore both and carry on. "I think it would be good to know…just in case."

"Kai won't like it, Myla." Aye argues.

"Kai isn't home and never has to know," I assure him.

He looks doubtful, but I can also see that he knows I'm right, even if he doesn't want to admit it.

"Fine, we'll go to the range, but you have to swear to do everything I tell you to do," Aye negotiates.

"Swear." I cross my fingers over my heart.

He mutters something under his breath then looks at Frank. "If she gets hurt, I'm blaming you." He points at Frank's chest.

"Sure," Frank says then smiles at me and winks.

"This is going to be bad. I'll go get the car," Aye mumbles, leaving the kitchen.

"It will be fine," Frank states.

I hope so.

"I CAN'T BELIEVE you shot me," Frank groans, lying back on the stretcher.

"It's barely a scratch." Aye rolls his eyes.

I squeeze Frank's hand, because even if it is just a scratch, he is right. I just shot him.

"A bullet hit me," Frank growls.

Aye just shakes his head.

"All right. You're free to go," the EMT says after placing a Band-Aid over the small wound.

"Are you sure that's safe? What if I have a concussion?" Frank asks.

The EMT looks at him like he has lost his mind.

"Come on, Frank. Let's get you home so you can lie down and rest," I interject.

"That's probably smart. I'm a little tired," he tells me, and I fight not to laugh at him. "And you should call me Uncle Frank." His arm goes around my shoulders and I feel myself stumble slightly from his weight.

"Okay, Uncle Frank." I tilt my head to look up at him.

He smiles, but then his face goes serious. "Don't tell Kai about this," he pleads.

I press my lips together to keep from laughing and nod my head once. Then I help him the rest of the way out to the car. No way would I tell Kai about this. I could only imagine his reaction.

Kai

AS SOON AS I get off the plane in Vegas, I head to the car that is waiting for me. Frank Jr., my uncle's son, is standing outside with his arms crossed over his chest and a look of displeasure on his face. He looks just like my uncle, but where Frank Sr. is slightly crazy, Junior is serious and has been my right arm since I was just a little kid.

"Brother," he rumbles, greeting me with a handshake and a half hug.

"How's it going?"

"Could be better, but then you know that or you wouldn't be here," he says.

"Did you get in touch with Rosenblum?" I ask him, opening the back door to the car and tossing my bag inside before heading to the driver's seat.

"He's meeting us there," he mutters once we're both seated.

I start the car but pull my phone out of my pocket, sending a quick text to Aye to let him know that I'm on the ground and ask him what Myla's doing. His text of, *Good. She's in the kitchen baking*, comes in almost immediately. I ease back in my seat, put the car in drive, and head for the police station downtown.

"My dad phoned this afternoon when you were in the air. Said he got shot today," Junior says nonchalantly.

My eyebrows pull together. If something happened, I would have been notified at the time.

"Did he shoot himself?" I half joke.

"Said your wife shot him."

I slam on the brakes, look over at my cousin, and pull my phone out, dialing my uncle's number before putting it to my ear.

"You land?" he asks on the first ring, sounding normal.

"About ten minutes ago."

"Good. Myla's safe and in my direct line of vision. I will keep you up to date on her whereabouts."

I grit my teeth and growl, "Heard you got shot today."

"Dammit, woman. I told you not to tell him you shot me," he complains.

I hear Myla in the background reply, "I haven't even talked to him!"

"How the fuck did Myla shoot you, Frank?" I bark.

"She wanted to learn how to shoot a gun," he says, and I hear Myla ask him what I'm saying.

"Goddammit, Frank! What the fuck were you thinking?" I holler.

"How was I supposed to know she was such a bad shot?" he protests.

"I'm going to kill you, Frank. Swear to Christ, when I get home, I'm going to kill you."

"Hey, now. I should be the one complaining. After all, I did get shot today."

"Where's Aye?" I demand, and the phone goes quiet for a moment.

"You don't even have to say it," Aye sighs.

"Apparently, I do. What the fuck were you guys doing?"

"Frank said it would be good for Myla to learn how to shoot, she agreed, and I agreed with them. The plan was good, man. Just the situation got fucked up."

"Do *not*...under any circumstance...leave Myla in Frank's care. You got me?"

"You know I wouldn't," he assures me.

"Good. Now, how bad was he hurt?"

"Grazed," he whispers, and I can only imagine my uncle eating that shit up like it was a near-fatal wound.

"Put Myla on."

"Hello," she says softly.

"No guns, *makamae*," I tell her firmly and hear her move around for a moment.

Then her soft, sweet voice slides down the line, wrapping around me. "I thought it would be good to know how to use a gun…just in case."

"If you still feel that way when I get home, I will teach you how to use one safely," I promise.

"Don't be mad at Uncle Frank. He was just trying to help."

"You shot him, which means you could have shot yourself, so he may have been trying to help, but he wasn't thinking clearly."

"In all fairness, I didn't know the gun was going to jump like it did," she confides.

I do not even want to imagine the kind of gun she was using that would *jump* the way she described. "No more guns."

"No more guns," she repeats. "Love you," she whispers after a moment.

I let those two words wash over me before replying just as quietly. "You too, *makamae*. Be good, and I'll call you when I can."

"Promise," she says before I click the phone off.

"I'm going to kill your dad one of these days," I tell my cousin.

"He tries." He shakes his head.

"He's crazy."

"True," he mumbles.

My uncle is a good man, but fuck if he isn't constantly causing drama. I stop at a red light and rub my hands over my face, thinking about everything that has happened and the battle I still have on my hands.

"How's Myla?"

"Good," I say, telling him the truth. She has put everything in prospective for me, and I know that, one day, when we're sitting on the beach, watching our babies play in the ocean, I will look back on these times and know that all the bullshit I had to deal with was worth it.

"So, you guys are for real?"

I look over at my cousin, a man I love like my brother, and speak the only truth I know. "There was never a time when it wasn't real. Even when I was fighting it, I still knew I would fight *for* it."

He grunts and shakes his head as the light turns green and I take off again.

Once we arrive at the police station, I see Richard Rosenblum, my attorney, standing near the front doors with his phone to his ear. We park, get out of the car, and head up the stairs.

"Just got off the phone with Judge Connell and explained that they have been keeping a client here without any explanation. He said he would be calling the chief now, so hopefully, by the time we get up there, they will have this shit sorted out."

"Nice to see you too, Rich," I mutter, but I feel my lips twitch. Rich, and his father before him, has worked with my family since I can remember.

"Yeah, yeah. We can catch up with a beer after we get your man out." He smiles as Junior opens the door and we all walk inside. Rich leads us to an elevator, then up another set of stairs, and into a large waiting room. "Wait here," he tells us.

I nod and watch him go to the desk and begin talking to the woman sitting there. When she picks up the phone, he shakes his head and says something that has her sitting up a little taller and glaring at him. I watch her mouth move but can't make out any words as she speaks to someone on the line before hanging up and saying something to Rich. He shakes his head and walks back over to us.

"The chief's in a meeting."

"Seriously?" Junior says, voicing my own question.

"My guess is he's on the phone with the judge. We'll give him a few minutes. After that, I'll make another call."

We sit there for another five minutes, and then one of the doors opens up and Pika comes walking out looking a little worse for wear. His clothes are wrinkled and his hair is in disarray, but he doesn't appear to be hurt in any way. He walks over to us as Rich walks over to the side to question the officer who brought him out.

"Glad to see you, man. A jail cell is not my ideal location to catch up on sleep," he grumbles, shaking my hand then doing the same to Junior.

"Did they say anything to you?" I ask.

He looks over his shoulder then back at me. I can tell he doesn't want to get into it here.

"We'll talk once we're out of the building."

I nod as Rich comes over to us. "Told me they can't talk to me." He shakes his head and looks at Pika. "We need to have a word once we're outside."

Pika nods, and we all leave, heading out to the large SUV we arrived in.

"You wanna tell me what all that was about?" Rich asks.

Pika rolls his head around his shoulders and looks at me. "Appears that someone knew I was keeping an eye on Paulie and Thad."

"What does that mean?" Rich asks, unaware of the weight of the situation.

Pika looks at Rich then back at me for permission, so I nod for him to continue.

"I was following Thad on his way to Paulie's house when, halfway there, the cops pulled me over. I didn't think much about it until they told me I was under arrest as a suspect in a burglary that happened in the area." He pauses, shaking his head. "I explained to them that I was nowhere around the area until that moment and they had the wrong guy. They explained that I fit the description of the suspect who was reportedly spotted in the area and I would need to go down to the station.

"Now, I may not be black, but my skin color is on the dark side of the color spectrum, so I did what they asked and went with them. I didn't think anything was strange until they kept me in lockup without even a phone call."

"This is bullshit," Rich says.

"This just proves there are a lot of dirty cops in this town, and the few who aren't dirty are afraid of what will happen if they try to go against the grain," Pika says.

"You want to fill me in on what's happening?" Rich asks.

I look around then back at him. "Not here," I reply.

"Let's meet at my dad's office in an hour," he offers.

"Pika can get a shower and something to eat before we meet you over there," I agree.

"See you then," Rich says, walking to his car as we all get in the SUV.

"Thanks for coming and getting me."

I look in the rearview mirror at Pika and shake my head. It's not his fault he has feelings for Myla; there isn't any helping it. If you're in her presence for a mere moment, you feel clean, and for men like us, that does something for your soul.

"We're family," I tell him simply.

He nods, and I look back at the road.

Once we get to my condo, Pika goes upstairs and showers. When he comes down, I'm on the phone with Kenton Mayson.

"You're sure Amidio is the one who was sanctioned to do the hit?" I question, 'cause if so, that is not good at all.

A few years ago, I would have said that that didn't matter, but now, it does. The man has gone crazy. There are whispers that he started using meth and that's why he's had a sudden change in personality, but I just thought all of those demons he had been carrying around had begun picking away at his conscience and what was left of his soul.

"That's the word on the street, so that's what I'm going to believe. They say there was some big real estate deal about to go down and not all the players thought it was a good idea. When they didn't back down and set up the meeting anyways, they decided to take out the threat indefinitely," Kenton explains.

That sounds about right. Real estate is huge, not only for the market value, but also for the street value. If you have a piece of property in a prime location where you could put girls, guns, or drugs, you could take over a city. That is the exact reason why I am never going to let Myla touch the property her parents left to her.

"I'm going to put in a call and see what I can do. For now, just keep your woman close."

"You know I will," I reply.

He hangs up, and I look at Junior then Pika.

"We may have to come back to the mainland for a bit. I'm going to need you guys to get everything set up for Myla here in Vegas. I want to find a house near the city, but far enough out that we have at least fifteen acres. I need you guys to make sure it's secure. Do whatever updates you need to do to it before I bring her here from Hawaii."

"What's going on?" Pika asks.

"I believe the relationship between Paulie and his son is about to change drastically."

Understanding flashes through Pika's eyes before he asks, "How long do you think we've got?"

"Not sure. I know it will take a couple of months to get stuff set up, and I won't bring her here until I know the new house is secure. This situation has been in the works for a while, so we have time, but I need to be here when shit goes down."

"Honestly, I'm surprised he's waited this long," Junior mutters and leaves the room with his phone in his hand.

"What do we need to do?" Pika questions.

"We need to figure out who all the players are before we make our move. From what I understand, Thad told Paulie Jr. he knew who Myla's parents were. Paulie, being who he is, knew that, if he could marry her, he would gain access to all of the land and properties her father had. In turn, he would become more powerful than his father, finally getting what he has wanted since he was sixteen."

"Why would Thad be involved? What does he have to gain from the

OBLIGATION

situation?"

"That's what I want to know," I mutter, running a hand over my jaw.

"She's afraid of him," Pika says quietly.

"She is. She hasn't spoken to me about why she fears him, but I know she does. She moved in with his family when she was young. She wasn't even really old enough to build real memories of her biological parents at that point, so all I can think is he scared her and she never got over it," I say, but something in my gut tells me that her fear has a much larger foundation than that.

"I don't know, man." Pika shakes his head.

I know he has seen the fear that comes into her eyes even when just her brother's name is brought up.

My jaw clenches and I growl, "Let me worry about Myla."

"Done," he mutters, holding up his hands, hearing the warning in my voice.

"We need to meet Rich," Junior says, coming back into the room.

"Let's go," I say.

We go out to the car, and this time, Junior gets behind the wheel and Pika hops in the back seat. When we arrive at the law firm, Rich and his father are both waiting. I let them know as much as I can. Rich's father has been taking care of my family since before I was born, but I trust *anyone* only so much.

"Are you heading back home?" Rich asks.

I look at him and shake my head. "No, I need to find a house here in Vegas before I leave."

"You've got your condo," he says, confused.

"I can't control the building. I need to find something out of town that has a few acres."

"I know an agent. I'll get you the info."

"Thanks," I mutter, shaking his hand before heading back out to the car.

I now have a few days to get things done before heading back to

Hawaii and explaining to Myla why we will be staying in Vegas for a while. I know she feels safe at home, and I hate taking her out of that environment, but I need to be here, and I won't be here without her.

Over the next two days, I look at over two dozen houses, and I am just about to give up and go home to my wife when I finally find a house I know Myla will love. It's a two-story adobe-style home on twenty acres. The house is much smaller than our house in Hawaii, but its open floor plan and updates are perfect for what we need, and I know my men can make it secure enough for us to live there comfortably while staying in Vegas.

I WALK INTO the house and go to the kitchen, wanting to grab a bottle of water before heading to find Myla. She doesn't know I'm home yet. We spoke earlier in the afternoon, and I told her I would see her tomorrow, but after signing the contract on the house, I got on the plane to come home. My body felt like I was going through withdrawals from being away from her.

I open the fridge, and I'm grabbing a bottle of water when something catches my attention out of the corner of my eye. I stand to my full height and flip the overhead light on. My eyes take in a cake that looks like it could grace the cover of a cookbook. I walk towards it and take in all the detailing. The white frosting looks smooth yet creamy. Three layers sit tiered one on top of the other, each layer displaying a single flower so perfect that, if you were not looking closely, you would believe they were real.

"You didn't tell me it was your birthday. Uncle Frank mentioned it, and I couldn't believe that I didn't know."

I look from the cake to my woman, my wife, who is wearing a pair of light sleep pants and a tank top. Her shoulder is resting against the doorjamb, her arms crossed under her breasts, lifting them higher, and the mass of hair she normally keeps tied up is down around her shoulders, framing her face.

"I never celebrate it," I tell her, and I honestly didn't even remember it's my birthday until this moment.

"That's what they said, but I wanted to make you a cake anyways." She shrugs.

I like that. I could imagine her floating around the kitchen, baking a cake with a smile on her face—the smile I only ever see on her when she's doing something she loves.

"You gonna feed me a piece?"

Her eyes go half-mast, and that look has my cock jerking in my pants. I step towards her, placing a hand on her hip, then look over her shoulder, seeing my uncle standing in the hall.

"Frank, you're dismissed."

He smiles and shakes his head, knowing exactly why I'm being so short with him.

"Thanks, Uncle Frank," Myla tells him then turns red when he gives her a wink.

Once I know he's out of earshot, I use my hand on her hip to pull her closer to me. "Missed you, *makamae*," I whisper against her mouth before kissing and licking the seam of her lips.

Her mouth opens and her body melts against mine as her taste floods my system. Her nails dig into my skin through the material of my dress shirt. With my mouth still on hers, I lead her backwards to the counter, lifting her up, spreading her thighs, and making room for my hips.

"I missed you too," she hisses as I nip at the skin on her neck and make my way over the swells of her breasts. She grabs my hair, causing me to growl as she pulls my mouth away from her skin. "Hold on," she whimpers.

I lift my head to look into her eyes. "What?" I question, breathing heavily.

She pushes my chest, and I regretfully help her off the counter and watch her as she goes to the fridge and reaches on top of it. Then she pulls a small box down before she turns the lights off. I wonder what she's doing, and then I see a flicker of light as a single candle on the top of the cake is lit.

"You have to make your wish," she tells me shyly.

I look at her beautiful face, which is only lit by the small candle, and wonder, not for the first time, what the fuck I did to please the gods so.

"I already got my wish," I tell her gruffly.

Her eyes go soft and her hair moves slightly as she shakes her head. "Do you know the reason you blow out a candle on a cake on your birthday?" she questions, carrying the cake towards me.

I shake my head.

"In ancient Greece, they did it to pay tribute to the goddess Artemis. They made a round cake to represent the shape of the moon and added candles to represent the moonlight. Later, people believed that, when the candle was blown out, your wish would go to the gods to grant. Some people believe the smoke from the candles will chase away evil spirits for another year. There is tradition in everything, every event, every holiday, and this is one tradition I want to share with you and, someday, share with our children."

Oh yeah, I like this. I don't know what I did to deserve having this for the rest of my life, but I know I will find a way to be worthy of it. I walk towards her, not even thinking about my wish, knowing what it is before I step in front of her and blow out the candle. I take the cake from her hands and gently set it on the counter before turning back to face her. Then I pull her by the waist, sliding my hands under her tank top, around her back, down over her ass, and inside her pants.

I slowly pull the thin material of her sleep pants over her hips and ass then down her thighs until gravity takes over and they fall to the floor. Then I travel my hand up over the curve of her hips and the dip of her waist until my hands meet the material of her tank top, pushing it up her sides and over her head.

"This is how you should always greet me," I say, bending and brushing my lips against her ear, feeling her shiver.

"There are too many people around," she moans as my hand slides around and down her belly.

My fingers slide between her folds then circle her clit. She's right; there are always too many fucking people around. But I know we are alone right now. I lift her up on the counter and hear her gasp when her skin touches the cool granite.

"What kind of cake did you make me?" I lean back and swipe my finger through the creamy white frosting.

"French vanilla with a mango center."

I hold my finger out and her tongue comes out. Her eyes lock with mine as she licks the frosting off slowly.

"You don't want any?" she asks.

I smile and lean back, taking another swipe of icing. This time, I gently smear it on the tips of her breasts before lowering my head and pulling first one then the other nipple into my mouth. Her body arches under me, and her feet dig into my back. I pull my mouth from her breast and kiss down to her belly button.

"It's good," I whisper against her lower stomach.

Her stomach quivers, and I nip the skin over her lower belly before locking my gaze with hers.

"But I've had better." I swipe my tongue over her clit before pulling it into my mouth with a gentle tug.

Her body starts shaking, and I pull away, breathing against her perfect core. Her eyes lock with mine and heat. I stand and slowly take my tie and shirt off before dropping them to the floor. The heels of her feet go to the counter, which opens her up to me. I growl in approval, quickly unhook my belt just enough to release my cock from the confines of my pants, and then slide the head through her wet folds twice before slowly edging inside her.

"Kai," hisses from her lips. Her back arches and her chest rises, causing my hips to buck and my length to slide in even deeper.

I have dreamt about her since I've been gone, and I haven't even used my hand to relieve the tension that has been building from waking up without her, so I know I will not be able to hold back the release I already feel building.

I roll my hips forward, and her hands come up to my shoulders. Fuck. She looks like some kind of pagan sacrifice spread open before me, her legs wide, her head back, the length of her hair touching the counter, and the moonlight bouncing off her features. I put a hand on her ass to keep her in place while my thumb goes to her clit, circling it. Her head lifts and her eyes meet mine as I begin pounding into her hard, each thrust causing her to tighten around me.

"You need to come." I slap her thigh, causing her to get wetter as her head falls back and her hands slip off my shoulders.

She lies on the counter, her back arches, and her hands roam up her stomach to hold on to her breasts, her fingers pulling on her nipples. Fucking beautiful. I have never seen anything more erotic than her writhing on the counter, getting off on the way I'm fucking her.

My thrusts speed up, and her hand travels down to where mine is rolling over her clit. Her legs wrap tighter around my hips as her pussy begins to convulse, her orgasm milking mine from me.

I lay my head on her chest, trying to catch my breath as I listen to the sound of her heavy breathing and enjoy the feel of her heart. I feel her shaking, and I wonder if she's crying. When I look up at her, her head is back and there is a stunning smile on her face, which I can see even in the moonlight.

"I'm going to get offended in a minute," I tell her.

Her head tilts down and our eyes lock. "Don't. That was awesome."

I chuckle and pull my weight off her, helping her to sit up while simultaneously sliding out of her. "Why were you laughing?"

"It's nothing." She closes her eyes.

I look down, seeing that I have once again fucked up and not worn a condom. I have never had this issue before her, and I don't understand what it says about her that she has the ability to cause me to be so reckless. Not that I would mind her ending up pregnant, but I know that that's not something she is comfortable with at this time, and I respect and love her enough to give that to her—at least for the time being.

"Tell me?" I pick my shirt up and help her slip it on.

"Just…at the rate we're going, I will never be able to start birth control."

"Pardon?"

She bites her lip then looks around before looking at me. "The doctor said I couldn't start until after I have my period." Her brow furrows and then her eyes get big.

"What?"

"Oh no," she whispers, covering her mouth.

"Myla, what?"

"I'm late," she breathes as all the color drains out of her face.

"Late for what?" I question, still confused.

"Oh no, oh no, oh no…" she chants, her eyes still locked with mine. Then it hits me.

Late. She is late for her period.

I feel my body lighten, but then I take in her ashen expression and instantly become concerned. "Talk to me," I tell her gently while tucking myself back into my slacks.

"It's too soon. We're not ready."

"It's not too soon." I gently place my hand on her stomach, overwhelmed by the thought that my child could be growing in there right now.

"We need to go to the store," she says, moving my hand and jumping off the counter.

"I'll send someone."

"No," she pleads, grabbing me with both hands. "If I am, I don't want anyone to know."

"We, *makamae*," I growl.

"What?" She shakes her head, looking around the kitchen.

"That's *my* son growing inside you. You're not in this alone, nor will you ever be."

"Kai." She shakes her head and tears begin to fill her eyes.

"This is our moment, and we won't share it with anyone else, but this is about both of us," I tell her firmly.

"You're right," she whispers. "I just… I just never planned for this. For *any* of this."

I catch a tear as it falls and remind her softly, "I never planned for any of this, either."

"I know." She closes her eyes then opens them back up. "I need to know if I am."

"I'll take you to the drugstore. We don't even know if you are, so you may still get your wish." I hear the deadness in my tone as I lead her back to our room. I grab a clean shirt as she quickly gets dressed.

The trip to and from the store is silent. I'm trying not to be pissed about this situation. I understand there is a lot to take into consideration, but I'm angry that she acts as if it would be the end of the world to have my child.

"Let me do that," I tell her, noticing that she is shaking. I take the box from her hand and open it up.

"What if it's negative?" she whispers, looking at the test.

I fight back the words that are on the tip of my tongue, and when she speaks, I'm glad I did.

"On the way to the store, I imagined what it would be like to know that I was pregnant. I was still scared, but there was also excitement mixed in there. Now, if I go and take this test and it's negative, I think I may be disappointed."

The anger that was building simmers down. I tilt her chin up so that I can look her in the eyes. "There's always someday, Myla."

She nods and walks to the bathroom, pausing to look at me over her shoulder before walking in and closing the door. It feels like forever that she is out of my sight, so when the door opens and she walks out, I pull her into an embrace.

"Do you have a watch?" she asks quietly.

"Yeah."

"We're supposed to wait three minutes," she whispers before burying her face in my chest.

I look at my watch, set the timer, wrap my arms around her, and then wait. When the alarm goes off, I press a kiss to the top of her head before she pulls away. She comes back a second later, holding the test in her hand.

I can't read the look on her face, so I hold out my hand to take the test from her. "What does it mean?" I ask, seeing two pink lines.

"I'm pregnant."

I look from the test to her and smile. "Yeah?" I question, my smile getting bigger.

Her face softens and she leans forward, taking the test out of my hand and looking at it again. "You're happy about this?"

"Yes," I tell her, not even a single ounce of doubt in my head. I know that this is right.

"I'm pregnant," she repeats then looks up from the test, her gaze meeting mine. "I feel excited. Is that weird?"

I exhale a breath, the stress I was feeling immediately leaving my chest. "It's not weird," I assure her then smile when she jumps up, wrapping her legs around my waist.

"This is crazy."

She is right about that, but since the moment I saw her in Seattle, our relationship has been crazy.

"Now let's go have some cake since you already gave me my wish," I tell her, and her face goes soft and her hands come up to either side of my face.

"Let's have cake," she whispers, pressing a soft kiss to my lips.

Chapter 13

Oh Baby

Myla

SINCE FINDING OUT I am pregnant, all the plans for going to Vegas were put on hold. Kai didn't want to risk something happening to the baby or me, and to be honest, it was one less thing for me to worry about. I hated the idea of being in an unfamiliar place, where I didn't have anyone to lean on. Kai's family has become mine during my time since I moved to Hawaii, and his mom is excited to be a grandmother. Even though I am just weeks along, I don't want to take that from her. Especially when we didn't know how long we would be in Vegas.

Now, as I look down at the water and watch Kai come out of the ocean looking like a warrior ready for battle, my insides become liquid. I never in my wildest dreams would have believed that someone like him would be my husband and the father of my child, but things always have a way of working out, just like they are supposed to.

He prowls towards me, the ocean water still running over the contours of his skin, and doesn't stop until he's caging me in, one hand on each side of the lounger I'm lying on.

"You should go inside." He kisses my nose then my lips as his hand at my side moves to lie on my lower stomach.

"I'm comfortable." I smile, stretching up and kissing him.

"Have you been drinking water?" he mutters as his fingers play along the edge of my swim bottoms.

"Yes." I roll my eyes when his eyes stay locked on where his fingers are touching me.

"It's hot out today." He finally brings his eyes up to mine and I notice they are darker than normal.

"Honey, we're in Hawaii. It's always hot."

His eyes go soft, and he presses another kiss to my lips. "I'm going to see about getting a chair that has a cover over it."

"I like the sun," I complain.

I love that he cares about me, but I swear, since we found out about the baby, he has been high-strung and doing everything within his power to drive me absolutely bonkers.

"It's not good for you, *makamae*."

"Kai." I shake my head.

He brings his hand up, his fingers tracing the edge of the top of my bikini, pulling it down slightly so the skin that is still untouched by the sun is exposed.

"Let's go inside." His finger runs under the material and over my nipple, causing me to gasp. "I'm hungry." He licks his lips, and my eyes follow his tongue. That liquid heat in my belly expands and spreads between my legs. "Myla." My name comes out like a warning as I lift my hand from my lap, running it over his abs and along the elastic of his shorts.

It's so difficult to keep my hands off him, and over the last couple of weeks, my need for him has only gotten worse. Luckily for me, Kai never denies me anything.

"I can see that you're wet," he whispers near my ear.

I pull away to look into his eyes. His gaze is locked between my legs, and I notice the damp spot on the piece of material.

He pulls his lower lip into his mouth, and his fingers flex into my skin. His face lowers towards my belly and he places a kiss there. Then he sucks, making my belly clench and more wetness spread between my legs.

"I can smell you." He nips lower on my stomach, right above my mound.

My hand tangles in his hair and I try to pull him away.

"*TU Kai*," he rumbles, making me squirm. "Up," he says.

I don't even realize he's lifting me until my ass is off the lounger and my arms are forced to wrap around his neck so that I don't fall to the ground.

I cling to him as he carries me inside to the bedroom. He kicks the door shut with his foot and carries me to the bed, gently setting me down before stepping back and pulling his shorts off. I lick my lips when his cock bobs against his stomach as he steps in front of me. When he pulls the string on each side of my waist, my bottoms drop to the bed, and then his hands quickly remove my top.

"Um," I whisper as he gets on the bed and adjusts me so that I'm facing the headboard and my pussy is right over his mouth.

"Feed me, *makamae*."

I look down at him and my hands press against the wall as I exhale slowly before lowering my hips. His eyes, which are locked on mine, heat, and I pause, leaning back so I can fully see his face and not just his eyes. His hands go around my thighs, and he pulls me down onto his waiting mouth.

At the first touch of his tongue, I watch his eyes close like he just tasted the most amazing thing he has ever eaten. When he licks me again, his tongue swirls around my clit, and his fingers dig into my thighs, pulling me deeper into his mouth.

"Kai," I whimper.

"Ride my tongue, baby," he growls, causing my pussy to contract and my hips to rock against his mouth.

My hands go to my breasts and I pull my nipples, which have become extra sensitive. I'm so lost in the way my body is feeling that I'm startled when Kai's mouth leaves me.

"Turn around."

It takes a moment to get adjusted, but when I do, my hands go to his stomach and run down his abs. One hand wraps around his cock and the other holds his heavy sac as I lower my face and lick the head of his cock, tasting the salty taste of him on my tongue.

His hips lift, and I suddenly feel powerful. Even with his mouth devouring me, I'm in control of the way he feels. I lower my mouth just enough to swirl my tongue around the head of his shaft, not going any farther down, even when his hips lift like he's begging me to. I remove my mouth and slowly slide my hand up and down, enjoying the feel of him in my hand, the way he feels smooth and hard.

I lick the head again, only this time, I take him to the back of my throat and moan when he rewards me with his fingers entering me. I lift then lower my mouth; each action is rewarded with a pull or a tug from his mouth. I'm getting close and know that, when I finally fall over the edge, I am going to be lost.

When his fingers begin moving faster, I whimper around him and start moving faster. I know that, when he comes, I will come too. I begin using my hand in sync with my mouth then gently cup his balls.

That's when it happens. His mouth latches on to me, quickly flicking my clit. I cry out around his cock, and the taste of him erupts on my tongue. I swallow him down as lights flash behind my closed lids, and my body explodes in the most mind-blowing orgasm I have ever had. It is like nothing I have ever felt before.

I lay my head on his thigh, taking large gulps of air while trying to get my body under control. He rolls me to my side then turns around to lie the way I'm facing, wrapping his arms around me, pulling me into his chest, and running his hand up and down my back while our breathing returns to normal.

"That was insane," I tell him, lifting my head and resting my chin on his chest.

His head tilts down so that his eyes meet mine, and a look I have never seen before fills his eyes.

"You come hard, *Makamae*, every time I eat you, but that time, you soaked my face."

I lower my face so that he can't see how red I am, but his hand tugs on my hair, lifting my face up until our gaze locks again.

"It's beautiful knowing I have that kind of control over you," he says softly.

He's right. When we're together, I find it easy to hand everything over to him. *I love knowing he'll take care of me*, I think as I drift off to sleep.

"TAMMY!" I CALL out when I see my lawyer—or, I guess, ex-lawyer—walking across the street.

Her head turns, she looks between Kai and me, and I see something in her eyes, but from the distance between us, I can't make it out.

"Myla." She smiles, schooling her face and walking towards us.

I look up at Kai to see if he noticed anything strange. His jaw is clenching, and the vein I have occasionally seen pop out of his neck when he's mad is displayed above the collar of his white shirt.

"How are you, Myla?"

I swing my head to Tammy and smile, stepping away from Kai to embrace her. "Good. How are you?" I question, stepping back.

Her eyes go from me to Kai, and she swallows then smiles. "Really good. I'm seeing someone," she says then looks up at Kai before bringing her eyes back to me.

"Sorry for being so rude. This is my husband, Kai. Kai, this is Tammy," I say.

Tammy smiles, but Kai doesn't say anything.

"So, you're seeing someone? That's nice." I smile awkwardly and feel Kai move slightly behind me.

"Sorry, *makamae*, but we need to hurry," Kai says.

I look up at him and nod before looking at Tammy once again. "Sorry. We have a doctor's appointment today to find out what we're having. He's a little anxious." I grin, setting a hand on my stomach.

You have to look close to see that I'm pregnant, but there is a roundness that wasn't there before, and today, we just hit our fifteenth week, so we will finally know for sure what we are having. Though Kai swears that it's a boy.

"You're pregnant," Tammy whispers, looking at Kai, me, and then my belly.

"That's why you didn't follow through with the divorce," she says, and I feel myself turn red. Her hand covers her mouth. "Sorry. I didn't mean that."

My gut clenches and my stomach is starting to feel sick. "We didn't know at that time." I shake my head, feeling like I need to make it clear that we had agreed to be together before we found out we were having a baby.

"I gotta go," she says, and I watch her leave in a hurry.

I turn to face Kai and search his face for a moment before letting my eyes drop to the ground. "That's your ex-girlfriend, isn't it?" I whisper, feeling like a complete idiot. And a bitch—an idiotic bitch.

"She is," he confirms, making me feel worse.

"I'm sorry," I whisper, watching as my tears fall to the concrete at my feet.

"You have nothing to be sorry about, Myla." He tilts my head back to meet his eyes. "We were over long before you came into the picture."

"She still loves you," I tell him, but he shakes his head.

"She liked the idea of being with someone more than the actual part about having a relationship."

"What?" I ask, feeling my brow crease.

"She is one of the only lawyers in town. She has an important job, and that was always more important to her than building a relationship with me. I accepted that, and I also accepted that she wasn't my future. She's a sweet, beautiful woman, but she is married to her practice."

"You loved her."

"No, *makamae*." He runs his finger down the bridge of my nose. "I cared for her. She's a good person, but I never loved her. Love is an obsession that, no matter how hard you try, you can't fight. I love *you*."

"I hope that she finds that," I tell him.

His face goes soft and his fingers skim along the underside of my jaw. "I hope so too."

He takes my hand again and leads me down the street to the doctor's office. Once inside, we head straight to reception, where we're given a form to fill out before being taken back to one of the exam rooms. As soon as I'm settled on the table, the doctor comes in with a smile on her face. She's short, about five one, with jet-black hair that sits at the edge of her jaw, making her already striking Asian features stand out even more.

"Myla." She pats my leg then looks at Kai and mutters, "Hi."

Did I mention that she hates my husband? Okay, *hate* is a strong word; she strongly dislikes him. During my first visit, Kai freaked out when I started spotting after the internal exam. He threatened to have the clinic shut down. That did not go over well at all. I swear I thought the small woman was going to murder him. It took ten full minutes to get Kai calm enough to listen that I was okay and it was normal.

"How are you?" I ask her.

She smiles then looks at Kai and glares. "I've been good."

"That's good," I mutter, squeezing Kai's hand hard enough that I see his skin turn a shade lighter in color.

"Let me get stuff set up for the ultrasound," she says quietly, walking over to the sink to wash her hands.

"Sounds great." I put on my cheerful voice, and her face softens some, but then it goes hard when Kai moves and reminds her that he's still in the room with us.

When she comes back, she feels around on my belly for a moment then squirts the clear gel onto my skin and begins moving the device that looks like a remote control around on my stomach. The *swoosh, swoosh* sound comes before the rhythm of a quick heartbeat fills the room.

Kai's hand tightens around mine. This isn't the first time he has heard our baby's heartbeat, but even now, I can see the look of wonder in his expression as he searches the screen in front of the doctor.

I was scared when I realized I was late for my period, but the more I thought about it, and the more I thought about who the father of my child is, the more excited I became. I knew that Kai and I still have a lot to learn about each other, but I also knew there was no one else I would want to have a family with. I knew that Kai would always do everything within his power to protect me and any children we have together, and really, when you're looking for someone to be the father of your child, I think that is the most important quality there is.

"I need you to sit up a little for me," she says.

My back comes slightly off the table. Her hand presses around on my stomach before helping me lie back down.

"Let's see if that helped." She begins rolling the device around on my stomach again before looking up at me and smiling. "There you go." She gets a strange smile on her face then looks at Kai. "You're having a boy."

"I know," Kai tells her.

She narrows her eyes then looks at me like, *What the hell are you doing with a jerk like him?* All I can do is shrug, 'cause the way I see how Kai comes across to everyone else is *not at all* how he is to me. I can count on one hand the amount of times he's even slightly raised his voice at me.

"He's been saying for weeks that it's a boy." I smile, looking up at him.

His eyes come to me and his face lowers as he presses a kiss to my lips before he stands to his full height again.

"Would you like some pictures to take home with you?" she questions, ignoring my last comment.

"Yes, please," I whisper.

She begins clicking away on the screen as I try to see more. Once she's done, she prints off a few of the pictures and hands them to me before making her way out of the room without even saying goodbye.

"I think we're going to have to find a new doctor, or you're going to have to find a way to apologize to her somehow so that she doesn't make it uncomfortable for me to be here."

"You're uncomfortable?" he asks.

I look up at him and wonder if he's oblivious to what just happened. "Yes, I'm uncomfortable! It's awkward to be in the same room with you two."

"I'll apologize," he promises, taking the towel I was using to clean the gel off my stomach away from me and cleaning me up.

"I didn't even get to enjoy the moment," I pout. When his eyes change slightly, I immediately regret saying anything.

"Do you want her to come back and to do it again?"

"No." I shake my head frantically. "Just apologize to her."

"Told you I would," he mutters, but I can see it in his eyes that he doesn't want to.

"Good." I slip off the table and fix my pants, my mind finally focused on what the doctor said. "We're having a boy," I breathe, adjusting my clothes. "You're really not surprised that we're having a boy, are you?"

"No. I knew." He kisses the top of my head and opens the door.

"How?" I ask, pausing in the hall to search his face.

"Don't know. I just knew it was a boy."

"Strange." I shrug and begin walking again.

His arm goes around my shoulders, and we make a quick stop to schedule our next appointment before heading out to the car. We don't talk on the way back to the house, but our hands stay locked together on my lap, the fingers of my free hand running over his skin.

"Thank you," I tell him, looking down at our entwined fingers when he pulls up to the house and puts the car in park.

"For what?" he questions, confused.

I lift my head and look at him, thinking about all the things I want to say. "For giving me everything."

His eyebrows pinch, and I soften my voice.

"For marrying me, for loving me, for giving me a child. Even if I was never expecting any of this, I'm still thankful for all of it."

"The gods had written you into my destiny a long time ago, *maka-mae*," he says quietly. His face softens as he lifts my hand to his mouth, where he places a kiss on my ring.

Chapter 14

Explosion

"**P**IKA!" I YELL from upstairs when I see my friend sitting in the living room, looking out at the ocean.

His head turns towards me, and I carefully run down the stairs and throw myself into his arms. He catches me on a *humph* and gives me a squeeze before pulling away and removing his hands from me.

"How are you?" I smile, happy to see him.

"Good." He smiles back then looks me over, his eyes settling on my round stomach for a moment. "You look happy," he says as his eyes meet mine again.

"So happy," I whisper, and he nods as his face softens.

"Myla."

I turn my head to look at Kai and smile, putting a hand on my hip, giving him a mock glare. "You didn't tell me Pika was coming home."

"It slipped me. Can I please see you in my office for a moment?" he asks, and I notice the agitation in his voice as he speaks.

"Um…" I look at Pika then back at Kai, wondering why the guys are acting so strange. "Sure," I tell him then turn and give Pika another hug, whispering that I'm glad he's back before pulling away, but not without noticing the embrace is not shared and his hands stay at his sides. Before Kai came home all those months ago, I would often lean on Pika, so the distance he's putting between us is slightly unsettling.

"Myla," Kai growls.

I nod then head towards his office, wondering what the hell happened. He's standing in his doorway when I get there, and all I can do is pray that something bad hasn't happened. Things have been quiet lately, and I would like them to stay like that. As soon as I cross the threshold, he closes the door behind me and begins pacing back and forth.

"Is everything okay?" I whisper, sitting down in his chair and watching him.

"Do not touch Pika again."

Of all the things I thought he might want to talk to me about, this was never one of them. I study his face and notice that his jaw is tight and there is a slight tick in his right cheek—the tick he gets when he is pissed off.

"Can I ask you why?" I question softly, leaning back in the chair.

"Because I don't like it."

"Kai—"

"No, Myla. All I need you to say is that you won't touch him again."

"You act as if I tried to make out with him," I mutter.

"You threw yourself at him," he snarls, ripping a hand through his hair, his gaze going out the window.

"I missed him. He's my friend," I say softly, watching him.

He prowls towards me until his face is inches from mine. "Do not do it again. Got it?"

I lean back, struck by his words and the intensity in his voice. "Do not tell me what to do, and do not *ever* get in my face like that again." I go to stand and his hands go to either side of the chair, caging me in, forcing me to stay seated.

"You do it again, Myla, and I will send him away. And this time, it will be for good." His tone is so deadly that a chill slides down my spine.

I have never, not once, been afraid of Kai, but this guy in front of me right now is not the man I fell in love with. This guy is someone completely different—someone who I don't like very much. I want to ask him what happened and why he's acting like this, but instead, I nod and swallow the hurt down so that I can get away from him.

"I won't do it again," I whisper.

His position in front of me doesn't change, and he searches my face for a moment then leans in. When I see his intention, I turn my head just in time for his mouth to miss mine and his lips touch my cheek.

"Myla," he says softly, and that softness only helps to piss me off further.

"I don't feel well. I think I need to go lie down," I say, looking back into his eyes. Concern transforms his features and guilt settles in my gut, but I don't let that stop me.

"Let me help you to bed." He stands to his full height but doesn't step back.

"No. I'll be fine." I drag my eyes from him and use the wheels of the chair to scoot back enough to stand. I walk around him and pause when my hand touches the knob.

I turn my body around and straighten my shoulders, knowing that, if I just leave right now with the things he just said ringing in my ears, I won't be able to even look at him or myself in the mirror.

"I don't know what happened or why you're acting the way you are, but let me make one thing clear so this doesn't happen again." I inhale a deep breath, letting it out slowly, making sure the words are well defined in my head before I spew them out. "I'm not one of your men. I'm not someone you can boss around and tell what to do. I'm your wife by choice, and like all choices in life, they can always be changed. So if you ever talk to me like that again, we will be talking through a lawyer when you're done."

I turn, open the door, and step out, shutting it behind me before taking off to our room. As soon as I reach our door, I notice that Aye is standing in the hall. I give him a wave, walk into the room, close the door behind me, and lean my head back against the wood as tears begin to slide down my cheeks. I know that jealousy was fueling his emotions, but I just don't understand why.

Then his words filter into my mind. He said that he would send Pika away for good this time, meaning he had sent him away before. I had never even thought about Pika—or Aye, for that matter—in a sexual way. Kai had consumed my every thought from the moment I'd met him, and he'd continued to do so.

I step away from the door and begin pulling my clothes off as I step towards the bed. My reflection in the mirror over the dresser catches my attention, and I pause, looking at myself. My hand goes to my stomach and I lay my palm over our son, whispering a silent prayer that his dad and I can find a way to work things out.

I feel a flutter and press my hand closer to my stomach, trying to feel it again. I have never felt him move before, and a smile spreads across my lips when there's another flutter, this one stronger than the last. I go to the bed and lie down on my back, placing my hands on my stomach and smiling again when there's another movement. It feels like butterflies are dancing in my stomach, and I can imagine my tiny baby boy rolling and doing flips.

"Why are you smiling?"

"The baby's moving." I smile then press my lips together when I realize I have just spoken to Kai when, only moments before, I had plans to give him the silent treatment for a few days at least.

"You can feel him?" he asks, and I can actually feel him getting closer to me, his energy wrapping around me.

I don't want to answer him, but I can't help it. "I can feel him," I tell him, not opening my eyes.

The bed dips, and his hand slides under my palm to settle on my stomach. I place my hand at my side and silently lie there, listening to him breathe. I don't like feeling uncomfortable around him, but right now, I don't even want him to touch me.

"Do not ever threaten to leave me again."

My chest compresses, and I inhale through my nose at his words.

"I shouldn't have spoken to you the way I did."

Got that right, jerk, I think.

"Look at me, Myla."

I squeeze my eyes tighter in refusal, and his free hand comes up to hold my jaw.

"He told me he was in love with you," he snarls, and my eyes fly open. "Do you know how it feels to know that another man is in love with your wife?" His fingers at my jaw move so his thumb can run over my bottom lip. "Knowing that, when you were not around, she accepted comfort from him?"

"I nev—"

He cuts me off, pressing his thumb over my lips as his face dips closer to mine. "It doesn't matter. I've tried to tell myself that it didn't mean anything, that you didn't feel the same."

"Pika is a friend, the same as Aye," I whisper.

"I know this, Myla," he growls.

I scoot away from him leaning against the headboard.

"My world is consumed by you and thoughts of you. The idea of someone interested in you makes me fucking homicidal. Knowing that he's someone I consider a friend, someone I entrust with your well-being, does not make me feel better. Then seeing you happy to see him, watching your face light up when you realized he was back—it was like a fucking knife to my gut." He moves closer to me, and his body turns so that one hand goes on either side on my hips. "I reacted poorly, *makamae*," he says gently, and my heart hurts from the vulnerability I see in his eyes. I hate this.

"I don't even know what to say right now. You really scared me." I close my eyes then feel his arms wrap around my waist and his head lie gently on my stomach. We are going to have to find a way to work this out or it will be something that drives both him and me insane. "I love you and only you," I tell him, lifting my hands to run through his hair. "You said that I consume you. Well, you have consumed me too, from the moment I wake in the morning until I go to bed at night."

I take a breath and tug on his hair until his eyes come to me. "I love you, Kai. When you make me mad enough that I swear I could spit fire or happy enough that I feel like I'm walking on air, I'm always yours and no one else's." I whisper the last part.

His eyes search my face for a moment before he ducks his head, kisses my stomach, and then lifts up, taking my mouth in a kiss I feel throughout my body, one that causes the warmth to seep back in.

"I don't know how I will be able to handle your friendship with Pika, but for you, I'll try," he tells me, pushing my hair away from my face.

"If you would have explained to me what was going on without freaking out, I would have respected your feelings," I assure him, lifting my hands up to run along the underside of his jaw. "You have to learn to talk to me without talking *at* me."

"I'm working on it," he says, leaning down and pressing another kiss to my lips before rolling to his side and placing his hand on my belly. Then he looks up at me. "Did you really feel him move?" he questions as a look of fascination fills his eyes.

"I DID. IT was more of a flutter than anything, but I felt it."

"I missed it," he says, and I can see the disappointment in his eyes.

I shake my head. "No, you didn't. I don't think anyone can feel him moving yet but me," I tell him, running my hand over his hair.

"Next time, tell me when it happens so I can try," he says before he kisses my stomach again.

Then he rolls to his back and pulls me to lie at his side, being careful of my belly as he adjusts me until my body is draped over his. His hand runs lazily over my back, and before I know it, I fall asleep only to wake hours later to an empty bed.

I get up, find a shirt and a pair of sweats, and then make my way out of the bedroom. I pad across the house to Kai's office. His door is slightly ajar, so I walk in, finding him sitting at his desk, looking at the phone.

"What's wrong?" I ask him.

His head lifts and his eyes sweep over me before he takes my hand and gently pulls me into his lap.

"Kai," I whisper as his face goes into my neck and he inhales. "Talk to me."

"I need to make a phone call."

"Okay," I say, confused.

"A man I know told me a woman was hurt last night and she's in bad shape," he says quietly.

"What happened?" I ask, wrapping my arms around him.

He's quiet for a long time, and I think he's not going to talk to me. "She was shot at close range," he says.

Every muscle in my body goes tight. That is not what I thought he was going to say.

"Thankfully, she was right outside of the hospital when it happened, and they were able to get to her fast enough. She almost died." He whispers the last part as his arms go tighter around me. "This wasn't supposed to happen. The men involved agreed that she was off-limits."

"I'm so sorry."

"This is why I will fucking work myself to death until we don't have to worry about this kind of shit. She was innocent, just in the wrong place at the wrong time."

I can tell he's having a hard time keeping it together, so I get as close to him as I can. "What are you going to do?" I ask him softly while watching every emotion cross his face.

"When Kenton called a while back, he asked if I'd be willing to put in a call for him. I did, and it was agreed upon at that time that she would be off-limits. I set that meeting up."

I nod and hold his cheek.

"My guess is he wants to set up another meeting so that he can figure out what happened and why the order to leave her alone was ignored."

"Do you know why?" I ask.

"She witnessed a hit. She was the only living witness. The man who went after her is known for not always doing what he's told and going his own way. This time wasn't any different."

"Oh my God," I whisper as my heart breaks for her. "I know that you're torn about getting involved, but you should call him."

"I know, love."

He lays his forehead against mine and his hand over my stomach before lifting his head and kissing me. Then he adjusts me in his lap and picks up the phone, dialing a number then putting the phone to his ear.

"I was told you need to speak with me," he says, and I'm surprised by the coldness in his voice after the moment we just had. "I'm sorry about your situation, but—" he replies after a moment then is quiet again for a few seconds.

"You're putting me in a very bad position," he growls. Then his hand around me tightens even further before he snarls, "Kill every single motherfucker who even thought about hurting her."

I know he's talking about me when he says those words.

"I'll make the call, but you owe me," he replies, and I look at him, wondering why he would say that. His voice softens when he says, "I'm very sorry about what happened," before hanging up. "I have to go to Vegas," he tells me.

"I KNOW."

His nostrils flare, and he pulls me tighter against his body. "I know this is the place you feel the safest, but I need you to come with me."

"Of course," I assure him, sounding much braver than I feel.

"Nothing will happen to you. You have my word."

"I know," I whisper, wrapping myself tighter around him.

"This will not always be our life. I promise you," he vows.

"How did this become your life?" I ask softly, pulling away so I can see his face.

He exhales, lifts me off him to stand, and then takes my hand and begins leading me out of his office. I think he's taking me to bed, but instead, he leads me outside, down to one of the loungers that is set up near the water, and sits before pulling me to sit down between his legs.

"My family was involved with the mob since my great-grandfather first moved to America from Fiji. He started a business in Hawaii and knew that, if he wanted it to expand, then he would need people with money to back him. This was not easy. No one wanted to take a chance on him, and no one believed that his business would take off, but then one day, a man came to him with an offer. He would help him if my great-grandfather would, in return, do him a favor. Every month, he would receive a shipment, and that shipment would contain drugs or other items that would be distributed in the black market in Hawaii. My great-grandfather agreed, thinking his hands were clean and that, if anything ever came to light, he could say he was in no way involved.

"After a year, he got greedy and decided to begin moving some of his own items. Five years in, he was one of the wealthiest men in Hawaii. It was around that time that he met a young socialite, fell instantly in love with her, and demanded that she marry him."

I smile and shake my head.

"She made him realize what was really important, and he started becoming concerned with his business. He could no longer say that his hands were clean, so he began cutting his supplies down and trimming back on orders.

"He and my great-grandmother were married in a private ceremony on the beach, and nine months after they said their vows, my grandfather was born. He believed he had everything he could ever want. The day he went to pick up his wife and son from the hospital, his wife was murdered."

"No," I whisper.

"After that, my great-grandfather lost all hope and began doing everything within his power to take over and get rid of the men involved in killing his wife. He vowed that, one day, he would take control of all of them and then crush them. *I ulu no ka lālā i ke kumu.*"

"What does that mean?" I ask as his fingers slide away my tears.

"The branches grow because of the trunk." He tilts my head so that our gazes connect. "He died before his wish could be realized. My grandfather, father, and now I have become stronger than they are, and we have been slowly cutting their supplies, making them turn against each other. One day, they will fall, and I will be the only one standing."

I pray that he is right, that, when this is all over, we will all be standing. "I'm scared," I say, vocalizing my fear.

"A lot of thought has gone into this, Myla. This is not something that will just happen. This is something that has been planned for years. I will not say it's easy to do, but every day, we're one step closer."

He moves and helps me lie down next to him with my head in the crook of his arm and his hand resting on my belly. We lie there in silence, looking up at the night sky, then watch as the sun rises up over the ocean, and only then does he take me inside and climb into bed with me.

"WE'RE LANDING," KAI tells me, kissing my hair.

I lift my head, look around the plane, and feel lighter. After Kai told his mom and dad what was going on, they insisted they come with us to Vegas.

We didn't know how long we would be in Vegas, so having them with us puts my mind at ease. I also think Kai was relieved that his dad would be with his mom and me, someone he trusted completely, since, from what I understand, most of my time would be spent at the house while Kai takes care of business.

It takes another ten minutes for the plane to land. As soon as we touch down, Kai is up and getting a bag down from the overhead compartment, which he sets on the seat he was sitting in, and opens it up, pulling out some leather and slipping it on like a vest. I notice that it has a holster for a gun under one arm and then a place for a knife under the other. Once he has the holster in place, he pulls a large knife out of the bag then a gun, and he clicks them both in place. He then reaches up, pulls his suit jacket down, and pulls it on, hiding away the weapons.

"Do you always carry weapons like that?" I ask as the feeling of unease comes back.

His eyes come to me and go soft as he squats down in front of me. "I don't plan on anything happening, but I need to be cautious."

"Cautious is good."

He smiles and leans in to touch his forehead to mine. "You guys are my life, and I would die before something ever happens to either of you," he says as his hand comes up to hold my cheek.

"Don't say that," I whisper.

He grunts and presses a kiss to my forehead then lips. "I want you to stick close to Pika when I'm not around."

"I will," I say as everyone on the plane begins to stand and retrieve their things from the overhead bins.

He nods and kisses me once more before standing and helping me get my things together so we can get off the plane.

"Are you sure you don't want me with you?" Uncle Frank asks Kai, and I turn my head away from them to keep from laughing.

"Frank, I told you before that your son will be with me while I'm here."

"I think you should let me go with you. You never know what could go wrong."

"I know what could go wrong," Aye mutters and then winks at me when I laugh.

Uncle Frank is a good guy, but he is seriously a disaster waiting to happen.

"Fine. I'll help look out for Myla," he grumbles, grabbing his bag and heading off the plane.

"This is going to be a long trip," Kai's dad says, shaking his head, watching as Frank stomps down the plane stairs.

"He means well," Kai's mom says.

"He's still not helping me out. He will end up doing something stupid, and then I will have to clean up his mess," Kai replies.

"He thinks you're still mad about him teaching Myla to shoot a gun," Leia tells him.

"I *am* still mad about that, and he didn't teach Myla anything except that she should never agree with anything Uncle Frank says."

"Perhaps you're right," she concurs.

"I am right."

"He just wants to feel useful," his mom mutters, and his dad rolls his eyes.

"He's not going with me, and I don't care if he stomps around for the next few days. It's not happing," Kai says.

His mom nods then turns and walks off the plane.

"She's right, you know. Uncle Frank is just trying to help," I say quietly.

"That may be, but right now, I have my hands full and can't babysit him."

"I know," I mutter, walking out of the plane and into the sun. As soon as my eyes adjust to the light, I notice two large SUVs.

"We're riding with Junior," Kai tells me, leading me to one of the SUVs, where there's a large guy who looks like Uncle Frank standing with his arms crossed over his chest. "Brother," Kai says.

The guy uncrosses his arms and greets him with a half hug before stepping back, and I notice that he's one of the guys who was there when we got married.

"You remember Myla," Kai says, reintroducing me.

The guy leans in to kiss my cheek, saying, "Myla," quietly before pulling away.

"How have you been?" I ask as Kai opens the door.

"Been good." He shrugs, and I realize how different this guy is from his dad.

"That's good," I mumble when he doesn't say anything else.

Kai helps me into the car, and he and the Junior sit in the front seat talking quietly while I sit looking out the window in the back seat.

WHEN WE ARRIVE at the house, I'm stunned by how beautiful it is. Kai told me that he knew that it wasn't our house in Hawaii but it was good enough for us to stay in while we were in Vegas. My husband is obviously crazy because the house isn't just okay—it's beautiful. The outside is white, and the texture reminds me of icing. Around the windows are red shutters that match the red beams that are sticking out of the roof. When we get inside, I am even more blown away the floors, which are all white marble that is cool on the bottom of my bare feet. Everywhere I look, there are windows that display the vast desert landscape.

"It's beautiful," I whisper as Kai wraps his arms around me.

"I'm glad you think so." He kisses the back of my head then holds me like that until he tells me that it's time to leave.

Chapter 15

Demon slayer

I KISS KAI and get into the back of the SUV with Pika and Aye, watching as Kai walks towards a group of men. Even through the dark, I can see one of the men that he was walking towards is struggling to keep himself under control, and I know that is Kenton.

"Will they be okay?" I ask, not taking my eyes off them.

"You know they will." Aye answers.

I nod. He's right. Kai wouldn't be helping if he thought for one moment that something could go wrong.

I put my finger to the glass as we pull away, and then I see *him*. My gut goes tight and bile crawls up my throat, making it hard to breathe. I knew he was in Vegas, but the idea of seeing him never crossed my mind, not even once. Like he realizes that I'm near, his head turns and his eyes lock on me through the tinted glass. His face goes hard for a moment, but then a sinister smile appears on his mouth and he winks, lifting his chin. I swallow, turning away from the window as my hands begin to shake.

"You okay?" Pika asks.

I nod and lower my face to my lap, taking deep, silent breaths. I don't want them to call Kai and have him worried about me—not right now, not when he's dealing with something that needs his full attention.

"Myla, talk to me," he says gently, moving to sit closer to me.

I shake my head and scoot away from him. I do not want to be touched by anyone. I place my hands on my ever-expanding stomach and try to calm down. One thing I know is that freaking out would not be good for our son, and I would never do anything to endanger him.

"Do you want me to call Kai?" he questions.

My eyes lift to meet Pika's, and I know that it would be so easy to call my husband and have him make me feel better, but I can't.

"No, I just…" I pause. "I just have a bad case of heartburn," I lie.

He searches my face then nods once, and without another word, we take off back to the house. As soon as we get home, I go directly to our room, not even saying anything to the guys before putting PJs on and crawling into bed. I wake up when the bed dips and the scent of Kai fills my nose.

"Myla, I need you to wake up."

I roll over at the sound of pain in Kai's voice. I go to sit up, but his hand at my waist keeps me in place.

"Is everything okay?" I ask sleepily, pushing my hair out of my face.

He shakes his head, and anguish appears on his handsome face.

"What happened?"

"I need you to talk to me, Myla. Pika told me that you saw Thad tonight and immediately closed down. I know that this is something you don't want to talk about, but I need you to open up to me. I need you to make me understand why, even if his name is mentioned, fear floods your eyes and your body goes rigid. I'm honestly begging you to talk to me about it, to trust me with whatever it is. I do not want our child growing inside you to feel that energy, and I don't want that for *you*," he whispers quietly.

Each and every one of his words causes pain to expand in my chest. The only person I have ever spoken to about what happened was my therapist in college. But I know I need to open up to Kai. He deserves to understand, and it's not fair for me to keep even the darkest parts of my life from him.

"Please," he whispers sounding completely gutted.

"Will you lie with me?"

He nods and slips his clothes off before getting into bed with me. He wraps himself around me, and that feeling of safety gives me the courage I need. I swallow and squeeze my eyes closed. I hate that this is something I have to share with him. I don't want what Thad did to me to taint what we have. I open my eyes and look up at him.

"My life was amazing growing up. I know my real parents suffered, but they did give me to a family who loved me and wanted me."

His face goes soft, and his hand runs over my hair and down my back, pulling me closer.

"Did you know that my mom couldn't have more kids?" I ask.

He shakes his head no, and I continue.

"She and my dad had tried for more kids after having Rory and Thad, but it just never happened, so she gave up, just happy to have them. Then my dad came to her one day after talking with my father, and he told her about me and the situation with my parents." I pause and let out a breath. "She said yes immediately. She was excited to have another child, and even more excited to be getting a daughter. My life was good. There was never a time that I felt like I wasn't wanted or like they didn't love me," I stress, wanting him to know that this wasn't my parents' fault. None of this was their fault. They were victims as much as I was.

"I get that, Myla."

I TAKE A breath and let it out slowly, gathering the courage to say what I have to say next. "On my sixteenth birthday, my mom and dad took me and a group of my girlfriends out to dinner. Birthdays were always a big deal, but it was a school night, and I wouldn't be having my party until the weekend, so they wanted to do something small until my party." I lift my hand, tracing his lower lip. "I remember having so much fun that night. My friends and I were all boy-crazy at that point, and my dad was always a good sport, joking that he would invite whatever boy was near over to our table and introduce us to him. My dad was the best. Still is."

"He's a good man," he agrees, and I snuggle closer to him.

"That was the night my life changed...or life as I *knew* it, rather. When we got home, I went upstairs to my room, did my homework, and then went about getting ready for bed. My brother Rory came in and told me about some game he was going to be in that Friday and made sure I knew what was happening for the weekend. We had all the same friends, so my birthday party was going to end up being more than just the girls I hung out with. I was excited to have my first boy/girl party, and Rory was just as excited because he had a crush on one of my friends at the time.

"Not long after he left, my mom and dad came in and kissed me goodnight like they had always done. I was lying in bed thinking about how awesome my day had been when the door opened and a small beam of light shone in, only showing the outline of a figure. I wasn't even afraid." I feel tears fill my eyes and I rub my face against his chest.

"Thad came in, closing the door behind him, causing pitch blackness to fall over the room. I wasn't even worried that he didn't answer when I called his name, and I didn't even think to be nervous when he came and sat down on the bed next to me." I whisper the last part.

"Stop!" he thunders, making me jump.

But I don't quit. I can't. I need him to understand.

"He raped me for three years," I whisper. "It wasn't every night, but it was often."

"He's dead. I'm going to fucking rip off his dick and feed it to him. I swear to Christ, he will not be alive long."

"He told me he would kill my parents if I told them, and I believed him. I hated it, but I didn't know what to do. I felt like I was alone." I sit up and pull away until my back hits the headboard. "I stopped doing well in school. I stopped caring about life in general. All I wanted to do was get away. That's why, when I got accepted into culinary school, I took it and ran."

"I wish I would have known then," he growls.

"No one knew. I was worried about him killing the only people I considered family, two kind people who had accepted me with open arms into their family. I hated it, every second of it," I cry, covering my face with my hands.

"Come here, *makamae*," Kai says, pulling my hands away from my face and tugging me into his chest.

Even though he's comforting me, I can feel that every muscle in his body is taut, like he's preparing for battle.

"I'm sorry I didn't tell you. I just couldn't, no matter how many times I tried to convince myself to," I whisper.

"I know now," he whispers back as his hand at the back of my head travels down over my hair and to my back so that he can pull me closer to him. After a few minutes, he pulls my face away from his chest and tilts my head back to look at me. "I'm going to go get Mom so that she can stay with you while I'm gone," he says.

MY BODY INSTANTLY stills. "Where are you going?" I breathe out in a panic.

"I'll be back." He evades my question as I attempt to cling tighter to him. "I have to go, *makamae*. I'll be back. I promise." He kisses my hair then pulls me off him as I struggle to keep ahold of him. He walks to the door, leaving me on the bed sobbing.

A few minutes later, his mom comes in, crawls into bed with me, and holds me until I cry myself to sleep.

Kai

"GET UP AND get dressed." I kick Aye's bed then walk across the hall and do the same to Pika's.

It takes two minutes for them to come out of their rooms dressed and ready to go. I knew in my gut what was going on with Myla, but I didn't want to believe that something so fucking horrific could have happened to my beautiful girl.

"What's going on?" Pika is the first to ask as he tucks his gun into the back of his jeans.

"I need you two to help me track down Thad."

"What happened?" Aye asks, but when my eyes meet Pika's, I see understanding.

"We'll talk in the car," I mutter, heading towards the front of the house.

I know where Thad was a few hours ago when I saw him, and I don't want to miss the opportunity to get him while I can. And since he has been hanging out with Paulie Jr., there's a good chance he would hide him away if he found out I was looking for him.

"Now do you want to tell me what's happening?" Aye asks as soon as we're in the car and heading towards downtown.

"Fuck!" I roar, pounding the steering wheel as a fresh wave of rage begins to pump throughout my body. "What I'm going to tell you is never to fucking leave this car. Got me?" I say through clenched teeth.

"You got it," Aye says softly.

I see Pika nod out of the corner of my eye.

"I KNOW THAT each of you has been around when Thad's been brought up, and I know you have seen Myla's reaction to even his fucking name," I start, trying to take a calming breath as I feel my hands grab the steering wheel so hard that the rubber compresses under my touch. "He raped her."

I hear my voice crack, and I know I'm on the edge of losing it. Knowing that my wife—the woman I love, the mother of my child—suffered at the hands of someone like him causes my chest to crack open.

"You cannot be fucking serious!" Aye yells, punching the back of my seat so hard that I jerk forward from the blow.

"He's dead," Pika grits out.

I stop the car in the middle of the road and turn so that I can look at both of them. "He's mine. The only way you guys get a shot at him is if something goes wrong and I can't finish him myself."

"We both care about her," Aye says, but I shake my head.

"He's mine," I reiterate, and they both nod reluctantly.

I put the car in drive and head towards the warehouse we were at when I saw Thad earlier. The parking lot is empty except for a large, white van, and I know instantly that they are just here for cleanup. I pull my phone out and send a message to Kenton to tell him that I'm cashing in my marker. His man Justin will be able to get me whatever information I need almost instantly. It takes less than a minute for me to get a message back from Kenton, and less than three for Justin to send me everything I need to know about Thad.

I send a reply message, letting him know that the offer I gave him a year ago still stands. I tried to have the kid come work for me, but he wouldn't budge.

His reply of, *Sorry, Charlie,* almost makes me laugh. I have to respect that, because loyalty is rare these days. I put the car in drive and head towards the Strip. Thad used his credit card there twenty minutes ago, and based on the amount he withdrew, he was sitting at a table.

"He's at Bellagio," I say then look in the rearview mirror. "Aye, he doesn't know you, so I need you to get close to him once we're inside."

"What's the plan?" he asks, cracking his knuckles.

"I'm going to find a woman who will help me get him outside."

"Where do you want me?" Pika asks.

"I need you in the car," I tell him, and he nods.

We drive the rest of the way in silence. Every scenario is playing out in my head. It's not going to be easy to get him out alone, but I know men like him, and if I can make the offer sweet enough, he won't be able to resist.

When we pull up outside of the hotel, Pika comes around and hops behind the wheel as Aye and I make our way inside.

"Message me when you spot him," I tell Aye as I head in the direction of the bar.

It takes me less than ten minutes to find two women who are more than happy to take me up on my offer. I tell them that one of my frat buddies is in town and we're going to play a little joke on him. At first, they are slightly unsure, but after I pull out a wad of cash, they're more than willing to play along.

It takes another ten minutes to get a message from Aye about where Thad is, and just like I guessed, he's sitting at one of the blackjack tables. I send the two girls over to him, and they do just what I asked, both of them flirting and whispering in his ear. Even from across the room, I can see that he's eating that shit up.

Eventually, they convince him to go outside with them, and I know the exact moment it happens, 'cause he pulls one of the girls into his lap and grabs the other by the back of her head, kissing her then forcing her mouth to her friend's. They all stumble their way out of the casino as Aye and I follow behind them and make sure they stay on course.

Once we're outside, the girls do just as I said and get him into the back of the SUV, closing the doors. After a few seconds, I make my way over and open the back door, getting inside.

"What the fuck?" Thad shouts as both girls scramble out the other door.

Aye climbs inside to sit on the other side of Thad, who's in the process of pulling up his pants.

"Where to?" Pika asks as he pulls away from the curb.

"Dino's," I tell him, and he nods as we pull out onto the main road.

"I asked you *what the fuck?*" Thad shouts.

Aye puts his arm around his shoulders and pulls him back into him.

"Take off your shirt," I tell him.

He looks at me like I'm crazy as the weight of the situation finally begins settling in.

"I said…take off your shirt!" I roar.

He holds his hands up in front of him, unbuttons his shirt, and slips it off, handing it to me. I set the shirt in my lap and begin taking my cufflinks off. Then I roll up the sleeves of my own.

"I don't have a wire," he tells me.

I laugh in his face. Then I pull my knife out, stabbing him in the gut twice before pressing his shirt to his stomach to staunch the blood flow.

"You just stabbed me," he whispers.

I lift his face so that he's looking at me and not at the blood that's now turning his shirt red.

"I'm going to kill you tonight. I'm going to hurt you until you eventually pass out from blood loss, but then I'm going to wake you up and feed you your own fucking cock until you choke on it before taking your dead, lifeless body into the desert, where the fucking wild animals will fight over what's left of you!" I roar as my hand on his jaw tightens to the point that both pain and understanding fill his eyes.

"She told you," he says.

I lean forward until our noses are touching. "Yeah, she told me," I say, and I then lean back enough to elbow him in the face.

His body slumps forward, and I wipe my hands off before turning away from him to look out the window. I was raised to do this. Every cell in my body knows exactly what needs to be done, all of them preparing for what's to come, and when it's over, I know I'll go home to my wife and tell her that she never has to be afraid again because I slaughtered her demon.

I roll my window down as soon as we pull up outside Dino's. His front door opens and he steps out onto the porch. Dino is about three hundred pounds, six seven, with a bald head. As soon as he realizes who it is, he swings his shotgun up to rest on his shoulder.

"Haven't seen you in a while," he says, looking at the occupants of the car.

"It's been a while," I confirm.

Dino has a house in the desert on two hundred acres. About fifteen years ago, he had bomb shelters built into the ground around his property. These shelters are soundproof and safely enclosed, the perfect place to kill someone and take your time doing it.

"I need a room tonight," I say, getting out of the SUV and walking over to the porch.

"Sure thing." He greets me with a handshake and waves for Pika to follow him. "I'll lead you guy out," he mutters, getting onto a four-wheeler while I walk back over to the SUV and climb into the front seat.

"This place is fucking creepy," Aye mutters as we drive through the desert.

Every once in a while, we drive past a part of the sand that has a red light sticking up out of the ground, the light signifying that the room is occupied. There is only one reason to come here.

After driving for about thirty minutes, we come to a stop, and Dino gets off his four-wheeler, and I meet him at the door of the shelter.

"You know the rules. You're locked in until you call. There are clothes and supplies inside, and make sure you leave your keys in the car so I can have someone come out and pick it up."

"Got it," I mutter.

He opens the door and the smell of cleaning supplies hits my nose. I inhale one last breath of clean air before walking into the room behind Pika and Aye, who are carrying Thad.

"Call when you're done," Dino says, shutting the door and locking it behind us.

FOR THE NEXT six hours, I tortured him until he couldn't even hold his head up on his own. Then I cut off his dick and shoved it down his throat like I'd told him I would.

Call me evil, but when I walked away from his lifeless body, I felt cleaner.

There was one last piece of shit in the world preying on the innocent.

When we arrived home, I went to our room and got into the shower before getting into bed with Myla. The moment I lay down, her body curved against mine and she looked up at me with tears in her eyes.

"It's done," I tell her.

Her beautiful eyes close open, and she leans forward, pressing a kiss to my chest. I gather her closer to me, and with her wrapped in my arms and my hand on her belly, I feel my son move for the first time.

"He moved," I whisper in awe, waiting to see if I can feel him again.

"He's been doing it all night. It's almost like he's trying to tell me that it will all be okay," she whispers.

I exhale a long breath. "You have nothing to fear now, *makamae*," I tell her.

She nods her head against my chest, and I wait, listening as her breathing evens out before following her off to sleep.

Chapter 16

Redemption

WE'VE BEEN HOME from Vegas for three weeks, and I know it may make me a horrible person, but knowing that Thad is dead and can never hurt me or anyone else again makes me feel lighter. I still felt bad for my parents when they called to tell me that he had gone missing. I know they were heartbroken over the loss of their son. I wanted to tell them the kind of monster he was, to make them understand they shouldn't morn his loss, but I know that, in the end, it didn't matter. He had paid with his life for his crimes. I even got up enough courage to speak to my brother Royce, and even though the conversation was awkward, it felt good to talk to him.

My relationship with Kai has also changed since coming back to Hawaii. The wall that had been keeping us separated finally crumbled. He now knew everything there was to know about me, and I now know he will be there to help me battle any demons I may have.

I silently lie here, looking out at the ocean, willing myself to sleep, but I can't get over the feeling that something is going to happen. I know that something is brewing. I don't know what it is, but the energy over the last few days has changed, and Kai is more anxious than before. But every time I bring it up, he explains that, when the time is right, he will share it with me.

"I need to go out for a couple of hours, love," Kai says, coming into the room, where I have been lying down, trying to take a nap.

I turn my head on the pillow and take him in, noticing that he looks worried. "Do you want me to come with you?" I ask him.

He shakes his head, leans over me, and presses a kiss to my lips.

When he pulls back, his fingers run down my cheek.

"I won't be gone long," he says, but the anxiety I see in his eyes has the worry in my chest expanding.

"Is everything okay?"

"Everything's fine. You just rest."

I study his face and take notice of the way his jaw seems to be harder. "I love you," I tell him as I lift my hand to run my fingers down his jaw.

His eyes go soft and his face changes slightly. "I love you too. I'll be back," he tells me, and this time, I hear the conviction in his voice when the words leave his mouth.

"We'll be here waiting for you," I tell him instead of doing what I really want to do, which is attach myself to him, making it hard for him to leave without taking me with him.

His lips press against mine as his hand moves to my belly one last time before he leaves the room. It takes all of my strength to stay on the bed and not follow him out of the house.

Soon after he leaves, I get up and phone his mom to see if she knows anything about what's going on. She tells me that Kai didn't tell her anything and she is sure it is just the hormones that are making me feel like something is off. When I get off the phone with her, I go into the kitchen and start baking to help keep my mind busy until he comes home.

I LOOK AT the clock and then over at Pika, who has been hanging out with me since I got out of bed earlier. When I notice that he's looking at the clock as well, I give up and go get the phone. I have never called Kai when he has told me that he'll be working, but right now, I need to make sure he's okay so the feeling in my stomach will hopefully go away.

I wrap one arm around my waist and then use the other to dial his number before putting the phone to my ear. My eyes stay locked on Pika's, and I can see that he's waiting to get some relief as well.

"Kai—"

My heart soars then crashes to the ground when I realize it's only the message for his voicemail. "Hey, I…I just wanted to make sure you are okay." I pause and let out a shaky breath as my head drops forward and tears fill my eyes. "Please come home," I whisper and then hang up. "He didn't answer," I tell Pika, placing the phone on the counter.

"I'M SURE HE'S okay."

"Me too," I agree halfheartedly.

"He's probably somewhere where he can't answer," he says, trying to convince both himself and me, but even as I nod, that pit in the bottom of my stomach gets bigger.

I pick the house phone up when it rings once, hoping that it's Kai telling me that he's okay and he's on his way home.

"Hello?"

"Honey, Meka's on her way to you now, and Bane and I are on our way," Leia says.

"What happened?" I ask as tears begin to fill my eyes. I know that whatever she is going to say is going to rip me apart.

"I don't know. No one knows exactly what happened. After you called me, I became concerned, so I asked Bane to look into what Kai was doing," she whispers. "He found out that Kai was meeting someone and they were taking the person's yacht out. Bane made Kai promise he would call in an hour, and when we didn't hear back from him, Bane called the coastguard. They told him that a Mayday was sent out, and when the coastguard arrived at the location, only pieces of boat were left. They think there was some kind of explosion."

"No." I close my eyes and my stomach dips as I try to avoid getting sick.

"They've been searching, but as of yet, they haven't found any survivors," she cries, and I collapse onto the couch behind me. "We're going to go over to the station and see if we can get any more information," she says, but her words begin to sound garbled, like I'm underwater.

I feel the phone slip out of my palm and hear Aye ask for Bane, but after that, everything becomes a blur until I hear my name yelled.

"Myla!"

I stand from where I was sitting on the couch as Meka comes rushing into the living room.

"Oh, God," she whimpers, rushing towards me with tears streaming down her cheeks.

"No," I breathe even though I just spoke to Kai's mom. I don't want to believe that it's true, but there is no denying the look in Meka's eyes as she looks at me.

"I'm sorry." She cries harder, and my chest compresses under the weight of devastation I feel.

My knees give out and I fall to the floor as a sob rips from my chest. I feel her wrap her slender arms around me, and her tears seep through the shirt I have on. I don't know how long we stay there in the middle of the living room crying, but after some time, I feel Pika and Aye pull us away from each other.

Aye helps me get settled on the couch just as Kai's mom and dad walk in, and a fresh wave of tears springs to my eyes.

"Honey," Leia says, coming to sit next to me.

Her hands go around me, and I know she is not here to tell me good news. It takes everything in me to focus on breathing, to remind myself that I have to breathe for our son. I cannot even begin to think of how I will make it without Kai. I don't know how I will live when I have to say goodbye to my soul.

"We didn't even pick a name," I whisper staring off into the ocean, which is turning orange as the sun begins to set.

"What, honey?" Kai's mom asks, using her hand on my cheek to turn my face towards her.

"We didn't even get a chance to pick a name." I shake my head. "Kai said he wanted to wait until after he was born so he was sure to get a name that fit him, and now, he won't be here to give him his name."

"Oh, Myla," she whispers. "Don't think about that right now. Right now, just pray that they find him." She chokes out the last part, and I can see it in her eyes that *she* doesn't even believe they will.

"I'm going to be sick." I get up, rush out of the room, and go to the toilet, the contents of my lunch coming up. I wait until the nausea passes before standing and going to the sink to splash some water on my face. The refection looking back at me when I look in the mirror is not one I have ever seen before, not even during the worst years of my life. No, the girl looking back at me looks lifeless.

"Can I come in?" comes from the other side of the door, along with a quiet tap.

"I'm coming," I say in a hoarse whisper. My throat feels like it's on fire from crying, and the passageway feels too tight to even take a complete breath.

As soon as I open the door, I come face-to-face with Aye, who looks me over from head to toe before pulling me into an embrace.

"He's a fighter," he tells me.

I nod, because that's true. I don't know what happened on that boat, but if there was a way for Kai to get out alive, he would, even if that meant swimming to shore.

Aye leads me back out to the living room and places me in a chair. He leaves and then comes back a few minutes later with a cup of tea and some saltine crackers before walking off to stand with Pika. I look at my two guys and close my eyes when I see not only them looking at me with concern, but also the pain I feel reflected in their eyes at the thought that they have lost their friend.

We all sit around the living room until the coastguard calls to say that they are calling off the search for the night due to a storm that was slowly making its way ashore. I lose it again. The idea of my beautiful husband in the middle of the ocean, with the only help available to him unable to reach him, causes me to lose the small thread of hope I was holding on to.

"Honey, why don't you go and try to get some sleep?"

I look from the ocean to Kai's mom and shake my head.

"You need to rest," she says gently as her eyes glance to my belly.

"Okay, but come get me if you hear anything please," I tell her.

She nods, murmuring that she promises.

As soon as I get to our room and open the door, I'm bombarded by his smell, and it takes everything in me not to turn around and run. I close the door behind me then go to the dresser and pull out one of his shirts, holding it to my nose and noticing that, even though his scent is lingering in the material, it doesn't smell completely like him.

I drop the shirt to the floor, walk over to his closet, and find his shirt from yesterday, one he put aside to have dry-cleaned. I put it to my nose and inhale a lungful of his scent, holding my breath until I feel light-headed. I only let it out when I have my clothes off and I'm slipping his shirt on. I walk over to our bed, pull back the covers, pull the phone off the nightstand, and then climb into bed, bringing the covers up and over my head as I dial his phone number. His name is the only thing he says, but the sound of his voice, repeating it over and over, eventually lulls me to sleep.

"*Makamae*," I hear whispered as I feel a finger run down my cheek.

I cuddle closer to the scent and warmth, not wanting to wake up if this is a dream.

"Wake up." This time, the voice is close to my ear, which causes goose bumps to break out along my skin.

"Kai?" I whisper, not wanting to open my eyes.

"Myla."

I feel fingers run up my thigh and a large hand curve around my ass. My eyes fly open, and a hand covers my mouth as I start to scream.

"Shh. It's okay. I'm here, but I need you to be quiet."

I nod, and he moves his hand away from my mouth. I look at him with just the help of the moonlight.

"Am I dreaming?" I whisper.

He shakes his head, and then I see that he has a few scratches on his face.

"Oh my God, you're hurt." I go to sit up and turn on the light, but he pins me to the bed.

"I'm fine. Just a few scratches."

"What's going on?" I ask him when I notice that he's acting strange.

"No one can know I'm alive, Myla. Not yet," he whispers, and I feel pain slice through my chest.

"What? Why?"

"I have the perfect opportunity to make a move. Everyone who was involved in what happened yesterday believes I'm dead. They won't be expecting me."

"Your mom and family?" I whisper as tears begin to fill my eyes again.

"I know this is going to be difficult for you to do, but I need your help," he says softly.

I know he wouldn't ask me to do this if he didn't have to, but that doesn't mean that it's going to be easy to lie to people who I know are completely heartbroken over the fact that they think their son, brother, and friend is dead.

"I had to see you before I left, but you can't tell anyone, *makamae*. Not yet," he whispers.

I know that this is him talking to me. This is him being honest. This is the thing I have needed from him all along, so now, I have to prove I can handle it.

"I won't tell anyone." I press a kiss to his chest, and the warm feel of his skin against my lips causes a sensation I thought I would never feel again.

His hand travels down over the curve of my ass, and he pulls me closer to him, so close that I can feel his erection against my belly.

"Kai," I hiss.

He rolls me onto my back. His hips settle between my thighs, and his arms go onto the bed on either side of me, making sure to keep his weight off my belly.

"I love you," he whispers fiercely, right before his mouth crashes down on mine and his taste explodes on my tongue.

I lift my hands and run my fingers through his hair as I kiss him back with everything I have, so grateful that I'm able to have this with him, that he's here with me now. He pulls his mouth from mine and kisses down my jaw and neck before pulling back enough to get the buttons of his shirt undone.

As soon as I'm exposed to him, his head drops down and his tongue licks my nipple before he pulls it into his mouth, sucking hard then doing the same to the other one. My body begins to wither under him as I fight hard not to scream out his name. He slowly licks down my body. Every inch of skin he touches feels like it's directly linked to my core. When he licks across the top of my pubic bone, I bite my lip so hard that I taste blood in my mouth.

"You smell so good, *makamae*. Sweet, like pineapple," he groans. Then his fingers hold the lips of my pussy open and his tongue begins flicking and licking my clit before he pulls it between his lips.

My hips begin to grind as I hiss out, "Please."

"Please what?" he asks. Then one finger slowly circles around my entrance while his tongue continues to torment me.

"I need more," I plead, looking down my body at him.

His eyes meet mine, and he enters me with two fingers, only to pull them out seconds later.

"Don't stop!" I cry. I know I'm going to come the minute his fingers touch that place inside me he seems to be the master of finding.

His mouth latches on to my clit, and his finger at my entrance dips in then out, the sensation causing a slow burn to begin.

"So close," he says.

I nod. Or I think I nod; everything seems blurry. Then I explode as his teeth graze my clit and his fingers fill me, both of them working in sync to pull me over the edge, and at the last second, I cover my mouth with my hand, muffling the scream that rips from my chest.

I feel lightheaded, and it takes a moment to come back to myself, but when I do, Kai is undressed and his hips are between mine. The moment our eyes lock, he presses inside me, filling me with one long stroke. My legs lift and wrap around his waist, and my hands travel up his back. I watch as his eyes get darker right before his head drops and he kisses me again, his tongue wrapping around mine as his hips rotate, the angle changing deep inside me on each stroke.

I moan into his mouth and press the heels of my feet into his back, lifting my hips up to meet him on each thrust. His pace picks up, and his mouth leaves mine so that he can lick down my neck, and then he bends and pulls one nipple into his mouth, making me turn my head and bite into the pillow to avoid screaming. I dig my nails into his back and use my leverage to fuck him, taking him all the way to the hilt each time, every stroke hitting that spot deep inside me that causes me to see stars.

"I'm going to come," I gasp.

"Let me feel it. Let me feel you milk me," he groans, and I lift my head and bite into his shoulder as my orgasm erupts through me.

I start to come back to myself when I feel his hips jerk and his face go into my neck, where he groans his release. I wrap myself tighter around him, and he shifts slightly to the side, pulling his weight off my belly. I lie there in awe, knowing that, earlier tonight, I thought I would never have this again.

"How did you get off the boat?" I ask as my mind begins to clear.

"Fucking Frank. I swear he doesn't listen, but this time, I'm glad he ignored my order. He knew who I was meeting with and insisted he follow us in another boat. I told him, 'Absolutely not,' because I didn't want the guys I was with to see him and get spooked, but lucky for me, he ignored me." He pauses and runs a hand down my cheek. "When we got out into the open seas, the guys jumped ship, leaving me alone on the yacht. I called for Mayday but knew something was up, so I took off all my clothes and got into the water right before the boat exploded. A few minutes after that happened, Frank pulled up on a small boat, looking smug. I told him then that no one could know I'm alive. Their stupid plan to kill me, and Frank's ignoring my order, gave me the perfect opportunity to finally clean up a situation that has been needing my attention for a while," he says carefully.

"You have to come back to me when this is over. I need you to be there when our little man is born so that you can give him his name," I say as tears fill my eyes.

"I'll be here for that," he promises, and his hips begin to rotate as he rocks in and out of me slowly.

He drops his forehead to mine until we both come together, my orgasm hitting me slowly as the feeling spreads through my body, making my whole being feel heavy and causing my eyes to close right before I hear Kai whisper, "I love you." I mumble the words back to him, and then I feel him button my shirt up and cover me up. I feel something slide onto my finger before I can no longer stay conscious.

When I wake up in the morning, the night before comes back to me, and tears begin to fill my eyes when I don't see Kai with me. But then I become aware of the wetness between my legs and I pull his shirt away from my chest, seeing that he left love bites around my nipples. I lie back down and pray that he comes back to me soon.

I roll over and begin to tuck my hand under my cheek when I notice that the ring I have on now has a band that wasn't there before tucked close to it. This one is the same gold as the original, but all around the band are round diamonds. I slip the ring off my finger and hold it up to look at it, but then an inscription on the inside catches my attention.

M & K ~ This is our story.

Tears fill my eyes as I slip the ring back in place. He is right. This is our story, and our story is just beginning.

Chapter 17

Sniper

Kai

I GET OFF the flight and fight my way towards the exit. I haven't flown commercial in years and had forgotten what a pain in the ass it is. I knew that, if I was going to get to Vegas unrecognized, I would need to make a few changes.

The first change was shaving my hair completely off and trading my suits for jeans and tees so that I matched the appearance of my new ID. The second was flying like any other middle-class citizen.

I had to make sure everyone I knew still believed that I'm dead. Growing up, I learned early on that, if an opportunity presented itself, you needed to take it immediately, so that's exactly what I did yesterday.

"So, how are we going in?" Frank asks, pulling a pair of dark shades over his eyes.

I look at him and wonder once again how the fuck he convinced me to let him come. "I told you you're staying at the hotel," I mutter, walking outside into the hot Las Vegas sun.

"I saved you yesterday," he reminds me for the hundredth time, and I grind my teeth together in annoyance.

He did save me. He also unknowingly helped me orchestrate the perfect plan, one that, until the ship I had been on blew up, making everyone believe I was dead, would never have been possible. Paulie Jr. had no idea that the idiots he'd sent to kill me were going to be the ones who helped me pull off his death.

"You're not coming," I say as I look around for Sven.

"You're going to let some guy you don't really know help you do this, but not the man who has been with you your whole life?" He shakes his head, muttering under his breath something about how my mom should have raised me better.

I ignore him and keep walking. Then I spot Sven posted up next to a small sports car.

"What's up, man? How have you been?" Sven greets us as soon as we're near.

"Good. How are things?" I shake his hand and place my small bag in the back seat. Then I lean the seat forward so that Uncle Frank can get in.

"You have got to be shitting me," Uncle Frank complains, looking at the seat then back at me.

"Sorry, man. My assistant is using my other car, so I had to bring this," Sven apologizes as my uncle stuffs himself into the small back seat then gripes when I put the front seat back in position so I can get in.

"Just ignore him," I tell Sven once we're all in the car.

"We still have some time to kill, so I figured we could all go to my house and get the details worked out before doing what you came here for," Sven says.

I nod then ask him about his club, which is close to the area of downtown that Paulie Sr. has recently started running drugs out of.

He tells me that the drugs have recently begun seeping into his club and a few women who have gone to the club have been roofied. When he went to the cops, he had a dead body and a note telling him to shut his mouth show up on his front step.

When we pull up at his house, I'm slightly taken aback by the normalcy of the area and home. I know that Sven has money, and a lot of it, so the fact that he's living in a neighborhood has me raising a brow.

"I have a penthouse but have recently been staying here," he mutters, shutting down the car.

I get out as well then lean the seat forward so Frank can get out before grabbing my bag from the back seat and following Sven up the front steps and into the house.

The house is large. The moment I enter, I walk into a large foyer that has a round staircase leading upstairs, and then there is a library off to one side and a living room on the other.

"Let me see if Mag's home," Sven murmurs.

We follow behind him through the living room and into a large, open kitchen that has a small dining room off to the side.

"Oh good. You're here. I got all the crap you asked for," a woman's voice says as we walk around the corner.

I wonder who she is. Her hair is dark brown, and it hangs down the middle of her back. She's slightly chubby, but she has curves in all the right places.

"Meat is not crap, Mag," Sven tells her, but I can see softness in his eyes as he looks at her.

"Stop calling me Mag. It's Maggie, for the millionth time, and meat is gross." She shakes her head then swings around to look at Uncle Frank and me when she realizes we're standing there. Her face is soft and round, but the color of her eyes is what makes her beautiful. They are so light that they look like honey. "You have zero manners." She looks at Sven again as she scolds him then looks at us, and her face transforms and a smile lights up her face. "He's rude. Sorry about that. I'm Maggie, this guy's assistant. Nice to meet you guys." She shakes my hand then takes Frank's, who holds on to her and pulls her closer.

"Nice to meet you, Maggie," my uncle says, kissing her hand.

"Aww, you're so cute." She pats his cheek then steps back and looks at Sven. "I'm going to head out. I have a date tonight."

I look at Sven, and his jaw begins to tick as he shakes his head.

"You need to work tonight," he tells her, but his jaw is so tight that I'm surprised the words even come out.

"I don't work nights." She laughs. "Nice meeting you guys," she says as she walks over to the counter, picking up her bag before walking out of the kitchen with Sven's eyes glued to her ass.

"I'll be right back," he growls then storms out of the kitchen after her. Then we hear the front door open and slam shut.

"That was awkward," Frank says, but I have a feeling I know what's going on.

Sven looks like the kind of guy who could walk into a room full of women and have his pick. Now, the woman he wants is not falling at his feet, so he has no idea what to do. It only takes a couple of minutes for the front door to open back up, and then the loud bang of it slamming echoes before we hear Sven storm into the kitchen.

"She makes me fucking mental," he growls, walking to the fridge and grabbing a beer. "I swear to fucking Christ I'm going to end up being put in a goddamn hospital because of her and the stress she causes me," he says before tilting the beer back and taking a large pull.

"You gonna be able to handle tonight?" I ask him after a moment.

He looks at me, and a different look fills his eye. "Fuck yes," he mutters, and I nod once. "Let me show you guys to your rooms." He walks out of the kitchen then leads us upstairs. "You guys can stay in these two rooms. Mag's room is down the hall next to mine," he says.

I start to laugh 'cause he is setting himself up for fucking mental issues.

"You don't even have to say it. I already fucking know," he grumbles then looks between Frank and me. "I'm gonna shower. We'll meet downstairs in an hour to talk about what the plan for the night is," he says, running a hand through his hair before walking off towards his room.

"That kid has it bad," Frank mumbles, shaking his head before walking into his room.

I turn and walk into my room and close the door behind me. I want to call and check on Myla, but I can't until this is done. I was going to leave her in the dark about what happened yesterday, but I knew, if I did that, she would be pissed, not only about what I was doing, but that she had been forced to believe I had died. I couldn't imagine someone telling me that she was dead and living with that news for even ten minutes.

I walk to the window and look out, and I see Maggie standing in the driveway and talking on the phone while looking at the house. My first instinct is that she somehow knows who I am, but then I see her wipe her cheeks and look up at the sky, saying something I can only make out as, "He's a jerk," before getting into her car, slamming the door, and backing out of the driveway.

I leave the window and sit on the bed, looking down at my hands and twisting my wedding band around my finger. I slip the ring off my finger and place it in my pocket. In a few hours, when I put it back on my hand, our whole future will look different. It will just be us.

I wait a few more minutes then go downstairs, where Sven and Uncle Frank are laughing in the living room when I walked in. Uncle Frank has that quality about him; he can always lighten up a situation. And as pissed off as he makes me sometimes, he is family, and he really did save my ass.

"Ready?" I ask.

Sven stands, and we walk into the dining room, where he has some papers spread out on the table.

"Justin did some searching and found out that Paulie is always at Steam on Fridays. I guess he buys out the VIP section and shows off how much money he has. He's always with these two guys." He hands me a picture. "This guy is missing"—e points at Thad—"but this guy is still around." He points at a man I have never seen before.

"Did Justin find any info on him?" I ask as I look at his picture.

"Nope. I guess he showed up a couple of years ago, and he and Junior have been tight since then. His name's Ivan."

"He's undercover," I mutter.

"What?" He takes the pictures and holds it up, looking at it. "We need another plan, because I can guarantee you they will be at that club together, and if he's undercover like you think he is, we can't risk him seeing anything."

I know he's right. I also know that the club would be the best location. Not only would his guard be down, but also, there would be so many people around that the risk of being seen would be minimal.

"Plan still stands," I tell him.

I can see that he's not convinced, but this is what I was raised to do. Long before I took over for my father, I was his watcher, the eyes in the back of his head. I knew exactly what someone would do before they did it, and that kind of conditioning doesn't go away.

We talk for a few more minutes before I head back up to the room and change. I put on a white tank and a dress shirt over it, and I keep the jeans I was already wearing on. Once I'm changed, Sven meets me downstairs dressed similar to me.

"Are you sure you don't want me to come? I can wait in the car," Uncle Frank mumbles, walking us to the door.

"We're not going to the grocery store," Sven says.

I shake my head.

"What if you need backup?"

"We won't," I assure him as we leave the house, shutting the door behind us and leaving my pouting uncle at home.

We drive to the club and park down the street. It is after midnight, but the sidewalks are still packed with people.

"Where's your club?" I ask when I notice this block has clubs lining the street.

"A block over. This area is new, but the nightlife here is one of the reasons people come to Vegas."

"This area is also connected to the mob," I tell him, and his eyes come to me as he runs a hand through his hair. "This street used to have nothing but old warehouses on it. Back in the day, a bunch of men bought up these lots, knowing that Vegas was going to expand. I wouldn't be surprised if Paulie actually owns the club we're going to."

"Justin didn't say that."

"Just because his name isn't on the papers doesn't mean anything, kid."

Once we reach the club, we go to the front of the line, where Sven knows one of the bouncers at the door, and they let us in without a word. Once we walk in the door, we know where the cameras are, so we avoid them at each turn.

From Justin's intel, we know that the club has three levels. The top is all VIP, which has smoked-glass panels with red backlights every twelve feet, making it look like a steamed shower with dancing people silhouetted behind the glass.

The second floor has the same panels, but these are blue and techno music is loudly pumping. The first floor is a large bar that goes around the whole perimeter of the room, with a dance floor in the middle.

"Let's head up and see the layout," I say.

We walk towards the stairs that will take us up a level. We know where Paulie would be hanging out, but seeing it on paper and being here in person are two different things.

"Sven?" a woman says halfway up the first flight of stairs.

"Hey, babe. I don't have time right now." He removes her hands from him then jogs to catch up with me.

"Sven," another woman says.

I look over at him and frown when he says the same thing he just said to the last one.

"Hey, stranger," a blonde says, stepping in front of him.

I shake my head. I have had my fair share of partners, but this is fucking ridiculous. No wonder Maggie is running away from him.

"It's not normally this bad," he tells me once he's free from yet another woman.

"I should have had you stay home with Frank," I mutter, looking around the second level.

"Fuck off," he grumbles then points toward VIP, where there is another set of stairs, this one blocked off by a red, velvet rope and a woman standing there with a clipboard in her hand.

"We need to get up there," I tell Sven.

He smiles and walks towards the rope. The woman's face lifts and she smiles as he gets near. I follow close behind him and hear her say his name. His hand goes to her waist, and he dips his head close to her ear.

She looks over at me then nods and pulls the rope. He kisses her cheek then says something else before we make our way up the last set of stairs.

We walk up to VIP and look around. There's a bar off to the side with steam rising up out of the glass behind the bar. Sven taps my shoulder and nods to the right. I see the guy from the photo, the one I swear is undercover. He's standing off to the side, his head lowered as he talks on the phone.

"Where's Paulie?" I question, knowing he has to be close.

I hear someone yell, "Fucker!" and I start toward the commotion while staying in the shadows.

Paulie is standing over some kid, who is lying on top of a busted-up glass table. His hands are in front of his face, and I can see that he's bleeding from open wounds on his arms. Paulie leans over him and spits, and then he starts to laugh before looking around at the people who have formed a circle, making sure they're laughing too.

"Get up and get out of here," Paulie says, kicking the guy, who rolls to his stomach before scrambling to his feet and taking off.

"That guy is a fucking dick," Sven says, and I can't agree more. He is a fucking egomaniac.

"We need to find our opening. You watch Ivan, and I'll keep an eye on Paulie."

He nods and walks off to the bar while I stay in the background. Every once in a while, a woman stumbles over, but as soon as they're in my space, I give them a look that has them turning around and finding another man to fuck with.

I still don't even understand how being with Myla came so easily. It's like the gods sent me everything I could have ever asked for in a wife, qualities I didn't even know I was looking for.

I watch as Paulie stands, pulls the blonde who's been all over him to her feet, and leads her towards the bar. My pulse starts to quicken as extra adrenaline begins pumping through my system. My eyes zero in on him as he leads the girl behind the bar and down a hall that is almost dark with strobe lights that flash every few seconds. I follow behind them; this is it—the opportunity I have been waiting for.

I watch as he picks the girl up. Her legs go around his waist, and one of his hands works between them. I get closer and pause when I feel a whiz slice through the sleeve of my shirt. I turn my head to see where it came from, and when I turn back around, Paulie is down on the ground. The blonde he was about to fuck up against the wall is screaming at the top of her lugs as she tries to stop the blood that is pooling out of his shirt.

Sniper.

I scan the area again, and then my eyes land on Sven. I have no idea what just happened, but we need to get out of here. Commotion begins to build around us as the crowd moves in on Paulie, who is still lying there, only blood is now bubbling out of his mouth. I lift my chin to Sven, and we both make our way outside. I see him moving quickly ahead of me. Just as I get to the club exit, the lights turn on. I step out onto the sidewalk and through the crowd that has begun to spill out of the club, and then I head towards the street we parked on. When I get there, I spot Sven.

"What the fuck happened?" he asks as we both get into the truck.

I ignore him, pull my off shirt, and look at the sleeve. There is a small tear in the fabric where the bullet that hit Paulie tore through.

"There was a sniper in there," I tell him as he stops at the stop light.

"Fuck. Do you know who it was?"

"No clue." I think, trying to pull up anyone I know with that kind of background.

"Where was Ivan?" Sven asks.

"He was still on the phone, and when Paulie went down, I saw him take off."

"What now?"

"I go home," I mutter, not knowing if I'm pissed or relieved.

"This isn't over," he reminds me.

"No, it's not, but now, we have to wait for his dad to make his move."

"How long will that take?" he sighs.

"No idea. The first thing he's going to want to do is figure out who took out his son...even if he knew the fucker was trying to take his seat."

"That does not make me feel better."

"Did you ever play with blocks when you were a kid?" I ask him.

He looks at me and shrugs. "Sure," he mutters, obviously wondering where I'm going with my question.

"What happens when you take out the block at the bottom of the building?"

"It falls?"

"No, it gets weak, and then, when you take another, and another, the structure continues to weaken until it eventually falls to pieces."

"How many more pieces until this is done?"

"One," I tell him, and the rest of the car ride is silent.

Once we arrive back at the house, we tell Uncle Frank what went down, and he has the same questions we do, but I have no answers.

Sven offers for us to stay, but there is no reason for me to stay in Vegas another night, so I decline his offer but do take him up on using his plane to get back to Hawaii. While we're getting out of his car at the airport, he gets a text and starts laughing. I don't expect him to share it, but he tilts his phone towards me and I can't help but grin.

Justin: *Tell Hawaii sorry about his shirt.*

I shake my head and move to the plane.

I WALK INTO my house, and everyone sitting in the living room stops to look at me, but my eyes are on Myla, whose eyes instantly fill with tears.

"*Makamae.*"

She comes to me, wrapping her arms around me, and the moment I have her in my arms, a sob tears from her that rips through me.

"I'm home. I told you I would be."

"I know!" she cries.

I tilt her head back and kiss her, absorbing her taste, letting her soak back into my system.

"I was so worried." She holds me tighter, and I do the same.

"Nothing could keep me from you. Not even the devil himself," I whisper into her ear.

She nods then lifts her tear-filled eyes to mine. "I love you."

"I love you too." I hold her face in my palms and kiss her again, the salty taste of her tears mixing in with her natural sweetness.

"Oh, God," my mom whimpers.

Myla wipes her cheeks then steps back.

"You're not dead?!" my sister cries.

I shake my head. "I had to take care of some business," I explain.

"I should kick your fucking ass," Pika yells, rushing towards me, and I brace myself, ready for impact.

"Pika, I knew all along!" Myla cries.

Pika stops halfway and looks at her.

"He came and saw me the night he went missing. I wanted to tell you guys, but I promised not to tell anyone," she whispers.

Aye glares at her. "You cried and screamed about keeping the search going. You flipped out whenever we talked about giving up and having a funeral."

She drops her head, looking at her feet. "I didn't want to have a funeral. I didn't want you guys to give up hope," she whispers.

"This isn't her fault. This is on me. I made her promise not to tell anyone." I go to her and wrap my arms around her. "I didn't want anyone to know what was going on. I couldn't risk anyone finding out I wasn't dead."

"I know that we raised you to always do what needs to be done, but this is going too far. Your mom was a wreck, and your sister and brother were devastated," my father scolds.

"Sorry, Dad, but I had to make sure that, when my son takes his first breath, nothing and no one can harm him," I explain, and I see understanding flash in my father's eyes.

"We thought you were dead. I believed I was going to have to plan a funeral then figure out how to get Myla through this pregnancy without her having a meltdown!" my mom shouts.

Guilt strikes me hard. She would have done it. She would have put her own pain away to make sure everyone else was taken care of.

"I love you, Mom," I tell her as she comes to me, wrapping her arms around me.

"You ever do anything like that again and I really will kill you," she says.

I hear some grunts of agreement around the room, but I ignore them.

"I needed to make things safe for my son," I repeat, and my mom nods against my chest.

Since Myla became my wife and we found out we're having a baby, I have worked tirelessly to make sure she can have a normal life and our boy has a chance to experience normalcy.

"I have been blessed to have you guys as my parents, but I don't want my kids growing up in a house where there has to be men with guns hanging around all the time. I want to enjoy my family."

"I can understand that, honey."

"Runt." I look at my baby sister, and she comes to me, winding her arms around Mom and me.

"Don't ever do that again," she whispers.

"I won't," I promise then look at my brother.

He closes his eyes then comes over to us. He wraps his arms around all of us, muttering that he's going to kick my ass.

"I'm sorry, guys, but thank you for taking care of Myla for me," I tell Aye and Pika.

"Always," Pika says, and for once, there is no feeling of jealousy— just gratefulness.

"You don't even have to thank me," Aye says.

I nod then step away from my mom, my sister, and me brother, and step towards my dad. Then I hug him like I haven't done since I was a kid.

"I love you, son, and I'm proud of the man you have become," he tells me.

I pat him on his back then step away and walk right to Myla to scoop her up.

"What are you doing?!" she shouts.

"We're going to bed," I tell her, looking at her beautiful face.

"Your family's here, and you just got home."

"I don't care." I lift my head and look at my family. "No offense, but I'm taking Myla to bed. You guys can stay or go," I tell them then turn and walk to our room, where I carefully set her on the bed then get down on my knees in front of her, lifting her shirt up so I can press my mouth to her stomach.

"You shaved your head," she says quietly, running her hands over my buzzed hair.

I close my eyes, relishing the feeling of her touching me. "Yeah."

"I'll miss your hair."

I open my eyes and smile. "Yeah?"

"Yeah," she repeats, resting her forehead against mine while her hands curve over my skull.

"It will grow back."

"You look good in jeans," she teases.

"Yeah?" I chuckle.

"Definitely," she whispers, placing her mouth on mine.

I let her take charge for a moment then push her to her back, taking over. This is what I would kill for—the woman under me and my child she is carrying. They make everything worthwhile.

Epilogue

Kai

"YOU CAN DO it, *makamae*," I tell Myla, kissing the top of her head while she bears down on another contraction.

"Oh, God, Kai!" she screams.

I wish I could take her pain away. Since the moment we arrived five hours ago, she has been in pain. They gave her the epidural as soon as we got here because she was already dilated five centimeters, but it only numbed the left side of her body.

"You're doing so good." I press my forehead to hers as she lies back on the bed, looking exhausted.

"One more, Myla," the doctor says.

I want to tell her to shut up, that my wife is exhausted, but when the nurse hands her a blanket, I relax.

"He's almost here," I tell her as her foot presses into my hand and she pushes again, her face turning so red that it looks purple.

"Five-count," the doctor says.

We all start counting. Once we reach five, Myla collapses back onto the bed, breathing heavily as a loud cry fills the room.

"I'm so proud of you," I whisper, kissing the skin above her ear as our son is placed on her chest.

"He's really here," she whispers, running her hand over his still-wet hair. "He is so beautiful." Her eyes lift to meet mine, and the wonder I see there takes my breath away.

I lean in and whisper against her lips, "He *is* beautiful."

His skin is lighter than mine but darker than Myla's. His hair is black, and it already has a little wave to it. His nose is wide—like mine and the rest of the men in my family.

"We need a name," she says.

I look at her then at our son. Since the moment we talked about naming him, I have said that I wanted to wait until we met him. I knew I wanted our son to have a strong name, a name that demanded respect, one that a good man, a man of honor, would have.

"What do you think of Maxim?" I ask her.

Tears fill her eyes as she looks down at him again and whispers, "Maxim," then kisses his head. "It's perfect."

"I'm going to take him and get him cleaned up," a nurse says softly.

I look at her then my son and want to say no, but I know she has a job to do.

"I'll bring him back," she assures me.

I nod, and Myla kisses his head once more before the nurse takes him from her arms.

"I can't believe he's here," she says as we watch the nurses clean him up.

I knew the moment I met Myla that she was going to change my life. I just had no idea to what extreme it would be. Not only did she make me a husband and father, but she made me want to be better, someone she would be proud to call hers.

"Love you, *makamae*," I tell her.

She shakes her head and lifts her hand to run down my jaw. "Love you too," she whispers.

One year later

Myla

"KAI!" I YELL as my hands go to the top of his head between my legs.

I woke up with Kai behind me on the bed. His hand was wrapped over my waist, his leg over the top of mine so I couldn't move as his fingers slid in and out of me, torturing me. When I was going to come from his fingers, he turned me over then tormented my breasts while holding my hands against my stomach.

Now, his head is between my legs, and I finally have the ability to touch him, but that doesn't mean he is giving me what I want.

"I really want to come," I tell him, and his fingers slowly slide into me, lifting up when they reach that beautiful spot. "Kai, please," I whisper.

That must be what he wanted, because his mouth latches on to my clit and his fingers pump quickly, making the orgasm that was building detonate. My legs start to shake, and my hands go to my sides on the bed, bunching up the sheets in my fists, My hips lift higher to his mouth as he drinks my orgasm, the strokes of his fingers and tongue slowing.

I try to get my body back under control as I feel his mouth on my belly. Then it's on my breast as he moves up my body until his hips are snugly between my thighs.

"Good morning." He smiles as his hand wraps around the back of my neck.

His mouth comes down on mine, stealing the last of my breath as he enters me with one long thrust. The taste of me and him is on my mouth as he consumes me. I lift my hands to his back as his hand travels down my side, over my hip, and then under, lifting my thigh higher as he goes deeper.

"Right there," I hiss when he hits that spot deep inside me that has my toes curling and my thighs squeezing his waist tighter.

"I feel it. Squeeze me."

He groans as his fingers dig into my skin and his hips pump faster. I lift my other leg higher and he wraps his arm under it, lifting up so he can pound harder.

"Oh, God!" I scream, putting my hands above my head, pressing my fingers against the wall.

He dips his head and pulls my nipple into his mouth, and I feel my pussy begin to pulse around him, pulling him deeper as my orgasm overtakes me. His hips jerk. Then he plants himself deep, his forehead falling to my collarbone as I feel his chest moving rapidly and the beat of his heart pounding against my sweat-soaked skin.

"That had to be it," he breathes, lifting his head to look at me.

"Be what?" I ask in a daze, my orgasm still lingering in my system.

"The time I got my girl."

I shake my head and start to laugh. We decided a while back that we would start trying for another baby, and since then, Kai has insisted he wants a girl. But unlike the first time we got pregnant, this time has seemed to be a little more work. Yesterday, when I took an ovulation test, Kai sent Maxim away to his parents' house for a few days when it came up positive in hopes that lots of sex during this time would get us what we wanted.

"It will happen," I tell him.

He rests his head against my chest again.

Four years later

WHAT WE DIDN'T know then was that Kai was right. That was the moment he got his girl.

I look down near the shore as Kai chases Melanie, our youngest. Her cries of joy and laughter fill the air as her long, curly, blond hair flies around her head.

"No, Daddy!" she screams, making me laugh.

Kai has been chasing her for the last few minutes, trying to get her to put her swim bottoms back on, but every time he gets close to catching her, she runs off again.

I take in the hotness that is my husband when he pauses, crossing his arms over his chest. His shirtless torso is defined by hard muscle covered by smooth, dark skin. His hair is down, and the shorts he has on show of the V of his hips. His eyes come to me and he shakes his head. I know what he's thinking. *She's cute, but a pain.* The moment he held her in his arms—actually, before that—she had him wrapped around her little finger. I guess that's not surprising since she is his only girl.

Melanie pauses, looks over her shoulder, realizing that her dad isn't chasing her, and then runs back past him just out of arm's reach before running towards me, screaming, "Sabe me, Mommy!"

I catch her in my arms, careful of my belly, and pat her cute, bottomless little toosh. "Easy, baby," I tell her, quietly pulling her close to my chest.

"SORRY," SHE SAYS, patting my belly, where her baby brother is growing.

"Got you." Kai chuckles, plucking her out of my arms and quickly putting her pants on her before she has a chance to wiggle away again.

"You know she's just going to take them off again."

"I know," he mutters, pulling me closer, kissing first my forehead then my lips. "Are you excited to see your mom and brother?" he asks, pulling me closer to his side.

"Yes! I can't wait to see all the kids together. And I know my mom is excited to be here for the baby shower," I tell him, leaning deeper into his side.

He kisses my hair again.

"What do you feel like doing for dinner?" I ask him after a moment.

His eyes come to me and go soft. This is what he worked so hard to achieve, and even though it is something so small, I know that these are the moments he is always thankful for.

"Whatever you want."

"Does that mean I'm cooking?" I ask, raising an eyebrow.

"Fine. I'll grill," he mutters, kissing the look off my face.

"Yum." I smile, and he shakes his head.

"You owe me a cake," he whispers.

I feel myself squirm at the word *cake*. Since having the house to ourselves, Kai has a lot of cake, and—lucky me—normally, I'm the plate he prefers.

"Daddy, come play with me!" our son Maxim shouts as he squats down in the sand in front of a castle he's working on.

"Yeah, Daddy! Come help us!" Melanie shouts, and I notice that she is, once again, naked.

"Go on, Daddy," I tell him, pressing into his side.

He turns towards me, where I'm sitting on the ground, and gets on his knees. Then he wraps his hand around the back of my head as he lays me back in the sand, taking my mouth in a kiss that steals my breath the same way he stole my heart.

"Love you," he whispers then jumps up, walking over to the kids before I can reply.

I look at my husband and my babies and thank my mom and dad, wherever they are. I know that it's because of them I have all of this.

The End

Have you or someone you know been the victim of sexual assault? If you need someone to talk to, there is someone available 24 hours a day, 7 days a week.

1.800.656.HOPE (4673) YOU ARE NOT ALONE

DISTRACTION

Sven and Maggie's story

I wake up with my head pounding, the feel of a bare leg over the top of mine, and a hand wrapped around my breast. I open one eye and close it immediately when I see dark, golden hair, a nose, and lips I know too well. *Sven* I try to recall last night, but my whole memory is blank. My heart starts to beat more rapidly as I notice that I'm completely naked—and so is the man asleep on top of me.

"What have I done?" I whisper as I recognize that the space between my legs is sore and wet.

Tears fill my eyes as I realize that the thing I promised myself I would only give to my husband has been given to a man who has had more partners in and out of his bed than he can even count. And the worst part is that I don't remember anything.

Acknowledgment

First I want to give thanks to God without him none of this would be possible.

Second I want to thank my husband for always being so supportive and cheering me on even when I want to throw in the towel.

To my editors Kayla, you know I adore you woman, Kai is all yours girl. Thank you for always knowing exactly what I'm trying to say. Mickey thanks for making sure that I'm always delivering nothing but the best to my readers. Thank you both for your keen eyes and attention to details, you each work so hard and I'm so thankful for that.

Thank you to my cover designer and friend Sara Eirew your designs and photography skills help to bring my characters alive. Your imagination and execution helps to complete the world that my guys exist in.

Thank you to TRSOR you girls are always so hard working I will forever be thankful for everything you do. Keep being trendsetters and changing the blog world, love you girls.

To my Beta's, I think I have said it a million time's but I couldn't ask for better, thank you all so much for always encouraging me. To my Aurora's Roses and Dirty Dozen I wish I could hug each and ever one of you. Know that you all make each day worth writing. To every Blog and reader thank you for taking the time to read and share my books. Without you all as an author I would have no voice. To my FBGM girls know that I'm always grateful to be on this journey with each of you.

XOXO Aurora

Other books by this Author

The Until Series

Until November – NOW AVAILABLE

Until Trevor – NOW AVAILABLE

Until Lilly – NOW AVAILABLE

Until Nico – NOW AVAILABLE

SECOND CHANCE HOLIDAY – NOW AVAILABLE

Underground Kings Series

Assumption – NOW AVAILABLE

Obligation – NOW AVAILABLE

Distraction – Coming Soon

UNTIL HER SERIES

UNTIL JULY – COMING SOON

UNTIL HIM SERIES

UNTIL JAX – COMING SOON

Alpha Law

Justified – NOW AVAILABLE

Liability – Coming Soon

Verdict – Coming Soon

CPSIA information can be obtained
at www.ICGtesting.com
Printed in the USA
BVOW09s1418180617
487201BV00002B/149/P